Hope you enjoy
the book!
Lee Sh——

Cycles of Death

****

By Lee Shearer

authorHOUSE®

AuthorHouse™
1663 Liberty Drive
Bloomington, IN 47403
www.authorhouse.com
Phone: 1-800-839-8640

First published by AuthorHouse 6/14/2010

ISBN: 978-1-4490-5992-7 (e)
ISBN: 978-1-4490-5990-3 (sc)
ISBN: 978-1-4490-5991-0 (hc)

Library of Congress Control Number: 2010901175

Printed in the United States of America
Bloomington, Indiana

This book is printed on acid-free paper.

TWO GREY GEESE
A FINAL FLIGHT

While on an autumn weekend walk,
I came upon an icy farmer's pond.
There floated two aged, grey geese,
with feathers ruffled by the wind.

In unison, they quickly moved away,
performing as if in a rhythmic ballet,
while turning their backs to the wind.

Two gray wing tips gently touched,
as their heads twisted in unison.

Each gazed into their mate's eyes,
recalling hatches flown but still loved,
fallen friends gone but remembered,
and endless miles flown touching wings.

The wind's force sharply cooled.
They snuggled as one for body heat,
united as they had always been in life.

In the distance, a hunter's gun barked.
They winced and turned into the wind.

With paining wings they moved,
rising towards the darkening sky,
always glancing to their wing mate,
wondering if this was a final flight.

Now each morning I see a rising sun,
I glance at graying hair and wrinkled brow
and sense the endless stains of aging.

I look with love at my sleeping mate,
is this day the start of our final flight?

Lee Shearer 4/30/85

A SPECIAL THANKS TO MY WIFE DIANNA. SHE GAVE ME UNWAIVERED ENCOURAGEMENT. SHE IS THE INSPIRATION FOR THE PREVIOUS POEM AND HAS BEEN MY WINGMATE THROUGH MANY FLIGHTS. ALSO, THANKS TO NICHOLAS SHEARER OF DALLAS, TEXAS FOR HIS WORK ON THE GRAPHICS. HE IS A TALENTED YOUNG MAN.

Table of Contents

**SEX WITHOUT LOVE IS AN EMPTY EXPERIENCE, BUT
AS EMPTY EXPERIENCES GO ITS ONE OF THE BEST.**

Woody Allen

Chapter One

****

**SHE GAZED INTO THE MIRROR, ADMIRING HER OWN NEARLY
NAKED BODY.** Not bad for a sixty year old, she mused. She was
correct in her assessment. Her stomach muscles were rippling, her
belly flat, her breasts were firm and erect and her thighs and buns were
slim and void of any of the cottage cheese texture dimples that plague
so many women her age. Her superb body was the product of endless
hours of work outs, weight training, a Spartan diet, good genes and a
gifted plastic surgeon.

She felt the spring breeze flow softly over her body creating a
tingling sensation over her entire body. The smell of nature's perfume
emerging from the spring flowers drifted ever so slightly throughout
her bedroom. She was as excited as a teenage girl anxiously awaiting
another date with her first sex partner. Even though this was far from
her first sex partner, the anticipation was still there; twenty prior
partners had not diminished the thrill. Rita had long ago concluded
that a night of sexual pleasure was merely good therapy for slowing
the aging process. Her philosophy was part of her self-developed anti-
aging formula; even if you are getting older you can slow the process
if you think, act, look and feel young. Besides, the thrill of satisfying
another much younger man was good for her ego.

This latest virile stud was tall, well muscled, young, hung and good
looking. His limited IQ was of only slight concern. She loved the

1

feeling of an ego rush of sending him home limp and smiling after a few very active hours with her. She admitted that after the sex was done, there wasn't much to do with him, except to contemplate and discuss the next best experimental position. Nonetheless, she knew he was very satisfying for her. She was not looking for a PhD at this stage of her life.

She seldom thought about her prior years as the pampered princess trophy wife of a local lawyer. His good looks, endless sexual appetite, quickly amassed wealth and very unhealthy habits were far in the past. She often found herself, at moments like this, reliving their brief but exhilarating years together. Those moments always ended with a smile and a few tears. However, every day the sizable estate he had left her brought a big smile to her beautifully curved, surgically modified, mouth.

The sound of an approaching person came over her security system, followed by the clicking of her electric entrance keypad at the front door of her large modernistic home. She moved about with the effortless grace of a ballet star. She glided from her oversized, pure white bedroom, with excessive gold fixtures, to the stark black carpet of her bedroom, where every accessory, including the bedspread, was brilliant red.

She looked at herself in the full length wall-sized mirror located opposite the balcony to the room. She slid the balcony doors open to allow the gentle fragrance of the night to enter her sexual playroom. All ten scented candles were checked to confirm their location would provide the proper mood, and also display her bronzed well muscled body through her transparent black, full length negligee. A scan of her wavy shoulder-length black hair confirmed the properly fluffed appearance. A quick check of her expensive jewelry assured it would be displayed in a stylish manner. Every detail was in place. She then laid in a seductive pose on the bed waiting for his arrival.

Her heart began to flutter as she heard the front door open and close quietly as he entered her house. She breathed deep. She was in no mood for small talk and fumbling foreplay. She did not invite him here for his wit and jokes. Raw, long-lasting, strong, deep-probing sex was her sole focus and his sole value.

He moved down the hall flicking off the lights as he moved towards the familiar bedroom. As he entered, he flung his clothes in every direction and blew out the methodically placed candles.

The crude S.O.B. was ruining her ambiance, but she was not about to object; not yet. She watched as his silhouette rushed to her in the darkness of the room. His powerful hands began the familiar massage of her calves, buns and thighs. She sighed; this night would not need the KY jelly.

His panting breath caused a flash of heat to surge through every inch of her body; particularly through her inner thigh area. He was clearly the best trained and best performer of the several young studs that had shared this room. His strong hand-probing touch brought rhythmic pants from deep within her. His aggressive exploration of her erogenous zones went on endlessly. Stranger sex is always initially exhilarating, but would he ever move beyond the groping? Her desire to have him in her, for the purpose of satisfying her, pulsated in repeated, strong and violent waves.

She could stand it no longer. As was her nature, she took control and reached down for him. He was long but limp, which are awful adjectives at this stage of lust. God, this is going to be like pushing a rope uphill, she thought. However, she knew she had all the tricks to solve this temporary problem. She put her well-contoured mouth to work and produced an instant miracle. She used every move she knew, and a few variations borrowed from a Paris Hilton web site, to assure a long lasting resurrection of her recently rejuvenated lover's best part.

He, at last, responded with animal vigor and began to satisfy her. They rolled about and repeatedly changed positions without a missed stroke. God, these young dicks are good for an ego, she thought. After her multiple orgasms, she realized, he was still not satisfied. In fact, she felt a limp feeling in her. Oh, what the hell, with a few swishes of her talented tongue, she knew she could make his little Richard rise again.

She rolled off him and took him deep within her mouth for another oral resuscitation. During all of her aggressive movements to stimulate him, she did not even notice the slight pain behind her right ear. She suddenly felt her heart accelerate its beating; her neck veins began to bulge, her vision started to become dark, her breathing was difficult.

Her big, deep brown eyes looked up at her lover with a quizzical look of surprise and shock. Her beautiful lips were frozen open as she had attempted to draw a last breath.

He slid from beneath her dead weight, dressed her in her expensive black negligee and placed her in bed. Her head was propped up with pillows, her hair combed to perfection and her hands placed across her lap. When this scene was set, he searched the room. He pocketed a few thousand in cash, diamonds and gold jewelry, but left the bulk of her jewelry behind to avoid any suspicion of robbery being involved in this untimely death.

His search became very focused as he looked for the trophy. After a short time, he found it among a pile of sportswear that could be a year's inventory for most Sport's Authority stores.

He took a deep smell and knew it was hers. He quickly placed it in his coat, checked that he had left nothing behind and departed. Lord, sex with these golden oldies was stimulating, they worked hard to satisfy. But watching them die was even more exhilarating.

GOLF IS A GAME WHERE GUTS AND BLIND DEVOTION WILL ALWAYS NET YOU ABSOLUTELY NOTHING BUT AN ULCER.

Tommy Bolt

Chapter Two

****

THE SAME AFTERNOON THAT THE MORTUARY SERVICE WAS REMOVING RITA KEYES BODY FROM HER BEDROOM, I WAS PLAYING GOLF. Rita's stiffening body was found by her maid, the afternoon after her death. There was no reason to call the police for the obviously quiet death of a sixty year old woman. Her tragic death on May 15, 2009, was at that time unknown to me. However, this untimely event was the start of an evolving series of occurrences that would lead me, Lee Scott, from life as a semi-retired, conservative law-abiding attorney into becoming an unremorseful multiple felon.

I was finishing my fifth round of golf for the week, as I carefully analyzed the 17th hole on Des Moines Golf and Country Club's North Course. The heat waves rising from the severely undulating green caused distortions in the blue sky over the well-manicured surface. In front of the green, stood an acre-sized sand trap with numerous tall stands of prairie grass emerging from mounded grassy surfaces located in the middle of this vicious trap.

Our game was, as usual, extremely competitive, and filled with good humor, mediocre talent, and extremely bad sportsmanship. I knew that with a great seven iron shot, I could take command of the game. I could have Matt and Morgan whining and ready to double the size of the bet as we went to the 18th hole.

God, I love this game!

After a smooth take away, at the top of my backswing, I felt the dreaded lurch. I moved forward slightly. Predictably, the ball flew short of the green into the cavernous bunker. God, I hate this game. It's stupid!

"Nice move, Tiger" came the shout from my partner, Doug Vallie.

He then commenced to cover my rotten shot by his own LUFU (look up fuck up) which converted into a worm-burning ball.

"Guess we need to press partner?" I growled.

The day was beautiful for early spring. The breeze was only ten mph instead of the typical spring gust of twenty-five mph. The air was filled with many species of birds returning from their migrations. They were darting about in all directions; building nests and collecting food for their new flocks. Their shrill cries filled the area with so many sounds; I had the impression of being inside a huge aviary. The sweet fragrances of the fresh cut new grass, the emerging spring tulips and daffodils and the budding trees floated in the breeze. It's great to be alive on a day like this, especially when you are about to win a hundred dollars from your friends.

On the tee of the 18th hole, we pressed, doubling the bet, and provided a few unprofessional gratuitous comments to our opponents regarding how their luck was about to change. Because of my caring, nurturing nature, I volunteered to help Matt with his swing thoughts.

"In a two plane swing like yours, do you need to set your hands at the top of the swing at the ten o'clock position or the twelve o'clock position?"

Matt shook his head at my obvious and typical efforts to disrupt his game. Despite my insincere suggestions as to how to improve his swing and concentration at this crucial time, Matt hit a great drive; slight draw, down the middle. Morgan, under pressure, untypically executed the same perfect shot. Luckily, Doug and I were able to stay close to their drives with acceptable but not great shots; wimp fades to the right.

Doug and I each hit our third shot onto the extremely contoured par five green. All we had to do was two putt for pars. Morgan hit his third shot into the left green side sand bunker and Matt tried desperately to save the day by hitting a ball fifteen feet above the pin. Morgan then commenced to imitate a farmer trying to kill a snake as he failed three times to get the ball out of the deep sand trap.

"Fucking wet sand," Morgan mumbled as he picked up his ball in disgust. Doug and I fought desperately to stifle our laughs and two putted to par the hole. Unfortunately for the good guys, all that remained was for Matt to roll in a very straight downhill putt for a birdie and a sweep of all bets.

Matt eyed the putt, and then asked Morgan how he saw the break of the green. Morgan observed that it clearly went left two to three inches. Matt lined up his putter and hit the putt. It broke right and by the hole four feet.

"That downhill slope sure is severe. Serves you right for listening to a fifteen handicapper," I noted with a very big smirk.

After two more putts Matt wilted and left the green reaching for his money-clip.

God, I love this game!

As usual, we settled our bets over a very cold beer in a frosted mug in the 19th Hole Bar. Ours was a small group who played regularly, whenever four of the six of us were available. We were all over sixty years old, single for a variety of reasons, financially well off and working hard to stay in shape and maintain good health and attitudes.

We all wanted to be great golfers, but had each silently concluded this was an unattainable goal; golf was only good to fill up time on a slow day during your golden years. We used a round of golf as a way to joke, gamble and unmercifully heckle each other. It was also a good venue to keep engaged with each friend's business, social and romantic lives.

Morgan Snyder, one of today's opponents, had been my friend for thirty years. He was a retired computer genius who had made a couple of fortunes and lost half of them on three divorces. He was the group's GQ magazine person and always sported the best and latest attire.

As he ordered a second round of beers on my account number, Morgan noted, "this game is becoming a bore, let's do something different. All I do is pay you two jackals. We need a trip where lots of young ladies will find this big lump in my left pocket attractive."

"I assume that big bulge refers to a gangster size roll of cash? It's a good thing you banked your last big program sale. If it wasn't for that pocket wad of hundreds that you sport, you couldn't get a young lady to return a text message let alone screw you," piped in Doug.

This comment was far from true as Morgan was six foot two inches tall, two hundred pounds, in good shape, with totally white shoulder length hair often worn in a ponytail. His green eyes were piercing from behind a very tan weathered face and chiseled nose. His social and golf course conversations were comprised of endless one-line sarcastic jabs directed at himself and his good friends. He often insisted that when he was on a roll, his charm could get a whore to pay him for his charm, wit and prowess. He was clearly a dedicated, relentless womanizer and made no apologies for his propensities.

He had grown up in the small Iowa town of Boone. He was a legend for his basketball skills in the early sixties. He had scholarship offers to play for all the state colleges, but he rejected all of them. He went west and played a couple of years at Stanford. His mind soon became bored with basketball. He was befriended by several geeks who were working on improving computer hardware and developing various new programs and alternative operating systems. These geeks went on to become wealthy owners of cutting edge computer companies. Morgan was always around the perimeter of their work and achievements; never in the center. He often said if he wasn't so busy trying to commit suicide by fucking himself to death, he might have been part of the Microsoft and Apple wealth.

Morgan had developed his vast knowledge of computers and their programs and systems when the world of computer technology was evolving in its infancy stage. He made a fortune during the dot-com era by selling his dot-com system for assembling antique car and airplane data to a company that was in the process of going public. He put the cash into municipal bonds. Occasionally he financially backed another computer propeller head and as a result had made other fortunes from a couple of these investments. He was extremely charitable and had funded the education of at least five bright small town kids who had gone on to be extremely successful computer geeks. They repaid him by being part of his network of information on new developments and new devices.

I had been his lawyer for thirty years. Besides helping him make a lot of money, I had drafted and enforced three pre-nuptial agreements. He wanted to give me a power of attorney to institutionalize him if he ever announced another marriage.

Doug announced, "I have it on unquestionable authority that all the horny women our age or preferably a little younger are staying in shape with long workouts with their young trainer, and then they are off to a spa for pampering. A trip to a spa would be my vote for a change of pace,"

Doug was a small man with a gymnast's sinewy muscled body, gray streaked short cut black hair, and deep black eyes.

"I can imagine just laying back, surrounded by a spa full of wealthy ladies while my little body gets worked on, especially in some of the more neglected areas."

Approximately ten years before, Doug had joined our group. We knew little about his past. He often remarked that he moved to Des Moines because it was quiet, relaxing and the area was filled with very educated, decent people. The bureaucratic life in the government as an agricultural specialist had taken him all over the world, but the process had denied him the right to settle down and enjoy life. Besides, the structure had bored him. He wanted a steady life filled with a lot of diversions of his choosing. He have never been married, and vowed to us that he didn't want to experience wedded bliss.

Doug was a high energy person who was extremely competitive and very athletic. The game of golf, however, drove his competitive nature wild with frustration. Despite long and frequent practices and lessons, he was just another hack. Being a good athlete and being a good golfer do not go hand in hand.

"I am not sure I am into being poked, caressed, fondled and oiled by a bunch of chubby-cheeked farm gals or gay guys," mumbled Matt Fielding, squinting over his professorial glasses.

Matt's short, thin blond hair messed up by his golf hat was pointing in every direction. His disheveled hair combined with his blue bespectacled eyes, light complexion and chubby cheeks, gave the appearance of an eccentric college professor or an aged Al Franken. In fact, he was a world class inventor who had several patents to his credit. He always had plenty of money, and a Renaissance man attitude. He was typically game for any new idea. It was out of character for him to be so negative.

"Listen Matt, you need to get into the mood for having a new life experience. You may discover your feminine side with all of us. Maybe we all will discover we are single because we are gay and won't admit it," Morgan shot back at Matt.

"Do you suppose you could invent cologne that totally eliminated the need for foreplay before sex? It is clearly over-rated and wastes a lot of time," Morgan asked.

"Morgan, you know you don't need magic cologne to try to bed your share of ladies and avoid foreplay. That cash roll in your pocket provides all your charm. Besides, I suspect you don't waste a lot of your effort on trying to satisfy any of your partners," I laughed.

After a second beer, I proposed, "We are going to try the spa routine. If Doug guarantees that it is a sure-fire place to find the horny, rich females of this area, that's good enough for me. I'll check them out. Anyway, we need to locate a masseuse for our sore muscles while we train for RAGBRAI. A spa would be good for rehabilitating some of your old muscles from the fifty mile training rides I plan to initiate next week."

While I had their attention, I noted, "Let me remind you again that RAGBRAI is a week long, four hundred and fifty mile biking event across Iowa. It is a target rich environment for a bunch of good looking, charming lechers like us."

"This voyage across the hills and plains of Iowa involves a rolling crowd of about fifteen thousand bikers from all over the world partying across our great state. From my first hand reconnaissance, this event is composed fifty percent of families looking for a fun bonding experience, and forty percent of the crowd is predominantly ladies who are in great shape or at least trying to get in great shape. Nine percent of the riders are a bunch of overweight males who are too fat to complete the trip and stuff potatoes into their riding shorts to try to look attractive. The last one percent is composed of in-shape studs like us. Aren't any of you concerned that our presence will cause a feeding frenzy?"

"Ha" was the unanimous and immediate response.

We simultaneously got up and left on that profound and exaggerated thought. We went our separate ways. Another day wasted with four hours of golf followed by one hour of macho bragging and lying about our dwindling sexual prowess. Getting old and keeping a healthy ego takes work and a good imagination.

GETTING OLD IS NOT FOR SISSIES.

Pierce Brosnan

Chapter Three

****

I DEPARTED WITH MIXED FEELINGS. I felt like I'd had a shitty game of golf, but I had one hundred extra dollars in my pocket, thanks to a three-putt effort by Matt. It's fun to watch an opponent with a case of the yips trying to make a two foot putt. I felt a little guilt for pointing out, right before his putt, how happy I was that his yip problem had clearly been solved. What are good friends for except to build confidence?

My big mouth had resulted in my being assigned the task of locating and setting up the spa experience. I was also directed to get my ass in gear and complete and announce the plans and timetable for the training regimen for our RAGBRAI trip. Bossy old guys can be oppressive with their demands, especially when they have lost a bet and had two beers. It was two weeks till Memorial Day and RAGBRAI was the last week of July. There clearly was enough time to start the process of getting the fat melted off our aging pampered bodies and developing our muscles to a trail worthy status.

Doug had reluctantly agreed to procure a quality team bus. Everyone voted that the deal was a "no go" if we could not find a bus with air conditioning, a good shower, a couple of bathrooms and enough space for good food, wine and beer. A nymphomaniac driver clearly was a preference, but not a deal breaker. This was our idea of roughing it.

When I arrived home, I followed my usual routine of engaging in a real workout. Golf is for fun, not improving mental or physical health and definitely not for developing feelings of self worth. My boring routine involved working on the cardio system for forty-five minutes, hitting the weights for fifteen minutes and concluding with ten minutes of stretching. I didn't have any particular goals for following this routine. I was too old for marathons or triathlons. It was just my way of trying to maintain my fading muscle size and tones. I had tried every new gimmick and gadget and had resorted to the old tried and true methods; running, weights with plenty of sweat.

Thanks to this regime, I had kept my five foot ten, large boned frame from expanding beyond two hundred pounds despite being sixty-five years old. Keeping my body from deteriorating from the increasing impact of aging was a losing battle, but this routine made me feel like I was doing something to slow down the losing process.

This sweat-filled workout also helped me forget the frustrations of the stupid golf game that irritated me and consumed so much of my time. It helped remind me that golf was not the measure of my manhood. If it was, I would be a eunuch. If it wasn't for the male bonding, good humor and post game BS, golf would be as popular as curling.

After a good work out, I checked my voice mail. The first message was from Margaret, a plus size, single friend for many years. She was smart, interesting, kind and a saint in times of need. She was always calling when a new restaurant opened, or she had tried a new recipe. She loved food so well she hummed when it was served and as she took each bite. This was cute, but not sexually motivating. I decided I was not in the mood and hit the erase button.

The next call was from a very cute twenty-five year old attorney who I had helped land a job with a local law firm. She wanted to use her first pay check and take me out for drinks and dancing with a stop at her place afterwards for a night cap. I suspect that the last stop would be a long one which would be great for my ego and bad for my conscience.

Besides, I hate dancing.

The truth is I do not trust any young woman that tells me she finds me attractive. She is either stoking me for some self-serving motive, or she has a father complex issue. Neither of these options is good. I hit the erase button.

I listened to a few more calls and hit the "erase all" button. I was slowly slipping into a dark mood.

I knew I was not attracted long term to older women. I also knew I did not trust any younger women who found me alluring, witty, and lovable because of my balance sheet, financial achievements, and business reputation. I doubt I would be given a second look if I was a mid-level supervisor with credit card debt and employed by a local bank.

I knew I would likely spend the rest of my life alone. My grumpy, cynical side was oozing out of every pore.

I FIXED MYSELF A RYE WHISKEY MANHATTAN AS A REWARD FOR A GOOD WORKOUT AND SAT DOWN ON MY FAVORITE RECLINING CHAIR ON MY DECK. The ironwood deck was three hundred feet long and spanned over half of the length of my large prairie style home located at the top of a high ridge. I slowly gazed south across the five mile wide valley below as the fog from the cooling air commenced to condense over the warm river water slowly moving in the Raccoon River. Nature's sweet smells drifted up from the four acres of budding prairie flowers and prairie grass and combined with the aromas emitted from the spring flowers emerging from the berms below my deck. This multifaceted fragrance floated on the light breeze. Its bouquet was soporific. I fixed another rusty bullet.

The sounds of the night filled the air; crickets screeched, frogs crocking from their ponds, coyotes howled for their pack, and night birds chirped. I could not count the number of times I had sat in this same seat and absorbed these images in every season. It was always tranquilizing, hypnotizing and mesmerizing. The smell of an impending spring rain filled the air.

As I watched natures kaleidoscopes of another sunset develop, I poured another drink to further assist in resolving my decaying mood. I decided to make a few calls to several mature female friends to solicit their thoughts about the idea of taking six old single men to an upscale spa and to elicit their suggestions as to which spa made sense.

Several of these friends were more than a little apprehensive that we could really absorb the relaxing experience without grossing out the female customers. A couple were pleasantly surprised that we would try something new as most old guys are usually completely boring and rigid in their habits. I was slightly irritated at such a narrow female view, but unfortunately as usual, it was accurate.

The consensus was if we wanted a tasteful presentation, with a variety of different pampering treatments, we should go to The Painted Woods Spa. As an alternative, if we wanted a back rub, a pat on the ass by a scantily clad young tech school trained masseuse and a guaranteed happy ending; we should definitely go to the Spa by the River. This choice of selections was difficult, but after another rusty bullet, I decided we would take the high moral road. The thought of some young lovely tech giving my wrinkled, groping friends a happy ending after the spa experience was even more than my perverted imagination could endure. With that image in mind, I concluded I did not feel like being the pimp for these lechers.

After a quick dinner of left over almond encrusted tilapia, prepared the night before as part of a long considered seductive plan directed at my new female play toy, I opened a good pinot from Panther Creek. I walked out on the deck to watch deer grazing on the prairie as the moon rose and the building fog spread across the valley. The full moon and gentle breeze with a rising fog provided the illusion of millions of ghosts dancing across the valley floor. Maybe the self-medicating had worked. Unfortunately, the longer I sat and watched the dancing ghosts below me, the more my mood spiraled downward into a black cesspool of depression.

It had been four years since melanoma cancer had so slowly taken my soul mate away. The process had been painfully slow for her. I suffered with her every moment because of my helpless role. The chemo treatments, followed by the recovery and dashed hopes, was gut-wrenching. All I could do was try to be positive, be supportive, and be there. I knew the trail we were on and tried very hard not to display my fear, not to feel sorry for myself or to let my frequent dark moods show. Being a caregiver is a real bitch and has a long-term emotional impact. But, it beats being the victim of a disease that is so illogical in selecting its recipients. After my loss, I had quickly admitted a great deal about the real me.

I realized that I did not have the emotional energy to get deeply involved with another woman. I did not have the desire to get to know them, get to know their family, or get to appreciate what they liked. I did not need a companion to enjoy life. I was content to do what I wanted, when I wanted, and how I wanted. I clearly was too selfish for anyone who wanted a long-term relationship. It was extremely unlikely that I would change. While I recognized this attitude was unhealthy, I was okay with it and did not have any motivation to reconsider it. Aging men with flexible attitudes are a rare combination.

I was at peace with myself and vowed every day to enjoy life enough for two people. Tonight, I knew I was slipping into one of my "pity me" moods. I hated losing her. I hated not hearing her laugh. I hated not hearing about her day. I hated missing a hug and kiss at night. I hated the feeling of not having someone next to me with a special smell and chemistry. A few tears slid down to the grass below as I hung my head over the balcony. Life's not fair.

> HEROES ARE PEOPLE WHO RISE TO THE
> OCCASION AND SLIP QUIETLY AWAY.
>
> Tom Brokow

Chapter Four

****

THE BED WAS WHIRLING AND ROCKING. How dumb of me to wash down four big brown drinks with red wine. Self-medicating one's own mood swings is not bright, especially in light of the reality that I had learned that same lesson far too many times. Older doesn't always mean smarter.

I knew this spiraling voyage into a black mood all too well. I closed my eyes and lay back on my three pillows. My alcohol-soaked mind, between pangs of shooting pains and whirling dizziness, drifted back to a life-changing meeting that had occurred three years before.

In a world that has few heroes, Judge Nathan Wayne stood out larger than life to me. He had helped me move on with life after Terri's death. He was a true life hero, and my only object of hero worship. He was a small town farm boy from Storm Lake, Iowa. He had grown up in the post depression era where life on the farm was simple. The first goal was to raise enough grain and animals to feed the family, and the second goal was to have enough left over to sell for minimal essentials. Nathan grew to be a giant at six foot six. The hard farm work on long summer days had made his muscles sinewy and strong.

He persisted in going to school in an era where most boys dropped out to work after the eighth grade. He simply loved to learn about every new subject that he was introduced to in the classroom. Luck was with him as he was encouraged to go to college by a teacher who saw his potential.

At the University of Iowa in 1939, Nathan as a freshman was one of the key backup players on the Ironmen team. He was a part of the tough linemen who opened holes for Adel, Iowa running back, Nile Kinnick. That year Nile won the Heisman Trophy, Big Ten MVP, Walter Camp Award, and Maxwell Award. He was the first college athlete to win the Associated Press Male Athlete of the Year, beating out Joe DiMaggio, Joe Louis and Byron Nelson. His clean cut good looks, humble demeanor and articulate leadership made him his team's spiritual and emotional leader and everyone's hero.

His Heisman acceptance speech caused AP reporter Whitney Martin to write, "You realized the ovation wasn't alone for Nile Kinnick, the outstanding football player of the year, it was also for Nile Kinnick, typifying everything admirable in American youth."

Kinnick was the grandson of a former governor of Iowa. His speeches in 1940, on the eve of war while introducing Presidential candidate Wendell Willkie, sounded like the wise voice of a patriotic future president. One local Iowa newspaper predicted a run by Kinnick in 1956 when he would be eligible.

Nile passed on a professional football career and entered the navy after a year in law school. He was inducted three days before Pearl Harbor. He wrote his parents, "There is no reason in the world why we shouldn't fight for the preservation of a chance to live freely, no reason why we shouldn't suffer to uphold that which we want to endure. May God give me the courage to do my duty and not falter. Every man I've admired in history has willingly and courageously served in his country's armed forces in times of danger. It is not only a duty but an honor to follow their example the best I know how. May god give me the courage and ability to so conduct myself in every situation that my country, my family and my friends will be proud of me."

Nile died in 1943 when his plane crashed on a training mission in the Caribbean. He was never found and the world lost one of its best men, a common occurrence during that era. Kinnick's ten foot bronze statue, with brief case in one hand and an aviator jacket in the other, stands at the entrance to Kinnick Stadium in Iowa City and is passed by thousands every football Saturday. He is also honored at every Big Ten game's coin flip as the conference coin bears Kinnick's movie idol handsome face.

Nathan never tired of telling about his hero. Nile had played on a Junior Legion baseball team with future Hall of Fame pitcher Bob Feller, fondly referred to as the Heater from Van Meter. Nile's toughness was legendary. He played his junior year on a broken ankle. He played his senior year with broken ribs. But he was most admired by Nathan for his moral fiber to do what was right, moral and patriotic. His picture and a copy of his commencement speech are proudly displayed on Nathan's wall. The picture has a few visible stains, admittedly from Nathan's tears.

It was not surprising that when Nathan finished college in 1942, he enlisted in the Army. He was too big for the Army Air Corp. Like many land bound farm boys, he feared water, so the Navy wasn't an option. His clear leadership and physical size led him to the army's ninety day wonder program that made him an instant officer and gentleman.

Nathan walked with the sixth wave onto Omaha Beach on June 6, 1944. He recalled that only the crashing of the Atlantic waves and an occasional artillery explosion from the defending Germans broke the eerie silence. The carnage that he walked through was horrible; bodies, body parts and equipment lay in piles as a result of the defenders' efforts to stop them on the beach. He did not recognize anyone.

Nathan cried shamelessly, like a baby, as he walked forward through the remains of the best of a great generation's manhood. He realized that, but for a lucky decision by a ship-bound officer deciding which wave would include his unit, he likely would have been expended in those early waves of men. He could hardly imagine the fear that went through the minds of those brave soldiers as they rushed headlong into hell.

Nathan went through the war without a scratch. He saw combat action in numerous small towns across France and Germany. He left the service in 1945 as a changed person. He quickly exercised his GI rights and went to law school with a commitment to change the world for the better as a feeble reward to those men whose bad luck placed them in the wrong place at the wrong time and lost that chance forever.

As a young federal prosecutor in Des Moines, he quickly won a reputation as aggressive, hard working and unbending. In an area where the Kansas City mafia claimed control of this region of their domain, his efforts were fearless. Only his size, careful attention to safety details and an ivory handled forty-five caliber Colt revolver kept him from harm.

As time went on, he entered into the private practice of law and made very good money defending white collar criminals. Unexpectedly, he quit. He often said, "I looked in the mirror and did not like the guy looking back at me. I could not hide behind that lawyer code that everyone deserves a good defense as they are innocent till proven guilty. Some pond scum doesn't deserve my efforts to keep them free."

After a year of travel and reading, Nathan returned to the prosecutor's office until a wise governor made him a judge. His courtroom was always filled with crowds to watch his total control of each situation, his closing remarks to juries, and his sentencing lecture to any guilty criminal that had the misfortune to have him assigned as the sentencing judge.

His image and forceful presentations soon led him to the Supreme Court of Iowa. As a law and order advocate, after a long tenure, he was vilified by the growing number of liberal judges and lawyers of the 90's. The new governor's judicial appointments decisions lead Nathan to write flaming dissents to the Supreme Court's increasingly liberal decisions. He often repeated the old lawyers joke: what do you call the person who graduated in the bottom ten percent of their law school class, who was too lazy to put in long billable hours and had no clients? Answer? "Your Honor."

On January 2nd 2000, after cheering in the millennium, he walked into the ambitious young democratic Governor's office and handed in his three word resignation. I always wondered if, "I quit shit-head," are three or four words.

At age eighty, he decided to become a writer. After writing two books on the waning ethics of the judiciary and the growing trend of judicial law making, he quietly retired to a small farm. His long term bride died in her early eighties. Nathan stayed on the farm and was seldom seen in public.

I had the good fortune to have tried several winning cases before him in my early career. I also had the good fortune to handle several personal items for him, including the legal aspects of the books he published. His trust in me was always one of my prized possessions.

While his books did not make a lot of money, as it was difficult to find an interested agent, he was exhilarated by the writing process. I was honored when he would call me to debate some of his more extreme positions as I was more liberal in my views. I found myself frequently stopping by his farm to talk about a bevy of life's problems. We became very close. He was like a father, giving me his advice when he thought I needed it, even if I had not asked for it.

I often would stop for a drink and his advice when I found myself in a business situation where the practical solution was not clearly in compliance with the law. Not surprisingly, I felt rigidly observing the law made no sense, but valued his counsel. He always reminded me NECESSITAS NON HABET LEGEM. Necessity knows no law.

Nathan was by my side when I needed a friend and spiritual advisor after Terri died. My emotional stability was at an all time low when he arrived unannounced at my door. He was using a walker to brace his aging body and an oxygen tank to supplement oxygen to his lungs that were damaged from his unrelenting cigar smoking. His eyes were still deep brown and had a sharp clear focus.

"Lee, I haven't seen you in months. Can I come in and bore you with some advice and old lawyer's stories?"

"You don't need an invitation. Come on in. I'm experimenting with making pressed coffee and I need a guinea pig to run tests on. I warn you this pressing process will likely provide you with more grounds than usual, but the coffee flavor is really clear and strong."

As he came into my house, I noted he was thinner than I recalled and very gray. We slowly moved to the deck where as he attempted to sit. He fell hard into one of my chairs. His still large frame was clearly breaking down and each step was a challenge. He looked at me for several seconds with piercing eyes, a long gaze and a stern fix to his lips.

"I know you feel like shit, and by the way, you also look like shit. It's time to move ahead. You have a lot of life ahead of you. You can not dwell in the past any longer."

"You're right about my feelings and probably right about my appearance. I simply cannot get out of the past, or see anything I want to do in the future. Have you ever found yourself emotionally stuck in place, unable to move?"

"I know you are well off financially and still young enough to chase a little tail, but you have to figure out a way to live whatever number of years you are blessed with by having enthusiasm for every new dawn and satisfaction for every new sunset. It's not easy but just like death, it is part of life."

"I know you're right, but I am having a hard time finding how to be stimulated by anything. I play golf with some great friends, but that stupid golf game is not enough to live for and some days not even enough to wake up for. I do enjoy playing and listening to all the lies a bunch of middle age guys come up with, especially about their sexuality. We all act like sex is on our mind and agenda 24/7, but if we are honest, most of that is BS and was long ago deposited in our memory bank. We all, in fact, have growing fear of being alone and contradicting fear of recommitting to anyone. Can you ever trust someone again? Can you ever care about them and their feelings again? Isn't being alone better?"

"Lee, I am not going to try to advise you about your trust issues, or sexual prowess. You alone have to confront those matters. Living out your final years is not always a cakewalk. I find that the only way to go forward is to wake up every morning with a new goal and go to bed every night trying to figure out how to achieve that goal. The goal is irrelevant. The existence of a goal is everything. Consider that advice. It will keep you young."

"You will laugh at my latest fascination, Lee. I started watching those damned big grey geese that shit all over my fishing pond. I noticed how they would couple up in the spring and fall. I, however, also noticed there was always another group that didn't couple up but stood aside with their same gender. At first, I thought I had discovered a flock of gay geese that had come to Iowa to marry since our Supreme Court has legislated gay marriages were legal. Who needs congressmen when you have law-making judges? Despite my skepticism, I decided to read more about the habits of those shit machine geese."

"Grey Geese are rare. They are the true goose and most other types are variations of their gene pool. They are very territorial. They mate once for life. When they lose their wing mate, they group with their own sex for life. What struck me was, despite their pain from aging and their loneliness; they are always going on with life and flying with their flock on every new migration. Even as they can barely flap their wings, they keep on moving ahead with life and not laying down to die in peace. Seems to me we humans can learn from their example, wouldn't you agree?"

I was silent. After a deep sip of my freshly pressed coffee, I looked into his strong unblinking eyes.

"As usual, I am glad to see you, my friend. I think this old goose has again been helped by your wisdom. I really will try to move forward?"

After a couple cups of coffee, well laced with rum, Nathan struggled upright and left.

"Stop over soon. I'm on a new kick. I'm writing poems. Here is a draft of one about those shitting machine geese that I would like you to review and revise. Don't try screwing yourself to death before our next visit."

With that unnecessary gratuitous advice and a hearty laugh, followed by uncontrolled coughing, he shuffled away.

As I watched him move to his car, fighting with his walker for every step and gulping in oxygen from his tank, a few tears formed. Here was my hero, my role model, fighting to the bitter end to learn, to experience and to grow. Goodbye pity pot and hello life. I am back.

With that lesson from Nathan freshly recalled, I swung my wobbly legs and rolling stomach out of bed, and looked at a very haggard-looking face staring back from the mirror. I laughed and vowed to God never to do it again. I knew I was lying, but it sounded like an appropriate promise to God, just in case he was listening or gave a shit.

Chapter Five

****

**AFTER RECALLING NATHAN'S GOOD ADVICE AND EXAMPLE,
MY NEXT MOVE WAS FOR THREE ALEVE AND ICE WATER.** My
solution to my now infrequent "pity me" moods had left a severe
residual impact in my head. I slowly rolled out of bed and put on a
jogging suit, just in case I acquired the energy to punish myself for my
stupidity over drinking. The aroma and several fast gulps of coffee soon
brought my mind back into focus. As I stood on the deck watching the
sun cut through the fog, I remembered it's good to be alive and there is
a lot more ahead for this old guy. The sounds of the morning filled the
air: blue birds calling their mates, finches flitting about and chirping as
they fed in the prairie, robins chiming their songs as they built nests for
their new hatch and pheasants crying for their mates.

As I leaned back in my deck chair and savoring the strong coffee, I
enjoyed an aging man's tendency to allow his mind to drift and reflect
upon years that had sped by far too quickly.

I graduated from law school in 1967, just in time for the draft and
the opportunity to go to Southeast Asia. I enlisted and luckily got a
JAG appointment. My year in the heat of Saigon was spent defending
young soldiers from crimes and getting them out of the hands of local
police, which meant learning the art of bribery.

I was fortunate to never see a day of combat and only experienced two injuries. One injury was from a one inch piece of steel from a terrorist bombing and the other from an opium-crazed local police officer who thought my first bribe offer was a personal insult. I vividly recalled that as he drew his gun, I added a few more cases of Jack Daniels to the offer, as if I had forgotten. I got a gun butt to the head for my negotiations error.

Every day while I played lawyer in a combat zone, I knew I was lucky to have avoided the heat, bugs and eternal fright. Each time I saw a grunt, I saw the physical and mental toll that combat had imposed on America's brave soldiers.

After a year in Saigon, I finally returned to San Diego for my remaining two years and was assigned to handle defendants' appeals. In reality, I was a public defender for the already convicted soldiers. I soon understood there were three types of military criminals whose appeals were my daily chores.

The first type was the psychologically and morally underdeveloped. These young men had not been raised with any moral center to utilize as the basis for making a decision. Survival and taking what you could get away with was their only driving motivation. Once they were trained to kill and maim and realized such action garnered rewards for good work, an uncontrollable demon was unleashed.

The second type was the emotionally fragile person whose feelings and self-image were extremely low before entering service. They were cracked eggs waiting to implode. In this pitiful state, combined with the stress of combat, the fear for life, the loss of friends and the constant fear of inadequacy in performance, they eventually broke and the consequences were unpredictable.

These two types of cases seldom had any basis for an appeal. Most appeals were merely reviewed by the appeals tribunal, and I lost. But the military legal system could technically say that due process was provided the accused.

The third type of appeal was for the solid patriotic young man who was in the wrong place at the wrong time and got convicted for not stopping the crime in process. Henry Faber appeared to be such a person.

Henry was from Des Moines, Iowa. He enlisted in 1968 as a young, patriotic high school graduate. He was quickly promoted to corporal because of his solid cool behavior, uncommon for a nineteen year old. Near the end of his tour, his squad entered a village after suffering several casualties.

As Henry scouted the perimeter of the area with half his squad, a massive level of gun fire erupted from the center of the village and caused him to quickly circle back. He arrived at the source of the eruption and found fifteen dead citizens crumpled around several overturned vats of corn. Chinese-made grenades and rifles were strewn on the ground, partially covered with the village's corn supply cascading from the large broken urns. The crowd was in tears and wailing with ear splitting screams as they pointed toward five smoking gun toting grunts.

As Henry was screaming at his men about the revenge-sparked executions, he had a big bit of bad luck. A young navy boatman captain entered the camp from the nearby river. The unfortunate event was the arrival of a tall heroic looking boat captain, accompanied by a cameraman who was monumentalizing the captain's every move. Likely, he was either a celebrity or was planning on running for office. The cameraman caught dramatic pictures of the results, including Henry screaming and waving his rifle. This filmed evidence put Henry and the five shooters before a court-martial court. The young captain's version was sketchy, quite self-righteous, and yet it was enough to convict all six.

When the case file arrived on my desk, my review left me with the clear belief that Henry was innocent. During the review process, I found telephone numbers from multiple calls from an older brother named Rod Faber. RF, as he preferred to be called in lieu of his given name of Rodney Leroy Faber, was apparently well connected and had amassed significant wealth.

When I returned RF's calls, he was shocked that someone had finally answered him. After several long, rambling speeches on how inefficient the Army was, how it was rude to ignore numerous calls and that he was a big tax payer, he calmed down. He knew Henry wasn't the brightest light bulb, but he was convinced he could not kill that easily.

RF first offered me money as an incentive to get Henry freed, which I had to reluctantly refuse. He also offered significant political influence to get a rehearing, which I acknowledged would be important.

Most importantly, he offered to provide expert investigative assistance, which I quickly accepted.

In a shockingly short time frame, the political aspect miraculously developed, and we obtained an appeal for Henry separate from the other defendants. A few days later, the investigation uncovered new facts which helped to put an entirely different light on Henry's case.

In fact, the work of a young Des Moines police officer, Randall Walker, moonlighting during vacation won the case. He concluded that no eye witness could connect Henry to firing a single shot. Even the five guilty soldiers could not remember if Henry was present during the massacre. Surprisingly, the now politically active boat captain could no longer make the connection.

The most significant discovery was that one of the squad members, miraculously located by Walker in the southern Los Angeles barrios, confirmed Henry was not even in the area when the shots were fired. The defense in Saigon had not done their homework and had allowed Henry to be whitewashed as part of the trial of the murderous five.

I later learned, over too many beers with Walker, that Henry was a bit of a nut. There was some possibility that while he did not fire a shot, he may have been pointing out targets. I also learned that the boat captain's memory was blurred by a sizable political contribution to his first senate campaign.

Walker even mentioned that the witness from the LA barrio now had a great job at RF's San Diego truck terminal and drove a new pickup every year. I checked and all five participants had their sentences substantially reduced for good behavior and were on the street within two years after Henry's acquittal.

Whenever I pondered this bizarre outcome, I remembered Nathan Wayne's words, "Necessity knows no laws."

After my unexpected but obviously brilliant win of his appeal, Henry was freed and was quickly hired by his brother to operate their Fargo terminal. RF offered to set me up with a law firm and plenty of clients after military service if I would return to my native Iowa area. I told him that I still owed Uncle Sam eighteen months of devotion but I had his number, and I would call if I was interested.

Following this miraculous judicial result, I went on a two day celebration that would make a pirate proud. Unfortunately, I decided to explore some local bars in some bad areas and got beaten unconscious. When I awoke in the hospital, the short petite blond RN asked if my ribs hurt worse than my hung-over head and liquor-laden GI track.

She giggled when I asked if my balls were still intact as the last I remembered was a size eleven tennis shoe trying to use them for punting practice.

We had a short courtship, with an extremely sexually active component, before we moved in together. I artfully convinced her that the high level of sex was necessary as part of my therapy for a full recovery from the groin kicking. During our free time, we shared everything as if there was not enough time to find out about each other. Upon my discharge, we married, and I called RF. True to his word, he arranged for me to be hired by a first rate law firm in Des Moines.

My star was on the rise as RF kept his word and referred new clients to me in a steady stream. I litigated for a few years, but soon grew tired of the time-wasting discovery and motion practice that cost time and money and denied quick justice. So I changed my practice areas to commercial and transactional work.

Eventually, I tired of listening to fellow lawyers brag about their latest exploits and whine about their latest mistreatment by the partners and/or the courts. Law schools seldom produce a happy and content product. Again, true to his word, RF backed me, and I started a solo practice with a few great paying clients. My practice of doing business transactions on a participation basis was well received. Soon, I owned part of several businesses. Life was good.

Terri kept doing her care-giving work. In the early years, she was an RN and eventually, when money was less of an issue, she became a volunteer fund raiser for a medical center. We were socially very active, enjoyed many wonderful friends and traveled extensively. Most importantly, we designed and built our dream house on a hilltop ridge overlooking the Raccoon River Valley.

Twenty-seven years went by like a shooting star crossing the Iowa sky on a pitch black fall night. Then the dreaded "C" word entered our lives and ended what was like Camelot on the prairie. The outcome was certain. We clutched for every minute. We spent many hours just quietly looking at our view and the wildlife living on our prairie. Words were hard to find, but touches were easy to give and receive.

I STOPPED RELIVING THE PAST. This could only lead me into another black mood. So, in an attempt to get my whiskey-soaked mind operational again, I picked up the Des Moines Register which was, as usual, very thin as it was a week day. A quick scan of several young reporters' interpretations of the world's news and the sports page consumed very few minutes. Next, I followed my habit of checking on any friends in the obituary section. I was visibly shaken by what I saw.

The dark haired, beautiful smiling features of Rita Keyes were staring up at me. Her long, wavy black hair, dark brown eyes, perfect upturned nose and full lips, formed a seductive image. The picture looked more like an ad from a beauty magazine than the subject of an obituary column. The article was comprised of a short list of relatives, and a long list of grateful, now grieving charities. It announced she had died quietly at home.

Rita was the source of many unforgettable memories. Three years before, she was a significant part of my emotional recovery when she reintroduced me to the world of a single eligible male. She had rekindled my desire to live a long and full life during a few eventful days on the Register's Annual Great Bike Ride Across Iowa, aka RAGBRAI.

Rita was then in her late fifties. As a result of her many workouts and active life, she was in incredible physical shape. She was a bundle of energy and lived her life two hundred percent more actively than most people. How could this one of a kind light be extinguished so soon?

My coffee cup crashed to the floor.

THE YEARS BETWEEN FIFTY AND SEVENTY
ARE THE HARDEST. YOU ARE ALWAYS BEING
ASKED TO DO THINGS, AND YOU'RE NOT YET
DECREPIT ENOUGH TO TURN THEM DOWN.

T.S. Eliot

Chapter Six

****

AS YOU GET OLDER, EACH DEATH OF A FRIEND DREDGES UP
DEEP VIVID FEARS REGARDING YOUR OWN MORTALITY. For
at least two minutes, my gaze was fixed on the strikingly beautiful
picture of Rita staring up from the obituary column. The model quality
smile in the picture of a now very dead lady caused waves of fear and
questions about death pulsating through my mind. Is there a heaven?
Is there another side? Do you get the chance to see the departed love
ones again? Is death just like being a dead plant with a plunge into
nothingness?

I was frozen in place while I came to grips with the very personal
emotions racing through my mind as part of the aging process.
Someone once said we all start the dying process the day we are born.
That concept is true, but hard to accept.

My memories of Rita were as vivid as if they had occurred yesterday,
not three years ago. After Terri's death, I had spent most of a year trying
to rebuild my attitude. I was lucky as my money issues were nil. RF
tried to get me engaged in work only when I felt the need to exercise
my mind and have some business interrelations.

My golf buddies kept me involved in numerous trips and golf
games. Their camaraderie and friendly attention to my well being were

as much as friends could do to assist in my recovery. I had to do it at my own pace. They chided me continually to get on with finding some young tart who could take my repressed sexual life out of retirement. For a while I ignored this advice and worked on other interests: golf, drinking and pouting.

My golf game did not get particularly better because of my lack of skill, but my warm feelings for true friends grew. I did eventually take them up on solving my repressed sexual issues by allowing them to arrange a few short-lived relationships. My friends likely lost some female friends by arranging these disasters. These staged events always ended when my gullible partner figured out I was only after sex, not companionship. I didn't think I was that obvious, but they were right in their assessments.

After Nathan Wayne's lecture gave me a map out of the pity fields, I started to set the bottle aside and worked hard on transforming my five foot ten body back to the two hundred pound weight that best fit my frame. I ended my brief hippie era of growing long hair and a beard. After a close shave and a fashionable hair cut, I looked into the mirror for the first time in a long while; it was clear that the year had taken its toll.

My once black hair was predominately gray, new deep furrows were etched into my forehead, and the lines around my eyes were now extra-large sized crow's feet. I was a walking annuity for a plastic surgeon. This disgusting reflection from the mirror drove home the reality that I needed to get my health back under control and to forge a new mental attitude.

I was searching for weeks for new goals and purposes in life when an old friend, Dale Harmon, told me about RAGBRAI. This internationally known bike route traveled from the west coast of Iowa on the sandy banks of the Missouri River to the east coast of Iowa on the rocky shores of the Mississippi River. This event originated approximately thirty-five years ago when a few local newspaper reporters who were avid bike riders decided to get a few friends together and in late summer rode across the state and wrote about the process.

The stories of the reporter, concerning rural Iowa's beauty, the fun-loving people along the way and the spontaneous parties that developed, stimulated the start of a unique event. Each year thereafter, the number of riders increased as they moved like a swarm of locusts across the state. The number and type of venders grew in number, teams were formed, team costumes evolved, family groups used it as a reunion venue, and reports of the spontaneous parties grew in number and intensity. The rumors of nocturnal hanky-panky by consenting adults became legendary.

My accountant friend, Dale Harmon, owned a school bus converted exclusively for his team's use on RAGBRAI. The old, brown fifty-two passenger Ford bus was fully equipped with a retrofitted kitchen, sleeping area and external portable showers. Dale and his wife, Helga, annually took their family, extended family and long time friends with them on this excursion. The old bus was their mobile command center, motel and cafe all rolled into one. Each time we would see each other; Dale would tell and retell the funny experiences that had occurred on this rolling party.

With more than a little trepidation, I agreed to give it a whirl. I was extremely concerned whether a sixty year old, pampered lawyer could make this rigorous trip, but they kept reminding me it was an adventure, not a race. After sixty days of training, I threw my newly acquired Trex 840 on the Team Slow Poke bus and headed to Onawa, Iowa.

THE 1970 FORD SCHOOL BUS WAS LIKE AN OLD BUFFALO MOVING ACROSS THE ROLLING PRAIRIE, FOLLOWING INTERSTATE 80 WEST TO ONAWA ON THE LAST WEEK OF JULY 2005. Its deep brown exterior, with a full length yellow stripe, proudly displayed the Slow Poke name and team motto on each side. "Team Slow Poke-Stop us if you want one."

As we moved along Interstate 80, we were part of a sixty-five mph parade formed by team vehicles ranging from upscale RV's, and highly decorated mini-vans to ancient pickups with rusted toppers towing tarp-covered trailers full of riding and camping equipment. The common denominator was that everyone was smiling and waving at each other. Only in Iowa could this type of friendship between absolute strangers spontaneously develop.

RAGBRAI was always scheduled for the last week of July, typically the hottest and most humid week of the year. This week was no exception. As we moved along with the parade, I sat by an open window trying to stay cool in the non-air conditioned bus, watching the parties that were in newer, faster and air-conditioned transportation pass us. I waved with a meek smile as they passed by, looking very cool and comfortable. But the process was not totally wasted. We were nearly to Onawa and I had been mooned three times, had four ladies pull their tops up to display their various-sized assets and had been given the finger five times for gawking.

I was sweltering when an extremely buff forty-five year old man sat an ice cold beer down in front of me. Scott Norris extended a strong hand from his pop-eye sized arms.

"Get used to this heat. It will be like this all week. Man up. Despite all your gray hair, you look like you're in shape so you will adapt."

"Scott, good to see you haven't lost your sense of humor. By the way, what happened to you? Last time I saw you, your body looked like the Michelin Man. Now you look like a male pin-up for AARP."

"After wife number three ran off with a boys' band, I stopped with the Krispy Crème and Pepsi breakfast and lunch. I have really immersed myself into developing a healthy body. I'm even thinking about entering a senior division body building contest this fall."

Scott and I had known each other for several years. He was a very successful lobbyist and my clients had used him to guide their legislature through the local congress on several occasions for a very handsome fee. I also had helped him through three divorces. He was extremely gifted at making lobbying judgments and negotiating the numerous trade-offs involved with this profession. He was equally inept at judging women.

His first wife had barely said "I Do" when the hunger pangs developed and her weight sky-rocketed to Hindenburg proportions. The second wife was thin, beautiful and bi-polar. The third wife was twenty-five years younger than him. When she realized that he could not party all night and work all day, she left him for a traveling backup band trying to make a name for itself. The local group, Slip Knot, had inspired many bands of lesser talents to seek the road to the big time. She admitted as she left for the next road trip that she could not resist the rhythm of the drummer.

"Scott, does this process involve all of the tepee creeping I have heard about?"

"Unfortunately, the legends are likely larger than the reality. Most of these riders are here for the fun of a long, relaxing journey with friends and family and all the camaraderie of traveling with fifteen thousand partying people."

"However, there are a few, like myself, with diminished moral values, who do try to seduce any young female that feels the constant movement of the bike seat has created an itch that needs scratched."

I bent over with laughter and Scott got us another beer.

"I do have a little issue to deal with at the start of this trip. I had a good thing going at the end of last year with two ladies from Omaha, who rode with Team Skunk. We have stayed in touch and my evil mind has already laid out an agenda of debauchery. I hope I do not have to make a selection as they are both way above my league. I've sent them my agenda for the first few nights and have not yet received a rejection letter."

After another beer Scott continued, "Here is the problem. Last year, I was really shitty the way I was talking about my runaway teenage wife and women in general. On the last night of the trip, I was railing about women and how I never want to be involved again. Unfortunately my audience was a group of men from Team Gay Blades. I realized too late they thought I was gay when one of them hit on me. I gave him a line about being tired and went to bed. I've gotten a couple calls from him, and he has seduction on his mind and on my behind. I have to shut him down as soon as we hit Onawa. This might get ugly. He was not bashful about the activities he had in mind."

Scott's predicament was side-splitting. We both howled with laughter about the different scenarios to end his budding gay relationship before it ever started. Pretending the two of us had just come to Iowa and got married seemed to be Scott's best resolution. I pulled the plug on that idea when he suggested I wear a wedding veil when I was introduced.

"How about being direct? Just tell him you're saving your little unit for a couple of young Skunks. If that fails, fight. If you need help, I would hold his panties and bra."

From Scott's size, build and scarred eyebrows, I would bet on him in any brawl.

After three sweaty hours and three ice cold beers, we arrived at Onawa, a town of approximately five thousand people nestled in the Missouri River Valley at the base of the Loess Hills. The surrounding area was flat and totally covered by booming grain crops. As I got off the bus, I could not help but feel intimidated as I looked east towards the Loess Hills. These monstrous-sized hills were deposited by glaciers and winds thousands of years ago. They appeared extremely ominous as the setting sun reflected on their multi-angled slopes of various shades of green.

They appeared like mini mountains jumping up four to eight hundred feet from a flat plain. Their rich loess soil was deposited from sixty to two hundred feet in depth. Only in China are there loess hills possessing this depth of loess soil. The continuous tree covered bluffs were scarred by steep, water-created valleys that made them look impassable. They looked like an obstacle to bike around, not bike over to the eyes of this novice rider. Who says Iowa is flat? What had I gotten into?

The Harmons stressed to me that the goal of arriving early to the kick-off site was to meet old friends, relax, tell lies and rekindle friendships and affairs. I did not have any old friends or affairs to rekindle, so I put on my team shirt and started to mill about, trying to blend in with another ice cold Miller High Life in my fist.

The smells were akin to a county fair: barbecued pork ribs, braised beef, frying hamburger, funnel cakes and fresh pastries mixed with the pungent odor of freshly tapped beer and an occasional sweet, lingering haze of pot. The town's, eight lane wide center street, self-proclaimed as the widest center street in the state, was filled by the crowd of thousands. Everywhere I looked, I saw old friends embracing and smiling, even as the sweltering heat caused their jerseys to become soaked with sweat.

I moved to the west end of the square where the sound of Buddy Holly filled the air at deafening levels. Buddy's tragic death at Mason City, Iowa, after performing at The Surf in Clear Lake made his music a natural for the kickoff event. Everyone sang in unison when "Peggy Sue" and "That Will Be the Day When I Die" were played. The dancing was building in numbers and volume as the beer flow increased. To a sweaty, sober, alone, single, sixty year old, it looked more like a form of a tribal ritual than rock and roll dancing.

I knew this trip was going to be good when three female members of Team Nude stripped and started doing pole dances on the three flag poles flying flags for RAGBRAI, Iowa and USA. Their gymnastic skills were admired by every keen eyed male in the area.

God, it was great to see young people who are not afraid to show off their skills.

As I wandered around, my jersey logo, "Stop Me If you Want A Slow Poke" got me three female requests for more details, as well as one clear offer as to where I could put my slow poke from an offended boyfriend.

As I was grabbing a tenderloin sandwich and beer, I saw Scott talking to a very tall animated blonde man in a cute purple bike outfit. The younger, taller man was red in the face and was shaking a long finger in Scott's face. In a flash, the man was on his knees in pain as Scott had dislocated his shaking finger in one quick twist. Scott leaned over and said something as he walked away with two Team Skunk ladies by his side.

Obviously, Scott had successfully mediated his problem. Sometimes when logic, wit and charm fail, pure mean brute force is the only logical answer.

As the night cooled, I went back to the bus and erected my small tent and unrolled my sleeping bag, feeling more like a boring old man than a party animal. I poured myself a big glass of Crown Royal and laid back and gazed at the stars which appeared larger and brighter than I remembered. They sparkled like small beacons in the nearly black sky.

I started to sink into my "pity me" mood, but I took control and commanded myself to look ahead for adventure and not look back on what couldn't be changed. The Crown Royal burned in a pleasing way, and I settled down to rest for tomorrow. In the distance, the sounds of Dion and the Belmonts, Little Richard, Elvis, and Bobbie Vee endlessly filled the night with their classic sounds.

THE SOUNDS OF BIKERS TALKING, LAUGHING, AND JOKING AS THEY BROKE CAMP TO START THE FIRST DAY JARRED ME FROM A VERY GOOD DEEP SLEEP. The cheers, moans, and chatter filled the cool crisp morning air. I was excited. I checked all my gear and double checked my bike. I put on my jersey, slipped on a sleeveless wind breaker and put the mandatory Butt Balm cream in the appropriate places. I quickly devoured two fresh homemade donuts, compliments of Helga, who had found a family bakery open for the event. A large cup of OJ laced with vitamin B-12 left me wired and ready. I reviewed with Dale and Helga where I would locate the team bus at the day's end and left with my adrenaline pumping.

The first ten miles were extremely flat. Each side of the road was filled with the deep green of corn and bean crops producing never-ending record levels. Occasionally, the green was contrasted by golden oats and even deeper green six foot tall waving pampas grasses that lined the many drainage ditches.

Pampas grass was leftover from the pre-settler days when, according to my grandparents, it created a nearly impassable barrier to this land. Its wiry root system ran deep and spread wide as it grew in density. In early settler days, it formed a natural barrier to passage, except for paths created by the waves of buffalo that migrated through this land.

As I pedaled along, mindlessly keeping up with the flow of fellow bikers, I could image the sight of a gigantic lead buffalo bull plowing with his head down, guiding his herd to an open grazing area. It was in these open areas where the shorter sea grass grew and provided a feast for the herd. This grazing area also provided a feast for my native ancestors who laid in wait for the easy targets of young tender bulls. Tonka would soon serve up a feast back at the campground and provide a winter blanket for the tribal marksmen.

The morning air was clean and carried with it the smell of the freshly cut alfalfa, fast growing corn and beans, and the nearly ripe oats. The humidity emitted from the many fast metabolizing plants was increasing in volume, but as yet it was very tolerable.

I was absorbed in this serene setting when the whirring sound of playing cards in bicycle spokes and the booming sound of Freddie Mercury and Queen's singing "We Are the Champions" roared by me. Fifteen huge men, sporting three day old beard stubble, and wearing an array of formals, tights and bras, and party dresses passed by at breakneck speed. I had just been passed by Team Drag Queen. The boom box, pulled in a cart behind the last bike, shifted to "Bohemian

Rhapsody" as they shot around the next curve.

As I rounded that same curve, I came upon a large tent by the road with over three hundred bikes strewn on the ground. The smell of pancakes, cooking bacon, coffee and sweet syrup filled the air. Naturally, the first vendor on the route had to be the Pancake Man. Under the tent, his operation was made up of a thirty foot long, metal conveyor belt which passed over numerous jets of blue flame. His cute, wholesome, farm girl assistants, with matching denim shorts and scanty halter tops, squirted pancake mix in rows of four at the start of the conveyor belt.

At the end of the conveyor, the Man himself flipped perfectly shaped pancakes onto the eager rider's plates already filled with freshly cooked bacon, hash browns and toast. Occasionally, he would display his skills and with a triple flip, deposit a hot cake onto the helmet of a boisterous patron or down the bra of an overly flirtatious female. I nearly stopped for a plate of those calorie-laden cakes, but the fear of eating too much and getting sick carried me on to the next stop.

My first stop for food was in the small town of Turin. The entire population of seventy- five citizens lined the main street and waved at the thousands of zany bikers' costumes and slogans. I stopped at a once proud block building bearing the chiseled name, Turin State Bank. A fresh baked cookie and coffee for one dollar was impossible to pass up.

One aged, tall, thin citizen came over to me. He was dressed in bib overalls and a red plaid short sleeve shirt.

"By the way you are gawking you have never seen a near ghost town."

"Sorry, I didn't mean to insult your town. It has such a stately bank and a great looking B&B; it's hard to understand why it is drifting into the dust."

"This town was like a hundred others. It was created as a railroad stop and grain pickup site. When the tycoons in Chicago moved the railroad to better routes, no one found alternative business. As time passed, more people started to drive away to work; then they just moved away. The town disintegrated like a rock falling apart; very slowly."

"For something unique, you might follow that young lady heading north on the dirt trail to the Turin Gravel Pits." He pointed at a lone rider with his long arthritically deformed finger.

"They've found some very interesting prehistoric bones in those pits, I am told. In fact, it has been the site of a lot of exploration lately. They found bones of a giant Jefferson ground sloth, a mastodon, dire wolf, musk-ox and river otter. We have people stay at the B&B all summer to go up there and pick around to see what treasures they can find."

He sipped deep on his coffee. "That rider headed north on that dirt trail is writing a book on the Loess Hills and how they were created. I think she said her name was Cornelia Mutel. She said she called these hills Fragile Giants in her book. Apparently the development of these hills is quite a mystery. Whether the seas, the wind or the glaciers created them is the topic of a big debate among the geologists.

Between sips he pondered, "Guess I never wondered how they came about, but they sure are interesting."

"I think I will pass on the dig, but thanks for the history," I said.

I looked at his proud face and searched for something positive to say about his town. I was at a loss, so I just shook his hand, said good bye and bought another cookie. What a terrible feeling it must be to be trapped in a dying town without a way out or the desire to move on before it collapses.

As I left Turin, I noticed with some concern that the closer I got to the Loess Hills, the more they looked like impassable mountains looming ominously in front of me.

Suddenly, the road rounded a corner and instead of climbing a mountain, we were biking up a broad, gradually sloped valley. I was elated that I didn't have to try to ride over those monsters. The valley was at least three miles wide and was filled with impressive crops. On each side, the hills jutted up hundreds of feet with steep cliffs and tree-lined crests. We biked on a decaying highway paralleling a river that had ages ago decided to follow the valley downstream to the Missouri River.

After eight miles, I caught up with a group of ten ladies who were pedaling at a leisurely pace. All were in very tight blue riding shorts and red bras. They were what I would politically correctly describe as full-bodied. The sound of Rickie Nelson's "Party Girl" came from their mobile boom box affixed on the rear of a tandem bike. They were all purposely overly made-up, wearing gaudy items of jewelry and sported exaggerated fluffed and back-combed hair styles. For the first time in four decades, I saw a couple of beehive hair-dos.

While they were large framed, they did not appear obese and, in fact, were attractive despite their over the top handiwork. As I passed them, I heard and memorized a few offers as to where to meet that night for a slow poke. I had just met Team Bittie Bitches. They may have been bitches, but they weren't bittie.

As I approached the small town of Castana, I heard the sounds of the Iowa-raised Everly Brothers songs from a mile away. I had to be careful as I weaved through the crowd as over a thousand of their bikes were strewn randomly on the ground. The two local taverns were operating at standing room only capacity. The local park beer garden was in full operation at 9 am.

The local sandwiches were impressive. I gave in and had a freshly barbequed steak sandwich covered with fried peppers and onions and a Miller. Like a voyeur, I watched the crowd quickly fill a freshly erected dance floor adjacent to the bandstand in the park. The dancers were instantly engaged in various modes of dancing, grinding and near copulating to the rhythm of the Shenandoah, Iowa, Everly's "Wake-Up Little Susie."

As I was absorbing the activities around me, a buzzing sound entered the town. Team Killer Bees had arrived. Forty riders, all in black with gold striped uniforms, complete with antennas on their helmets and stingers attached to the rear of their biking shorts, came to an immediate stop. They were right out of the SNL John Beluchi skit.

The swarm quickly surrounded three members of Team Nude and humped and bumped them with animalistic enthusiasm. The human swarm on signal stopped, left the three victims and biked away in pursuit of another victim. The stung girls were all covered with fake tattoos and stickers in some very sensitive and intimate areas announcing, "I've been stung by a killer bee, and I loved it."

As I stood by my bike sipping the rest of my Miller High Life and laughing at the Killer Bees attacks, I felt a sharp sting on my left buttock. I turned and I found myself surrounded by eight beauties who were all dressed in black spandex shorts and very tight, deep cleavage cut black bras. They were all well over fifty years old, perfectly made up, tanned and sporting drop dead bodies with ample, but likely augmented, breasts filling the cups of their bras. I had just met Team Black Widow.

This was looking like a great day!

I looked down to see the reason for the sharp pain. Its source was a spider headed pin attaching a sticker to my rear pronouncing that I had been stung by a Black Widow. They all laughed at the surprised look on my face. A small, dark haired cutie wearing at least one hundred thousand dollars of diamond baubles around her neck and on her ears came up and nuzzled against my wounded rear.

Rita Keyes, with the sweet voice of a teenage virgin, whispered that if I wanted to survive, I would need to be at the Black Widow RV by six o'clock in order to have the venom removed. I gave her my cell number and wrote hers on my hand. I assured her that I wanted to live and would be there with plenty of time to spare in order to have the proper examination and treatment for the venom. They rode away giggling like teenagers.

I pinched myself in the area of my wound to make sure this dream was real. An old mans fantasy had come true.

The rest of the day passed quickly as I rode mindlessly over some very steep hills, anticipating the night's stop and a rendezvous with the Black Widows. As I neared Wall Lake, I caught up to Helga Harmon.

Helga said. "Glad you're still with us. Those hills from Battle Creek to Wall Lake were terrible. They go up four hundred feet and immediately drop to a valley. You really learn how to operate your bike's twenty-one gears and build up your leg muscles."

"We're coming up on Wall Lake. It has about eight hundred residents. It's like a lot of these towns; dying, but proud. Its claim to fame is the Williams Brothers who travelled all over Iowa in the fifties. Eventually, Andy broke off and became a big hit. He talks nostalgically about his home town, but like all escapees from these dying towns, he is glad he got out."

Helga continued. "These people are so nice; they are hard working, honest and friendly to a fault. But here they are stuck in a town where the passing of this gaggle of idiots on bikes is the biggest event of the year."

Riding with Helga was like riding with a tour guide for Iowa. She was a tall, large woman with big shoulders, a red Norwegian complexion, blue eyes and long blond hair which was always in a long pony tail. She was a loving lady who had really taken me under her motherly wing.

"We're coming up on our first overnight stop at Lake View. This town was originally called Fletcher after one of its founders, James Fletcher. He was quite an early settler entrepreneur. He cut a deal with the railroad to allow him to build a railroad siding at this location and precluded others nearby from having similar stops. He selected this location because of Black Hawk Lake, a deep glacial lake. It's named after the Indian chief who terrorized and dominated this area for years before Iowa became a state."

Despite my warm feelings for Helga, I became extremely bored with history lessons after hearing about the twenty various Indian wars and broken peace treaties that impacted this area. My great grandmother was a Winnebago tribe member, and I had heard the other side's version of this story.

I politely told Helga to go on ahead and I would catch up as I desperately needed to stop to use one of the blue outdoor toilets at a rest stop. I picked the longest line filled with female users to assure that Helga had a long lead.

"Sweet, but boring," I thought to myself as I watched her ride away.

My mind was not into history lessons, but was more focused on lust and debauchery with the Black Widows. Like most men, my brain was now clearly located in my biking shorts, and it was operating in high gear, despite being sweaty and covered with Butt Balm.

Chapter Seven

****

AFTER BEING STUNG BY A CUTE SPIDER, MY ADRENAL GLAND
WAS RAPIDLY PUMPING AND MY TESTOSTERONE LEVEL WAS
INCREASING BY THE MINUTE. My male ego had been gently
stroked and brought back to life. The rest of the day and seventy-five
miles went by quickly; my imagination was functioning in high gear.

After arriving at the final stop for the day at Lake View, I grabbed
an ice cold beer and fell on the ground in exhaustion. I had never felt
more relaxed and alive. I quickly engaged in the Slow Poke members'
day-end ritual of exchanging stories of the day on the trail. Everyone
tried to top the prior story and the good humor and banter was
nonstop.

I won the award for the grossest event when I told them about how
the Mutton Man had seduced me to his tent with his slogan; "You ain't
seen nuttin till you tried our mutton." The fried mutton chop, coated
with mint jelly, had mixed slowly in my stomach, combining with the
steak with peppers and onions sandwich, cookies and beer.

The combination erupted in my intestines like a pipe bomb. I
had jumped into a corn field just before the eruption occurred. As I
emerged from the five feet tall corn field wearing an embarrassed smile,
I saw four other riders exiting the same field with the same sheepish
look. I made a note to suggest to my doctor friends that mutton, beef,
onion, peppers, cookies and beer can be a great laxative before a colon

examination.

It was good planning by the RAGBRAI committee to have cornfields located very near to the roads.

I became a best friend in a day to the Slow Pokes. Iowa people are unique in the way they open up and welcome you into their lives. When I gathered enough energy to clean up, I wobbled towards the makeshift showers hanging from the Slow Poke bus. Dale apologized that they had nearly used up the sun-warmed shower water held in several twenty gallon, black plastic containers.

He didn't realize my goal was not to relax with warm water, but to invigorate myself for a long night. The cold shower was wonderfully energizing. Now all I had to do was find the Black Widows. I decided to kick back and wait.

I dozed off as I lay on my sleeping bag, listening to the young boy's afternoon riding experience behind Team Nude. He was as excited as the day he saw his first Penthouse magazines centerfold.

When my cell phone buzzed, I jumped awake from my nap. A soft sexy voice announced that the Spider's lair was open for visitors and told me the location. I hopped on my bike and said a quick farewell to the Slow Pokes.

There is no fool like an old fool.

The Spider's lair was a far cry from the Slow Poke bus. It was a fifty foot long converted Greyhound bus, painted black with several spider logos on each side. Outside the main door to the bus, affectionately labeled "The Spidermobile", were two tables set with white linen. They displayed several platters of cheese, salami, and fruit placed between multiple large scented candles. Several vases of freshly picked wildflowers and multiple bottles of Belvedere Vodka and La Crema wines resting in silver ice buckets provided the setting with a Martha Stewart touch.

The real eye-catching aspect of this scene was the Spiders themselves. They were all dressed in fresh black shorts, tailored perfectly to display their well trained and tanned legs, and very sheer black blouses. Not a bra in sight.

I am sure that I looked like the little boy in "Willy Wonka" who discovered the final Wonka bar gold certificate as I pedaled into a man's version of Toys R Us.

As I dismounted from my bike, I received a soft long hug and a nice wet kiss on the cheek from Rita. She introduced me to her good friends, Mona Lee and Carole Picket. We then commenced the ritual of getting to know each other while downing a couple ice cold vodkas and some snacks.

Unfortunately two six foot five inch tall younger men arrived. One was tanned, and blue eyed with nearly white hair. His right hand sported a finger in a splint. I recognized him as Scott Norris's antagonist from the night before. The other hunk was dark, tanned to an even deeper hue, with brown eyes and jet black shoulder length hair. They were very well muscled and the six pack muscles of their abs were obvious.

Carole seemed almost giddy and announced she needed to see her new masseuse for a scheduled back rub and darted to the side of the dark haired young hunk. I watched the blonde talk to a few of the Spiders, and then he disappeared when a couple of extremely muscled chaps from Team Gay Blades road up.

Rita and I wandered over to a tree trunk bench and sat down. She was flirtatious and charming. Her near black eyes danced. Her wavy, dark, long hair flitted. Her artificially plump perfect lips outlined with red lipstick were seductive. It was impossible to keep my eyes off the see-through black blouse and the ample mounds that were struggling to erupt through the material.

I checked to make sure I wasn't drooling or gazing too long. A drooling old man would not be cool.

In a few minutes, I learned that Rita was the widow of a local attorney who I had known by reputation. He bought real estate on a down cycle in the eighties and sold it all in the nineties to a REIT that fortunately paid too much. He and Rita were social animals. They never missed a gala or benefit program. Unfortunately, his smoking, hard drinking, lack of exercise and bad genes caught up to him.

Paul Keyes had died two years ago while having sex with his young secretary. Likely, Rita's enthusiasm for life, hard partying and endless libido helped hasten his early demise. The strain of keeping up with a twenty year old secretary's needs clearly had added to his stress. He had left Rita mad and embarrassed, but a wealthy lady. She was zealously devoted to keeping her body, face and attitude young. She was clearly succeeding.

I devoted very little time to explaining about myself as my lust meter was registering high. She surprisingly knew quite a lot about me, including my approximate age. She was most complementary which, of course, was well received by a lustful old fart. As we were talking, I noticed the dark haired young stud and Carole disappear into the Spidermobile. The fact that he had his hands down the back of her shorts and her hand was on his crotch as they walked together was convincing proof that this was not a trip for a simple massage. This massage would be nose to nose and toes to toes.

I jumped with a sharp pain on my penis. I looked down to find the source was another spider headed pin with its customary announcement of being stung by a Black Widow. Rita was giggling and had a coy teenage virgin smile on her face.

"You realize you could die if that venom is not removed quickly? I am very good at venom removal. Would you like to follow me and I will save your life?"

I nodded like a bobble doll.

We entered one of the Spidermobile bedrooms. It consisted of a wall to wall bed covered in black silk sheets and topped with brilliant red pillows. There were scented mood candles already placed on the shelf opposite the fully mirrored wall located at the foot of the bed. I could hear Carole moaning down the hall. She was really enjoying the massage.

Suddenly Rita was out of her clothes and had commenced to suck the venom out of my wound. I realized I was very lucky to have had a trained medical expert present to handle this delicate procedure.

Altogether too soon, the venom was removed. With an extremely soft touch she rubbed my aching legs and back. As I lay back soaking in the smells, feels, tingles and emotions of the moment, I knew that an enthusiastic payback was expected.

With Rita's nurturing touch in all the right places, I was able to accommodate her expectation. I lost track of her orgasms as she was the most physically active sex partner of my life. I was glad there wasn't a trampoline or swing set nearby as Rita would have developed a use and my aging spine was not up to the stress.

The process went on all night and I was proud of my

performance.

Who needs those little blue pills?

For men, sex acts like a tranquilizer. I was dead asleep when I heard the Spiders chattering and giggling outside as they prepared to start the day. I quickly dressed and headed towards the Slow Poke bus in order to start the day with my team, as was the custom.

I gulped down a pint of water to replenish my low fluid level, grabbed a granola bar and banana and hit the trail. I felt like a fifteen year old who had just lost his virginity at a church camp. I wanted to brag, but had no one who cared. I slowly mounted my bike to start the day's sixty-mile leg, committed to consuming only healthy foods, fruit drinks, wheat laden juices, vitamin B-12 supplements and power bars.

Midway through the morning, I broke my healthy and unrealistic commitment. I stopped to make the acquaintance of the Pork Chop Man. I rationalized that a little protein would be good for rebuilding testosterone. His hoarse voice could be heard for miles away, calling the riders to his red school bus decorated with white pictures of hogs in various forms of play. The smell of the burning corn cob fire and barbequed chops drifted for miles. The aroma had the riders salivating like Pavlov's dog when they topped the highest hill where his operation was located for the day.

I downed one of the ½ pound chops and bought another for later in the day. I justified the second chop. I knew I needed more protein intake as I would, with a little luck, be called upon to render another nocturnal gymnastic performance.

Other than my rationalized stop with the Pork Chop Man, I ate and drank like a monk on a pilgrimage to the Holy Land until the day-end party, which was traditionally located at the last town before the day's final stop. By the time I arrived, over two thousand bikers surrounded the location at a four building town called Sly, Iowa.

This near ghost town consisted of three homes and a single story brick-sided bar with a sagging roof in a nearly collapsed state. The town was surrounded on all sides by tall, deep green waving corn fields. People of all ages and shapes were dancing on the grounds behind the bar, the sagging roof of the bar and the top of their RV's, vans or bus's which encircled the bar.

On top of the roof danced the fabled Chicken Man. He was a

thin young man with no shirt, tight biking shorts, and a rubber cap that was shaped like a rooster's comb. He held a beer in each hand as he danced down the sagging roof line to the rhythm of Louie-Louie. Unfortunately, he did not see the roof's end and fell feet first into a bright blue portable toilet.

Everyone held their breath till one hand emerged holding up a beer bottle swinging to the rhythm of the music. A mother somewhere must surely be proud.

The temporary plastic water slide down the hill behind the bar was in heavy demand as the icy water was a welcomed relief from another sweltering day with over ninety degree temperature and eighty degree humidity.

All of a sudden, everyone made room for the tall, bald, portly nude man and a shapely nude sixty year old, bleached blonde as they hit the slide hand-in- hand. Her erect nipples and his nearly hidden penis were vivid proof of the cold temperature of the slide water.

Everyone cheered with gusto at each of their several trips down the one hundred foot long slide. Love is always something to cheer.

The sounds of Freddie Boom-Boom Cannon, Del Shannon and Sam Cooke blasted across the dance grounds, carrying for miles across the waving green crops. The riders were tired, but the day's end was near and they were just getting their second breath. I watched for a few minutes and was about to move on as dancing did not interest me.

Besides, I had lust in my heart and on my mind.

My interest in dancing suddenly escalated when I saw the Black Widows in the center of the dance area. I put on my best rock and roll moves and danced into the fray, heading directly towards the Black Widows. I must have been pathetic, as Mona saw me trying to do The Twist while moving in their direction, and took pity on me. She quickly dragged me into a line dancing to the "Oh Macarena" song. Even I could follow the choreographic moves of that song. I was also equally adept at the Village People's YMCA song with all its moves symbolizing the letters of YMCA.

Rita saw my pathetic efforts and broke away from a crowd of young law students from Team Justice for All. Their puzzled looks at being abandoned when Rita chose to come over to the gray haired, awkward dancer were priceless. I think they were after more than justice with

Rita.

Never trust lawyers, especially horny young lawyers.

After an hour at Sly, I had it with my feeble dancing skills and left. I hoped Rita would remember my parting whisper to call when she had arrived in Fort Dodge. She was amazing as her energy was endless. A mile from the final stop, I caught up to Team Slow Poke. I received my daily history lesson from Helga.

"This once booming town has been slowly decaying. It was initially built as a protective fort for people attempting to settle and develop this area when the western land rush occurred in the 1840's. More than a few Scandinavian settlers frequently sought safety in the old fort from the Sioux and Winnebago warriors who claimed this area, until they signed treaties giving it away.

Helga hardly slowed down as we climbed a steep hill. "The town developed into a rail center for meat packing and grain processing. Many ancillary service and agri-manufacturing businesses developed. As the union meat packing industry in the 1970's became over priced, the trend of closing plants and moving to non-union sites descended with brute force on Fort Dodge. The climb back is very slow, but these proud people were determined, just like the early settlers."

Like the first night, after a cold shower and a couple of beers, I was falling asleep during my history lesson about tomorrow's stops when my cell phone vibrated. I politely told Helga I had to see a new friend, and she winked as I quickly mounted my bike for a rendezvous with lust.

When I arrived, the same party was in process. Rita and I had a drink and a nice tight hug and laughed about the day's events. With a cute smile and stoke of my cheek, she suggest that I might be well advised to consider some dancing lessons if I went on the trip again.

I winked and said, "I have always relied on natural rhythm, not style."

"That's obvious. But your rhythm is set for the Samba mode, not rock and roll. Attempting to do the Peppermint Twist to a Samba beat gives away your age. Forget dancing; let's do something else to test that natural rhythm you're so proud of!"

I might be old, but I'm not slow. I recognized a great invitation that I could not possibly turn down. I promised her to work very hard on my rhythm in order to live up to her expectations. With a seductive smile from Rita, we grabbed another drink and moved away from the crowd towards the RV.

I was bothered when I saw the same tall dark stud moving in the same direction with his hands again down the back of Carole's biking shorts. Young, muscled and handsome males can be intimidating competition when viewed through sixty year old male eyes.

My only solace was I had years of cunning, lying, and trickery at my disposal, and they were all valuable assets in the art of seduction.

Rita and I spent another night in the RV. I tried very hard to keep up with her agile moves and energy. Her pilates, yoga and stretching lessons gave her a definite advantage. I even tried snuggling to gain a few minutes of recovery time. If there was a score board and judges were ranking our performances, Rita was near a clear ten, and I was likely a struggling five.

The same process unraveled on the third night. However, I was exhausted from riding in the heat and humidity. My ass and balls were sore. My crotch felt like I had sandpaper in the lining of my biking shorts as a result of three days on the bike seat, despite ample butt balm. I knew my performance was less than impressive; my testosterone tank was registering empty. The fourth night I laid in my tent and hoped the call would not come as all I wanted was sleep. The call never came. Never make a wish, as it might be granted.

THE TOWN OF WAVERLY WAS OUR FOURTH STOP. The day had been a repeat of the others as it relates to the scenery, rolling hills, laughing people and hospitable small towns.

I had drifted mindlessly into the riding process. My mind felt clear and mellow and my aching body was getting used to the rhythm of the trail. My body now rode mechanically; legs pumping with a steady rhythm, back arched forward at a proper angle to avoid pain and provide power, eyes ahead ten yards to check for obstacles and hands shifting gears without thinking as the grade changed.

God was I at peace!

As I lay on the ground, supported by my rolled bedding, sipping a cold beer after a cold shower, I mused about the call that never came from Rita. I think I was more relieved than rejected. Helga sat by me, sipping her first beer and nibbling on an apple as she gave me the daily lesson about this location.

"Waverly is the county seat for Bremer County and has over nine thousand proud citizens. The homes feature many stately stone block buildings. Wartburg College looks more like a series of castles than a college. It is named after a castle located in Eisenach, Germany, a sister city of Waverly. In the 1840's, Iowa was being settled and Waverly was a safe site for brave settlers. Chief Black Hawk, in the war of 1839, was forced to sell the area."

Helga paused for a deep sip of ice cold beer. "When Iowa became a state, it cleared the area of the Winnebago Indians and moved them to Long Prairie, Minnesota. This tribe could never stay peaceful and never picked a winning side. It was forcefully moved four other times. Today the Winnebago tribe resides at a reservation in Nebraska overlooking the Missouri River. They are trying to recapture their wealth one card at a time through a local casino."

Helga left me alone while she created a healthy dinner of salad and fried chicken. She was slightly miffed that she had no takers on her offer to show them the first school built in 1858 and the cabins of early settlers, Frederick Cretzmer and William Harmon.

I settled back and deeply breathed in the evening air. I knew the relationship with Rita was ended. For this sixty year old guy, it had been a wonderful ego booster. But in reality, there wasn't much to talk about after a few nights, and I realized that younger guys brought more to her party than I could deliver, even in my own self-inflated dreams.

Facing this part of aging isn't for the insecure.

The next day Helga caught me by midday. She was anxious to deliver her route guide wisdom earlier than usual.

"We are coming up on Oelwein. It was founded in 1872 when the Rock Island Railroad located a site to allow its trains to take on coal and water on the farm of Gustav Oelwein. By the turn of the century, its population was over five thousand citizens. It was a rail center with its own round house where trains could be redirected to various route. It was a grain collection and packing house center. When the union packing houses were closed and the farm crisis descended, the town collapsed."

"This past winter, I read a lot of news articles about the

methamphetamine industry in small town Iowa. At first, I thought it was the product of some young liberal news writers' over-exaggerated imagination. This spring at an Iowa Writers Work Shop event for budding historical writers, I met a young writer named Nick Reding who had spent a couple years in Oelwein gathering facts for a book he was writing named "Methland."

"He contended that Oelwein and Ottumwa were huge manufacturing centers for meth. Meth manufacturing in small towns is easy. One key ingredient, ammonia based fertilizer, is readily available. In addition, access to the other main ingredients, Sudafed and Contact, were equally easy, as their sale in small towns was seldom regulated."

"It doesn't take a PhD in psychology to conclude that combining the availability of such key material with a populace that is depressed, trapped, without hope and poor, is a lethal combination. Nick allowed me to read an early draft of his book. These two Iowa towns were not unique, but they were examples of the rural country town's decay and frustration and the spread of the meth epidemic."

I kept Helga's graphic description of the meth problem in mind when I entered Oelwein later that day. I knew quite a little about Nazi Gold, the most popular and available meth. I had watched the son of a dear client drift helplessly into a mind-numbed state. The sudden rush of pleasure as endorphins are released in mass by the drug effect creates an instant addiction that is hard to shake. No one tells the user about bleeding skin sores as pores open up to expel the drug, vast areas of the brain depleted of neurotransmitters, internal organs shrunken from dehydration or endless bouts with hallucinations and paranoia.

I rode into town and quietly stopped at the Do Drop Inn Tavern. There were a few riders in a booth having a mid-day Bloody Mary to drive away the demons from the previous night's parties. But they were extremely quiet. Several locals sat at the bar, totally uninterested in the RAGBRAI process and the participants who were in their bar. Their long deep stares, twitching eyes and sniffing noses were unnerving. I left when I computed the teeth to tattoo ratio was one for one. This was no country for an old man.

I WAS ENTHUSED THAT THE LAST DAY HAD ARRIVED. THE FINAL DAY'S TRADITIONAL TIRE DIPPING CEREMONY AND

CLOSING DAY PARTY WAS NEAR.

I was tired, sore and worn out. Scott Norris however felt like his already powerful legs were akin to pistons in a racing engine. He never thought of the pedaling process. His legs simply reacted and drove him by other riders. He ascended the steep hills entering Dubuque with several lower gears unused. He descended those same steep hills at break-neck speed approaching forty mph. The cool morning air and breeze caused an ecstatic adrenaline rush throughout his body. His endorphins were in high emission mode. He was exhilarated. This RAGBRAI trip had a rocky start with the finger twisting fight with the big, pissed off blonde man, but the past few days were extremely upbeat and unforgettable.

Norris was happy, his relationship with friends, both new and old, had grown. He had experienced a unique bonding event. He physically and mentally felt in his best condition in decades. It had been a long time since he had laughed so much and felt so accepted and unrestrained.

He had also found a lady that might be the real deal. She was a marketing executive at a local Des Moines bank. She was nearly his age, divorced, without children, attractive, confident and did not appear in need of a male relationship. This latter point was the main attraction. Scott vowed he was through with needy people.

The last slope up to the final hill into Dubuque was intense with a forty degree grade. As Scott topped the last hill, he waived as he passed me. I was in low gear working desperately to get to the top of the hill without a disgracing walk. The copse trees on his right side and sheer cliff on his left overlooking the majestic Mississippi River were breathtaking.

As he crested the hill, Norris spontaneously increased his pedaling rate and started downhill for the final rush to end the trip. Half way down the hill, he was reaching a level of speed that petrified even him. He simultaneously but gently squeezed the two handbrakes. NO. The rear brake lever went limp. He was in trouble. If he hit the front too hard he would cart wheel over the handlebars. He repeatedly tapped the front brake, trying futility to slow the increasing rate of speed.

From his left, he saw a dark gray blur fly in front of him directly into his front tire's spokes. Scott Norris's last vision of life was the sudden dramatic halt of his bike as the trash bag wrapped into his bike's spokes, abruptly stopped any forward movement. Instantly, he was airborne, flying weightlessly for thirty feet headlong over a two hundred foot high cliff to the Mississippi River's rocky shore below. As the rocks and sand rushed up at him, he gasped in deep gulps of air and rolled into a ball to desperately attempt to break the fall. He failed.

I HAVE NEVER KILLED A MAN, BUT I HAVE READ MANY OBITUARIES WITH A LOT OF PLEASURE.

Clarence Darrow

Chapter Eight

****

THE RISING SUN WAS SLOWLY CUTTING THROUGH THE EARLY MORNING FOG. Doug Valli sipped his carrot and apple juice mixture directly from his blender as he cooled down from an early morning run. He was over sixty and was fighting the inevitable aging process. Running five days a week at least five miles helped, but every day it was getting harder to force his muscles to make another mile. However, the sweat dripping down his body felt good as did the feeling of renewed strength in his wiry muscles.

The sun, attempting to penetrate through the humidity, created a pink morning sky as he looked out of the expansive picture window of his double unit sized townhouse at Owls Head overlooking the Water Works Park. These two story townhouses utilized a Frank Lloyd Wright design, so the natural wood colors blended perfectly into the landscape.

The massive trees below Doug's balcony combined with the bud-filled berms to form an unusually vivid spectrum of color variations for late May. The spring of 2009 had arrived early, and the grasses, in varied shades of green, were growing lush and thick. Large herds of deer slowly roamed through these grasses, free of any fear of predators or mankind.

Doug felt at ease. He was a complex man who had made a living in an unorthodox fashion. He was at peace here. The people he met quickly viewed him as a friend. They seldom probed about his background.

This capital city was filled with big community culture and small town values. Simple events, like farmers' markets, were well attended as people sold their prime produce, plants, cut flowers and calorie-laden, tasty homemade foods. High quality civic center programs came from Broadway and Las Vegas. Highly honored, well known artists from all over attended a world class art festival. This was a great place to fade into with a new life and freedom from detection.

Doug looked into his bedroom. The ultramodern bed, with its mesh webbed steel beam frame, supported an oversized king size mattress. A bright blue silk bedspread was nearly covering his new friend's body. Her finely-featured face was death-like still, except for an occasional contented sigh.

The offset overhead penlights from the ceiling displayed the bed and her, as if she was the focus of a stage. At the end of the bed sat four curved-back stainless steel chairs with bright red, blue, green and yellow cushions. They surrounded a four-by-four block of steel with varied shades of rust that served as a coffee table. The stark contrast of steel and the vivid colors of the accessories were a statement about the way he had led his life: strong, unbending, with a flair for the extreme.

As his young friend commenced to move about attempting to wake, he had a pang of guilt for taking advantage of a twenty-five year old farm girl. Quickly, without remorse, he got over the guilt and started to prepare breakfast. He knew he was too old to change.

Besides, the feel of a young lady beneath him made him feel young again, and the feel of one on top of him made him feel even younger.

With a series of precise moves that would have impressed Julia Childs, he cut up the onions and various types of peppers into precise-sized squares. He swirled the eggs into just a touch of sour cream, and then blended all of them. They were soon in a hot skillet and two omelets were under way. When finished, he carefully placed them into a warming oven.

He then moved to a room containing a large aquarium. The five hundred gallon glass tank of salt water was full of fish of multiple types that created a moving rainbow of colors. Beside the tank was a tropical rain forest tank with frogs, lizards and toads of varied types and colors moving among the ferns and algae. He quickly scooped up a purple dart frog, cut its head off and threw it into a sizzling pan. Within a minute it was cooked and the skin deftly removed. He put the skin in a small vile, and placed it into his travel bag.

When everything in the kitchen was cleaned, he tried to wake Mindy Browski. It was nearly time for her to get to her job at Principal Life Insurance Company.

She was like many young farm people who came to Des Moines: well educated in a small town school system, ready to work hard to succeed, unaware of what happened socially in the world outside a small town and full of energy and love of life. While she was naïve, she was striking; tall, long, straight black hair, deep brown eyes, freckles and a very firm athletic body.

Mindy's natural beauty and build were all fine virtues, but her endless appetite for sex was what made her so attractive to this horny old Sicilian. His guilty conscious was quickly disposed of and replaced by his own selfish needs. He kept reminding himself that he could never trust a young woman who said she found him attractive. That defied logic.

Every day he was amazed at her childlike thrill when experiencing new, fresh ideas, events and sensations that he had long ago experienced. Her flash of spontaneous love for life made him vicariously feel young. He knew their age difference likely doomed any long term relationship, but this time the feeling was unique. He had decided to follow the building relationship on whatever path it took him.

Besides, the sex was great, a real bonus for a man over sixty.

Despite a few gentle shakes, to arouse her, she simply would not move or awake. The night before had involved some very good red wine and creative sex. He took off his running gear and slipped his sweaty body next to hers. His hands caressed her back, rear and neck in an effort to wake her. She started to respond, and he also found himself responding. Soon they were entwined, and it was clear she would be late for work.

They showered and quietly ate a post-sex breakfast. She quickly readied herself, which wasn't hard when your beauty did not rely on heavy quantities of makeup. He dropped her off at the thirty-story headquarters building and proceeded to the airport. He had plenty of time.

He checked his tickets. His first stop was Chicago, then he moved to Miami and ultimately to Cabo San Lucas. It would be a full travel day, following indirect routes. He checked his multiple passports to make sure they coincided with the varied ticket names. Attention to detail had been his assurance of a long and prosperous life. He had plenty of time to relax, read and plan on how to best perform this vermin elimination project.

Today he would miss the golf game with his friends. He hated to miss the fun and the challenge, but he was beginning to hate the game. He was a natural athlete in every area. He had studied every part of this game. He knew every technique. Yet, he was still a hack. But in between consulting trips, he kept coming back for more frustration.

He made a quick call to a friend who knew a person who ran an RV rental operation and gave him the RAGBRAI dates. In a few minutes, the RV was booked as the owner saw the wisdom of cancelling a prior rental when he could make double the fee for this rental and also repay a favor to a well connected senior citizen.

MINDY ENTERED THE OFFICE WITH A POST-SEX SMILE. She loved growing up in Sioux, Iowa, but she also loved leaving it. She had been chased by every young stud in the county, but they all had the same goals: date her, screw her, get her pregnant and stay in the decaying area to raise a family. Mindy found this scenario far too boring.

Her brief fling with the local girls' softball coach, after the season ended, convinced her that this scenario must be created by a poison in the water. Coach Martin had provided her an education about sex with an older partner. However, she soon learned like most men, he was all macho talk, with a limited IQ and even less ambition.

She went to a local junior college and finished her marketing degree at Drake University. Since she had high grades and a high IQ, a job with Principal Life Insurance Company was not a surprise. This world-class company paid well, hired well and quickly promoted good people. She enthusiastically immersed herself into learning all about her new home, and soon she was involved as a volunteer in numerous civic projects and meeting many new friends. Small town Iowa was quickly viewed only in her rear view mirror.

At the Art Festival in June, Mindy was acting as a guide, leading tours of people in wheel chairs and walkers from a local care facility and explaining the art displays and the awards of the various artists. As she explained the perpetual metal movement art of Andrew Carson, she stumbled on a display tent anchor rope and catching her fall, bumped into a small, darkly tanned, well dressed gentleman. He caught her and broke the fall.

After a few polite comments about her near fall, he asked about her flock of very elderly patrons. He interjected himself when he assured her he would be delighted to tag along and give his insights on the various displays. His knowledge of art and artists dazzled the elderly groups, and his wit especially charmed the several blue haired ladies.

After the bus picked up her elderly flock, they had stopped for a couple glasses of wines. He was very particular on the type of wine, which was novel for her dates usually selected Budweiser or Millers. She had found his education and extensively witty discussion of the artists' work and their backgrounds fascinating. He was clearly not a product of education at Sioux High School.

They had several short dates to trendy bistros before the sex aspect of their relationship commenced. She could not remember if the first suggestion was his or hers. She admitted only to herself it was her idea, but she rationalized that he led her to that result with his seductive and suggestive comments. Clearly it was the horny, devious old fart's fault.

Where was this relationship going? He was still surprising her with new ideas, experiences and places. He was continuing to educate her about the world and world events. He read the paper for news, not just the sports page. He treated her with impeccable manners and respect. On top of it all, he smelled good, felt good, tasted good and performed at an amazing sexual level for someone nearly her dad's age. Life is full of surprises when you're young and naïve.

THE ONLY TIME MY PRAYERS ARE NEVER ANSWERED IS ON THE GOLF COURSE.

Billy Graham

Chapter Nine

****

AT TWENTY-FIVE MILES PER HOUR, THE BREEZE WAS TYPICAL FOR MAY. The sun was warm and the wind soughed through the many budding trees. The smell of freshly cut grass from the well-groomed golf course mixed with the pungent smell of freshly applied fertilizer. The sound of birds trilling and geese honking as they headed north combined with the Hispanic chatter of the busy grounds crew. It was a great golf day.

Despite the beauty of the day, I was still emotionally sour about Rita's death. Her funeral was two days away. My true reaction was not to go as it would leave me in a deep funk for days. I knew I would go. The closure concept of witnessing the funeral was a factor. The real truth was I wanted to say one last thank you to a person who deeply impacted my recovery.

Matt was gone, working on a new invention. Doug was off on another consulting trip. So the balance of our group, Lucas Waltz and Tim O'Brien, joined Morgan and me. Fresh money was always welcomed.

Lucas was a huge man, standing over six feet seven inches tall with a large frame, carrying a fit two hundred and fifty pounds. He always stood ramrod straight. He had a fair but well tanned complexion that fit perfectly with his close cropped blonde hair and deep blue eyes.

He would have made an Aryan poster child for the German Army in another time and place. He was always quiet about his past. He had a noticeable limp from a wound to his right leg and hip. He seldom spoke of how it happened; just that he had taken a nasty fall on an air excursion in Asia.

I had been his attorney for a long time, so I knew most of his background and respected his silence. He had served in the army as a consultant after his injury and during that time acquired a PhD in psychology. His research and writings on testing methods for the selection of leaders had earned him acclaim in the military and many consulting jobs after his army stint. He also had developed cutting edge material on psychological testing methods under various stress conditions. Those testing articles and methods led to periodic trips to the Pentagon on application issues regarding such tests. He was always quiet about his work.

He was a very complex person who had lost his wife a few years before on 9/11, and was very private about any new female relationships. With his friends, he was a constant source of new stories and jokes. Like all of us, he bragged and exaggerated a lot about his sexual prowess, but he never dropped names, just details.

He fortunately also had a good memory and only told the same story twice. Behind the jokes lingered a very lonely man who was struggling with what was the next chapter in his life.

Tim O'Brien was a retired logistics consultant. In the Air Force, he had mastered the art of mass movement of product in the cheapest and quickest fashion. Because efficiency and timeliness was not appreciated by many long term government employees, he left the military. He marketed his skills to many warehousing companies and producers. He found that he could make a fortune by working on a percentage of the savings or ownership in the company. Eventually, the demand for his time was overwhelming and his fortune grew beyond his expectations.

During one of his frequent trips, he came home early one evening. Unfortunately, he found his wife in her convertible, engaging in her newest novel improvement to deliver oral sex with the soccer coach of their two boys.

Urban legend has it that Tim's scream that he had a gun made a deep impression on the coach, as Mrs. O'Brien's mouth clamped shut like a bear trap. The coach, thereafter known as Coach Shorty, and Mrs. O'Brien ran off together, leaving Tim with two teenagers. He raised them and both were in professional schools.

For a considerable period of time, his bitterness towards women made him impossible to enjoy. A friendly intervention by his five best friends helped him focus on the future, not the past. He slowly stopped being so negative. Privately, we all decided he was out to punish the female gender by having as many affairs as possible and ending them just when the partner got serious.

His red hair and freckles, combined with his diminutive frame, made him look like a large Howdy Doody or Opey from Mayberry RFD. He was very competitive and an endless source of personal good-natured barbs.

Our golf game was its usual mix of great shoots followed by stupid ones. Our bad sportsmanship was the only consistent part of the game as we continued to set a new low in decorum for this gentlemen's game.

On the seventeenth hole, Luke killed a seven iron and put the ball in the center of the par three green which was one hundred and seventy yards away. Morgan and I both over-swung five irons and pushed our balls to the right, barely clearing the two acre sized sand trap in front of the green. Tim put his entire one hundred and fifty pounds into his five-wood only to see it gobbled up by a ten foot wide yucca plant in the middle of the sand trap.

"Those thorny spikes may hurt on your next back swing little fellow. Don't let one of them sting that little pecker of yours," giggled Morgan as Tim tried to find his ball, to no avail.

Tim gave up and left the hole for Luke to win.

Both Morgan and I chipped from off the green to within two feet of the pin. If you're a bad player and miss a lot of greens, you tend to become a good chipper because of the constant practice.

"Too bad Luke hasn't solved that awful case of the yips he had last week, he might make this putt," I commented to Morgan, just loud enough for Luke to hear.

Luke was intense, and he knew I was right. Under the exterior of his big athletic body was a yip-prone nervous system.

Luke gripped and re-gripped his hands to relax them for a smooth putting stroke. He promptly yipped as he touched the ball, and his five foot putt went eight feet beyond the hole.

Morgan and I had to turn our backs to avoid a display of childish laughter. We were good sports and congratulated him on making the third putt, which was at least two inches from the hole.

We were now tied, and the par five eighteenth hole would decide the day. Morgan and I both hit good drives. Luke killed his shot and it sailed over ours by fifty yards. Tim was beside himself and actually out drove both Morgan and me. His Howdy Doody smile was unusually irritating.

Morgan, Tim and I each laid-up short of the creek just in front of the green. Not Luke. He hit a five-wood onto the green two hundred and forty yards away. He promptly broke up in a fit of laughter as I dropped my shot into the creek in front of the green, and Morgan sailed his bladed shot over the green into an extremely difficult bunker. These acts of random stupidity would doom us to at least a bogie.

With a two putt performance from ten feet, Luke finished the game with a win. He wore a huge smile and was choking back a huge snicker. A big Nazi-appearing man trying to stifle a laugh can be totally obnoxious.

"Remind me, you two, where was it you got your short game lessons? I want to sign right up," giggled an obnoxious little Tim.

Ignoring Tim's repeated and stupid inquiries about my short game skill, I reached into my wallet, paid and moved to the 19th hole bar. Over an icy beer, we again discussed the RAGBRAI trip.

"I've worked out a four times a week riding schedule. We will work each week on short fast rides and then shift to developing stamina and trail-ready butts with a few long rides. If you can't meet these times, then train on your own. This is a great experience, but you need to be in shape to enjoy it."

"I thought this was more about parties, drinking and pussy?"

"Morgan, those are main attractions, but you have to be in shape to enjoy them. By the way, Doug left word he has the RV all arranged. He said it is loaded with extras. All we have to do now is find the nymphomaniac driver."

After a long cold sip, I said. "Incidentally, I've ordered the team jerseys. This is official. We are now Team Grey Geese."

I waited for their response with trepidation.

My name was promptly rejected and various alternatives suggested. I quickly rejected their suggested names like Big Dicks Dew Drop Inn, Tab A Looking for Slot B or You are Now Entering the Free Diddling Zone. None of them were acceptable for distinguished, sophisticated gentlemen our age. Besides, the jerseys were already ordered, complete with an extremely buff, well endowed gander on the back.

I explained to them how Nathan Wayne had given me the idea and gave them the short story about Nathan's research regarding Grey Geese. The guys seemed to accept my explanation. I made a mental note to never ask their opinion again on any issues about this trip.

Old men have too many irrelevant opinions, so why ask for them.

AFTER BEGRUDINGLY PAYING OFF MY BET, I LEFT. I went directly to the Painted Woods Spa to begin my exploration of what a spa day involved. The shopping area was made up of several clothing shops, restaurants, bars, art stores, a very high end furniture center, a coffee & blues house and very expensive jewelry stores. Its walkways wandered through an extremely large forest where the shops were located and designed to replicate small huts in an ancient forest. The area was filled with numerous smiling patrons grazing through this reclaimed forest filled with upscale goodies for all ages and tastes.

The warm, late spring gentle breeze and setting sun brought an extremely calm feeling to me; which was an unusual reaction after a day of bad golf.

Who really plays golf to relax?

As I entered the door to The Painted Woods Spa, the aroma of various creams, skin care products and herbs combined into a rush of scents. The sound of soft elevator music continued to set the mellow mood. I was greeted by the owner.

She was a forty year old general surgeon, turned entrepreneur, and doctor to the rich and beautiful. Dr. Shelly Keene was a family friend since she was very small. She was a very socially active person with three children, two dogs, a cat and a successful plastic surgeon husband. She was well dressed, poised and had a beautiful face, compliments of good genes, good care and a talented husband's handiwork.

With a sweet but professional voice Dr. Shelley started the tour.

"First, we will need to experience a tour of the spa in order to provide you with a feeling of the atmosphere of relaxation and tranquility we are trying to deliver."

We first stopped at the snack area. I had a choice of fresh fruits, dried fruits, sweet chocolate candy, petite pastries, herbal tea or wine. A nice cold Rombauer chardonnay was my choice.

"The clients' next moves to the changing area where they slip into a nice warm fluffy robe before they adjourn to the mood adjustment area."

In the mood adjustment area, I sat down in an overstuffed reclining chair and the dim lights, music and wine turned my body's metabolism down to turtle pace. The massage area was our next stop. Its private rooms all had their doors shut as patrons were being given a treatment. Other patrons were waiting and making their menu selections from a long list of various massages.

I noticed two tall, attractive blonde female massage therapists energetically discussing the virtues of the different types of massages to their waiting clientele. The owner's husband's surgical efforts were impressive as both had near perfect faces.

Two tall, muscular male massage therapists were aggressively working on advising two smiling elderly ladies about a deep back rub. I immediately recognized the white haired and black haired therapists from my RAGBRAI encounter three years before.

As we continued to tour the massage treatment area, the fragrant smell of cinnamon candles and heated herbal-laden oils floated from each room. When these scents were combined with the gentle sounds of water gently cascading over rocks in an adjacent fountain, my nervous system reacted as if I had received a main vein Ambien. This area hooked me for more return visits, especially if one of the beautiful blonde therapists could undertake resolving my ever present tight muscles.

My dirty old man imagination was alive with possibilities.

We moved on to the manicure and pedicure areas. The therapists were busy plying their trade and every chair was filled with men and women with relaxed smiles, sipping a glass of wine or the spa's special herbal tea. The gurgle of water rapidly rushing through the foot basins like a spring brook added to the soothing atmosphere.

Dr. Shelley noted, "We make sure all the water is maintained at one-hundred degrees, and is fully charged with extra oxygen plus our own brand of disinfectant. We take extreme measures to avoid any distribution of fungus or germs between clients and to give the rooms that fresh sea aroma you just experienced."

An ocean smell in Iowa seems okay to me.

"The next stop is the medical procedures area. I can perform Botox injections to give you a perpetual smile and also fill in valleys and crags brought on by smoking, wind or bad genes. With a few chemical or laser treatments, I can painlessly strip away that old rough skin and those unsightly blemishes that you have developed."

She continued, "You could use a little happier look by eliminating the lines on your forehead and around your eyes. It also would be good to remove a few brown spots that distract from your natural good looks. I could knock off ten years in a couple of sessions."

I knew she was embellishing about the natural good looks, but I admired a good sales job.

"While I'm here, give me a quick permanent smile."

With eight quick well placed shots of Botox, she finished. The soft hands, gentle voice and smile made it a very easy process.

"Within a few days, the wrinkles over your eyebrows will disappear and the crow's feet by your eyes will also be gone as the muscles relax. You will be handsome for about four months, and then you will need to see me again as you will start to look old again over a period of time. Those muscles naturally retract to their former length. It has been my experience that the duration between treatments will increase as the muscles become more relaxed."

I was hooked. Who wants to look old, even if you are old?

We then set about planning a menu for a day at the spa for Team Grey Geese.

"I recommend your group starts with a massage with heated oil while they are lying on heated rocks, followed by a facial to relax their facial muscles, and conclude with a pedicure and manicure. Botox is optional. You name your choice of wine."

I agreed with the recommendations of my hostess and selected a good Napa Valley White Oak Red Blend. We then went to the front desk to schedule the events with a petite little blond who could have been my granddaughter. I was very businesslike as I knew any efforts at flirtation would come off like a feeble fool.

As I neared the scheduling area a couple of the therapists were dabbing at their eyes as they ended the day with a little gossip.

"We just lost a good client and long time friend to a sudden heart attack." Dr. Shelley gently whispered to me.

"Who?" I asked.

"An energetic little lady named Rita Keyes." Dr. Shelley said as she gently wiped at the tears in her beautiful deep brown eyes.

"This is the second unexpected death in the last several months. Rita's friend, Mona Lee, just past passed away last winter. They were both so full of life and appeared to be in great health. Life can be so very cruel. These two lovely ladies made a lot of people happy."

Including a lot of young men half their ages, I quietly thought to myself.

I again felt that rush of fear regarding my own mortality rekindle within me. Mona Lee had also been part of my extremely fond experiences on my first RAGBRAI trip. I must have been out of town, or neglected to read the diminutive sized newspaper, as I had not known of her death.

The coincidence of these two deaths puzzled me. The common thread was RAGBRAI, this spa and my sport diddling both of them on that same trip. I doubt the thrill of my performance had brought on their apparent heart problems.

I left the spa with the menu in hand, and my mind in a fog. I felt a sudden light-headed flush caused by a feeling of personal loss, and the uncomfortable reminder that death is just around the corner at any time at my age. These depressing emotions made me very uneasy when they combined with my naturally skeptical instincts concerning two similar sudden deaths to seemingly healthy women. It simply didn't make sense that it was just one of those things.

SEX WITHOUT LOVE IS MERELY HEALTHY EXERCISE.
Robert A. Henlein

Chapter Ten

****

AS I DROVE HOME, I COULD NOT LEAVE BEHIND THE SUBJECT OF ANOTHER UNTIMELY DEATH. I had very fond memories of Mona Lee. It was so hard to believe that the grim reaper could be so malicious and prematurely snuffing out such a vivacious woman. For the second time in two days, my own mortality smashed me in the face like the stunning impact of a subzero blustery winter's day in Iowa.

I recalled several years earlier when after three straight nights in the Spider's lair, and two hundred miles across rolling hills, my body wanted only rest and undisturbed sleep. I was both happy and disappointed that I had not received a call from Rita. I went to the nearest church food stand for a dinner of chicken and noodles poured over mashed potatoes. I ate a double helping and crashed in my tent.

I knew I had avoided what every guy dreams about, but my testosterone tank was registering empty. My butt hurt, my thighs burned, my back ached, my head pounded, and humidity had taken its toll. Boy, was I having fun?

The next morning, I was energized and hit the trail after listening to Helga's history and geography lesson for this leg of the trip. With a double treatment of Butt Balm on my crotch and a big jolt of espresso, my body was doing surprising well and the ride seemed effortless.

A few miles into the trip, I started to notice dead animals posed in various creative forms like statues on the road. They all had stickers attached to them announcing that "Team Road Kill had arrived." Their dead animal art work included a squirrel one foot wide and one inch thick from tire traffic, propped up and waving at passersby; a bloated fox with a cigarette in his mouth and anus; a pheasant with an Iowa State pennant under its broken wing and a rigor mortis rigid raccoon setting upright with three cigarettes in its mouth, sporting broken sunglasses and holding a sign that read, "cigarettes can be hazardous to your health."

Their imaginative efforts demonstrated their macabre humor.

After approximately fifteen miles, I caught up to Team Nude. Ten very attractive young ladies were leisurely pedaling in a V formation. All had on college tee shirts, and no panties. I knew it would be embarrassing to accelerate and ride past their formation. Like any red blooded, middle-aged male, I could not possibly keep my eyes looking ahead. So I picked the only logical alternative and fell in behind them, eyes straight ahead slowly, carefully selecting the winner of the "Lee Scott's Award for Best Buns on RAGBRAI."

Unfortunately, the male crowd behind Team Nude expanded as quickly as a teenage boy's pecker reading his first Playboy magazine. It was too crowded for my rookie riding skills, so I passed them trying to look straight ahead.

"Good morning ladies. Any good views ahead or are they all behind me?" I quipped.

Young girls are cute when they giggle at such a lame attempt at humor by an old fart.

I took a break at the next town when I saw eight older ladies dressed in farm wife attire, playing songs on various homemade instruments: washboards, a butter churner with strings, gourds, and spoons. They were singing country songs made popular by the Carter Family and Hank Williams during the still-remembered depression era.

Ottumwa, Iowa native actor, Tom Arnold, and his team were in the middle, engaging in each song with great gusto. Homemade breads and foods of all tastes were being sold by their church at several booths erected around the stage.

"Hey everyone, stop right here and buy a few homemade snacks. These lovelies are going to have a wet tee-shirt contest after the next song," yelled Tom.

Riders, like lemmings, stopped, bought and joined in the singing.

This entire ride was spiritually uplifting, despite my bitching about a few painful areas, i.e. my entire body. People were happy, healthy and filled with good humor towards each other. Small town people lined the street in Wal-Mart folding chairs, shouting encouragement and waving American flags as an entourage of celebrating riders passed through their town. Every town had the hose squirting boys and the homemade food stands, all provided with never-ending Midwestern smiles. It was easy to feel your attitude improve and your energy level increase.

When I arrived at Manchester's park, the Team Slow Poke camp area was all set up and was fully occupied. I quickly grabbed a shower from the sun-heated water bags suspended from a tree limb before that warm liquid gold was exhausted. After a couple beers, I collapsed, feeling my leg muscles become like limp rags. Then my phone buzzed.

I knew it was trouble as the unidentified, soft female voice gave me directions to the Spidermobile's location. I hopped on my Trex and left the Slow Pokes. I was again in the mood for more nocturnal nonsense.

After I arrived at the Spider Lair, I met Spiders Betty and Dawn. They were like Rita, well preserved, well trained, well enhanced and charming. After a couple of martini, my horny, old-man syndrome started to regenerate and take control. I moved confidently to Rita's side. She gave me a pleasant smile, and a quick ice covered hello.

Without any explanation, Rita made a rapid departure from my feeble efforts at small talk and headed with a sensuous waggle towards the tall, dark haired, smug young man that I had previously seen with Carole a few nights before. I later learned his name was Steve Delong. I was beginning to develop a deep dislike for his smug grin and magnificent body.

My confidence had been gift wrapped and shoved up my very sore ass. I was feeling foolish because I was a sixty-one year old man trying to act young. I am sure I looked like a kid who had just discovered there was no Santa, when I felt a gentle nibble on my ear lobe and heard a whisper.

"I am glad you answered my call, come to my web, little fly." My spirits, plus another part of me, had a sudden awakening.

Mona took my hand and we walked around talking about the events of the day. Her description of the Team Rode Kill combination of a dead opossum and the dead cat posed in a macabre screwing position was hilarious. She had a tent for the night as others had priority on the Spidermobile rooms.

We eventually tired of small talk and went inside her tent and shared a glass of a very good Malbec wine. She was well shaped, smelled of expensive cologne and was well dressed. She was stunning in a pair of very short white shorts and a plaid blouse tied at the waist, displaying a very flat tummy. The blouse was totally unbuttoned, revealing ample deep cleavage. Her gray eyes and totally gray short cut hair was a perfect match. She had very few wrinkles except around her eyes that only appeared when she laughed, which was frequent, and charmingly spontaneous.

"You shouldn't feel bad. Rita is very partial to young studs and I am surprised she stayed interested in you for three nights. You must have put on quite a performance."

I momentarily felt better. But was that a complement or an insult?

"Personally, I like seasoned lovers as they have more experience, more desire to satisfy their partner and they are easily satisfied." I think this was not meant as an insult.

I quickly agreed with every word of Mona's brilliant and articulate observations as I knew if I played my cards right, I was about to be the victim of another Spider. I fought hard, but the Spider won. I was again convinced that a good night under the stars with another Spider, exploring varied positions and testing the full extent of our reduced flexibility, was simply good medicine for staying young. It was so medically sound that I tried multiple treatments.

I also made a mental note to try yoga, stretching classes and pilates. Screw golf lessons.

This nightly process went on for the rest of the trip. She was quite unique: well educated, well read, and an aspiring artist. She was a pampered princess who could become a professional impulse shopper. She had grown up in small town Iowa, liked her city life and never wanted to go back to the poverty situations of so many small town citizens.

After that RAGBRAI trip, I saw Mona a few times for lunch or a drink, but the meetings led nowhere. We had good chemistry, but I concluded the obvious; our feelings were superficial. The fact that she was married to a very wealthy, older land developer who was in ill-health may have been a deterrent to our relationship. Mona knew that she was just a heart attack away from twenty million dollars in inheritance. My charm, wit and growing love got trumped by money. What a shocker!

Marvin Lee did live for a couple more years, but finally passed away, leaving his trophy wife half the estate and his spendthrift son the balance. The local economy prospered from her power shopping and the son's stupid buying of every real estate deal he saw. He soon squandered his half and left with a boyfriend to Montana to find himself.

I never reconnected with Mona, which was too bad because I had many fond memories about our brief and torrid times together in a tent in the middle of Iowa on two, starry nights. I never, till then, appreciated that biking could be such great exercise and could lead to so many memorable friendships.

I let out an unaccustomed sigh. We might have had something going in our relationship, but it was the wrong time for both of us. I could not help smiling. The memories of Mona ignited my imagination and growing exaggerated expectations of a similar RAGBRAI trip. I hoped to again find friends like Rita and Mona. Unfortunately, that was not in the cards for this trip.

WHAT'S THE MATTER WITH REVENGE?
IT'S THE PERFECT WAY TO GET EVEN.

Archie Bunker (Carroll O'Conner)

Chapter Eleven

****

THE MEXICAN SUN WAS SEARING FOR LATE MAY. Sweat poured from the tourists as they departed the US Airways jet at the San Jose Cabo San Lucas International Airport.

The small, older man, wearing tan slacks, a flowered Tommy Bahama shirt, and a tan billed fishing hat with Ray-Ban Aviator glasses, shuffled with the crowd as they wandered through the arrival and immigration lines. His dark complexion, mustache and craggy skin, blended well with the many avid fishermen on the flight.

The immigration entrance process, as usual, was slow and inefficient, but friendly. Obviously, slow, inefficient work is not limited to USA government employees.

When he finished this process, he went directly for a cab. He always avoided the dozens of well dressed, overly zealous amigos inviting new arrivals to receive a free cab ride, a bottle of tequila, a bottle of scotch, a blanket, free food, and maybe a free tourist boat ride, only if you would come to a short educational meeting at a time share villa. The time share business in this area is big business and the marketing techniques make used car salesmen seem retiring and timid. Just like so many successful salesmen and politicians, they feel immune to any requirement to tell the truth.

The cab ride to the far southern end of the Cabo peninsula was efficient but still took forty-five minutes. The highways were well surfaced and maintained. This area was full of contradictions. On the left side, overlooking the flat calm azure color of the Sea of Cortez, were strikingly well groomed, very pricey golf courses and opulent hotels. On the right side stood stark poverty, rusting cars, falling roofs and ragged children in an arid desert. The new white concrete bridges extending over wide, normally dry rivers were impressive examples of modern span construction. Under these bridges sat rundown pickups, vans and cars with countless poor people milling around, operating a subculture complete with barter, sex, booze and drugs.

At the end of the ride, a quick check into the Hotel Martini went quietly and without incident. With a quick change into shorts and running gear, the well tanned older man jogged west onto the Pacific Coast beach. He ran by several multi-colored high-rises comprising the Playa Grande time share complex and the Finisteras Hotel. Both were on a private, expansive, white sand beach free of peddlers and beggars. The sound of the crashing waves and salty smell of the sea made his endorphins release at an accelerated pace. His jogging pace accelerated, and the smooth flowing strides showed he was still flexible and strong.

All the while he ran he was eyeing the extremely steep cliffs to his right. They were five hundred foot high cliffs composed of shear flat, grey stones. He was measuring the time it would take to climb to the top where Casa Del Gordo Gatos (House of the Fat Cats) was located on the highest peak.

These cliffs comprised the Pedregal area, where several mansions created an eclectic montage of architectural styles overlooking the crashing waves of the Pacific. Local rumors had them owned by only the rich and famous. The highest and most impressive building was Casa Del Gordo Gatos with a full two-story windowed wall overlooking the extraordinary view. It was built from local brown rocks and held a complex of twenty oversized guest rooms, a large bar, a spa and a five star restaurant.

Only the wealthy and connected could gain access, and then only with a recommendation from four prior patrons. Besides serving the premier foods in the area, it catered to every person's sexual cravings or fantasies with a high level of satisfaction and discreetly maintained privacy.

Years ago, scaling this cliff would have been an easy challenge, but this was a time when the reality of an aging body's limitations needed to control this decision. The well gated and guarded entrance could be breached by a little cunning, not brawn. The return jog was invigorating.

He was always mesmerized by the sight of the craggy rocks of El Arco standing majestically at the south end of the beach, with the waves crashing violently across its large jagged rock formation as the Pacific and the Sea of Cortez merged. As sunset was nearing, the whale watching cruises were rounding El Arco point, loaded with multi-cultured turistos in search of humpback sightings.

Even as he enjoyed the scenes and scents of this unique area, the jogger's mind was obsessed with rehearsals of every detail of his short stay and the steps necessary to safely carry out with perfection his client's assignment.

A quick jog up the Pedregal Hill where the Casa Del Gordo Gatos' gates stood confirmed that the guards were armed and looked very serious. He noted that the change of the servants' shifts still occurred promptly at three pm. The van carrying the evening shift entered after an inspection. It left ten minutes later loaded with the morning shift's workers.

Shortly after this exchange, three Cadillac SUVs entered the complex carrying fishermen back from a day-long battle with the many marlins that populated this area. All the fishermen were dressed in shorts and loose shirts, and were sunburned, sweaty, and drinking Pacifico. Their voices were loud and nonstop as they bragged with macho vulgarity about their exploits in hooking, boating and conquering a fish whose IQ was ten on its best day.

After making a mental note of the time of arrival of the conquering fishermen, the small mysterious man spent the rest of the day wandering the area looking for routes to and from the site, checking out streets and memorizing every building.

Attempting a siesta in the cool of his rather nondescript room failed. The recollections of his first visit to Cabo many years ago, with Marti, kept him awake. They had met after his second tour of Viet Nam. He was stationed in Camp Hodge in Virginia, reviewing new tactics on beating Charlie by buying the hearts and minds of the people.

Marti Cole was a PhD student at Georgetown when they first met. After a couple of dates to Georgetown, followed by a few nights of animal-like sex driven by too much alcohol, their relationship actually evolved into a real friendship.

The long weekend trip to Cabo was her first trip out of the States. Her energy was electrifying and transmitted to him as they walked the beach towards El Arco. She reveled in this adventure with her mystery man. At low tide, they walked around the huge rock structure that formed El Arco. This three hundred foot high, jagged rock had gained its fame from the movie, "Planet of the Apes," which concluded with Charlton Heston riding on a horse down this beach as he viewed the tilted and buried Statue of Liberty leaning against the mammoth El Arco. This masterpiece of nature served as their backdrop when they arrived at Lover's Beach in the shadow of El Arco where they spread their blanket for their first night in Cabo.

They truly were becoming soul mates. Their stay at this quiet, small fishing village allowed them to grow even closer. Days of leisure eating freshly caught shrimp and lobster properly washed down with local cervesas, followed by afternoons of snorkeling or just lying together on the beach, was a perfect romantic environment to shape their love.

He had screwed up big time. His promiscuous nature had led him to three short hormone driven flings. One was with a nurse at Walter Reed, where he was doing some back rehab. The second was with a consultant, who was presenting a two week seminar on new techniques in psychological warfare. The third was unfortunately with a Georgetown professor. Bad luck occurred when it turned out the professor was working with Marti on her PhD. Young women can't seem to keep a secret and are terribly unforgiving.

He knew when he lost her; he would never find another soul mate. Maybe that loss was his reason, or likely excuse, for never being able or wanting to commit to loving another woman. But, this was all long ago. It's hard to break an old dog from old habits.

At 11 pm, the alarm went off. He quietly slipped into his black running suit, and a pair of black running shoes. He jogged in the cool May night to the Playa Del Tonto, the main street leading away from the shadows of the Pedregal gate. It was not long before the small waiter, Samuel Carrozona, exited the security bus and walked sleepily along the path towards his home. He had just finished a night of food service at Casa Del Gordo Gatos. He had been identified in a prior trip as the perfect candidate. Following Samuel to his small home located just a few blocks from his job, without being seen, was quite easy for someone with extensive tracking skills.

When Samuel opened his door, he experienced the terrifying feel of the barrel of a Smith & Wesson thirty-eight caliber revolver pressed to his head. His fears were short lived. Instantly, he was deep asleep as a cloth, well soaked with ether, covered his nose and mouth. His wife experienced a similar fate.

When they awoke a few hours later, the two Carrozonas found themselves bound with plastic straps designed to hold, but not hurt them. Their mouths were taped shut, except for a straw which ran to a gallon of fresh water. They each wore a pair of Depends to protect them from a long confinement. Both looked at each other with fear as they knew they were hopelessly trapped.

The next day, the three SUVs left Casa Del Gordo Gatos with their hung over warriors, heading for another day of marlin massacring. As was expected, Harlan "The Hunk" Haluska was among the sportsmen. His six foot, eight inch three hundred fifty pound frame made him stand out like a zit on your prom date's forehead. Little did the Hunk know, the most important day of his life was about to occur.

BEING A HERO IS ONE OF THE SHORTEST LIVED PROFESSIONS ON EARTH.

Will Rogers

Chapter Twelve

****

HARLAN "THE HUNK" HAD LIVED THE LIFE OF A PAMPERED SPORTS AND MOVIE HERO. He was prosperous and famous, a football legend and movie hero by the time he was forty-five years old. He had grown up on the plains of Nebraska, near the small town of Grand Island.

The long hot days of farm work, followed by long cold winters on the prairie, involved endless work. This extremely arduous and boring routine had built his naturally huge muscles like steel. Those same days also led him to be driven to get away from the farm forever as soon as possible.

The Hunk's football skills led him to the University of Nebraska. The Nebraska fans loved their football, and their enthusiasm for their Big Red team was unparalleled. Their hero worship for local talent that would lead their team to victory was like the Roman's worship of gladiators. Harlan's good looks, bulk, intense drive and purely mean attitude quickly made him an All American. Every Big Red fan had a picture of the "Husker Hunk" on their son's wall.

His shoulder-length blonde hair bronzed skin and chiseled nose and chin, from his German genes, made him a stud in a pasture packed with home bred fillies. By the time he finished his tour of the then Big eight conference, he was bound for the NFL.

The Nebraska coaches were extremely glad to see him move on to greener pastures. The constant muscle building, steroids and worship of gridiron violence had made Harlan into a PR disaster waiting to erupt, or more accurately, get caught.

The cover-up of his drunken, alleged rape of three co-eds on the same night, at the same party, cost several full scholarships, plus a few life-time fifty yard line tickets as a settlement. Allegations of his sexual appetite and methods for obtaining satisfaction were quickly hushed by smart assistant coaches and alumni.

The disappearance of his hometown sweetheart after a homecoming party during his junior year further added to his deteriorating image. She was found floating in a nearby gravel pit two weeks later. The Hunk's bereaved performance at her funeral was repeatedly played on local television. His angry pledge at the post funeral gathering to never stop till he found her killer, and the lack of any evidence connecting him to the crime, caused the case to go cold. She had been brutally beaten, but her body was laced with meth. Susan Getting was soon forgotten by the local press and law enforcement with the belief that her death was an unfortunate by-product of drug use.

Over the next years, two more similar beating deaths of drug laced co-eds occurred. Their deaths were never connected to The Hunk. He was not even a person of interest as he was becoming increasingly known as an outspoken critic of drug use by teammates and friends. When he was in front of the media, he preached with great emotion how drugs were unnatural and made sane people crazy.

The NFL was just another playground for The Hunk. He earned a fortune. He was the team's poster child for how an NFL player should perform as he took violence on the field to a new level. Unfortunately, there were several other vicious drug-related deaths that followed him as he moved to three different teams. Owners spent fortunes making sure his ironclad defenses to any participation in such deaths were never challenged. His speeches against drug use continued to grow with increasing anger and self-righteousness.

During his last few years in the NFL, he took on a new persona. In every public appearance, he was immaculately dressed and his already chiseled face became even more handsome. A frequently broken nose was fixed, sagging eyelids were adjusted and his chin became very prominent with the help of an implant.

His public appearances at fund raisers became numerous. On each such occasion, he spoke with fire and brimstone passion about how drugs were to be avoided and distributors and users harshly punished. He always concluded with a sermon about how he had suffered a deep personal loss in his early years because of demon drugs.

When he retired from the gridiron, he quickly signed a movie contract, hired an agent and moved west. Hollywood loved the Hunk at first. His clean cut looks and now trim muscle-rippling body made him a natural action hero. He loved the life of a star. He reveled in making action films, and doing his own special effects. Most of all he loved the female extras.

After five years of making repeated box office busts, his luck ran out. Hollywood movers and shakers had agreed that despite good, rugged looks, makeup and endless coaching, he was simply too dumb to learn the art of acting. Despite endless voice coaching, he still sounded like a Nebraska farm boy.

He was also a pain in the ass with all his drinking and ass chasing. His luck, for the first time, failed him when a co-star charged him with being blind drunk and beating her into a six month hospital stay merely because she took a line of cocaine.

He was still possessed of some luck. When the police arrived at the scene they found the black and blue starlet tested positive for various illegal drugs. A subsequent sweep of her house disclosed a cache of drugs that could keep a rock band going for a month. Hunk's system was clean of drugs, but hit nearly four times the legal limit for alcohol. A few more shots of Captain Jack and he would have died of alcohol poisoning. His public display of his hatred for drug distributors and users ended the case and the actress's career. But Hollywood had enough of his antics, and his contracts were all cancelled.

The Hunk spent the next several years getting fat, chasing increasingly younger women, and engaging in every macho sport he heard about. A failed reality show ended his public life. The media unanimously concluded that being drunk, overweight, wrinkled, and stupid with a whiskey-soaked voice that sounded like a cast member of the Beverly Hillbillies had no market appeal.

The Hunk often whined, "If Ozzy Osborne could do it, why can't I be a reality star?"

Promptly at 3:30 pm, the SUVs delivered their load of wealthy, hard drinking, bragging fisherman to Casa Del Gordo Gatos. By 6 pm the cocktail party was in full swing. The Hunk was one of fifteen kings of entertainment and industry, sporting their latest young female, or in some cases male, admirer and drinking to excess. These young, trim female lovelies were all in scanty dresses, which displayed their wonderful bodies, especially their cleavage. Their faces were all perfectly cosmetically enhanced, compliments of the Pampered Harlot Spa, an amenity of the Casa Del Gordo Gatos.

Not even excessive makeup could cover up the puffed lip and eyes of Debra Vance, the Hunk's abundantly suntanned young companion. She could not have been over nineteen. She was slim and trim like all the others, but she had a very sad and scared look in her eyes. As she sat obediently down next to The Hunk, the small dark waiter approached them. He delivered their drink orders and presented a plate of three large sushi wraps to the Hunk and a shrimp cocktail to his companion.

"Mr. Hunk, my Jefe is un mucho fan of yours. He has watched everything you've ever done. He has your picture in his casa. He would like you to sample his new sushi specialty. If you approve he will name it "El Hunko Supremo. It's purple and black skin comes from a very scarce Brazilian frog and has been specially cooked to add an unforgettable flavor. He feels sure you will never forget this flavor."

The Hunk glanced at the waiter's name plate and in a drunken slur noted, "Well thank ya, little Sammie. Tell your boss the Hunk says mucho gracious."

With three quick gulps of sushi, washed down by a big Jack Daniels, he cleaned the silver serving plate. In thirty seconds, The Hunk felt a red hot flash of pain surge through every limb and organ. He was paralyzed. He could not scream, even though he felt pain beyond anything he had known. He could not move. He could not swallow. He could not breathe.

He was fading into darkness when the waiter whispered the last words he would ever hear. "Susan Getting's family sends its regards."

The little waiter screamed for help when The Hunk's body crashed to the ground like an imploding casino tower. As everyone rushed to help the fallen hero, the waiter exited by a back door and calmly rappelled down the cliff to the beach. He disappeared into the dark. After taking a cab to the airport and making sure the evening flight was on time, he called the police to rescue Samuel and his wife as the water and Depends would be nearly exhausted.

MEMORIAL SERVICES ARE THE COCKTAIL
PARTIES OF THE GERIATRIC SET.

Harold MacMillian

Chapter Thirteen

****

RITA'S FUNERAL WAS FILLED WITH TEARFUL PARTICIPANTS. Some tears fell from loving friends. Some fell from charity fund raisers because they had lost an easy touch. But most tears fell from the eyes of several young men who had lost their Mrs. Robinson. The sight of her still beautiful face in a coffin had a shocking impact on me. She was one of a kind, and she had left me with numerous unforgettable memories.

She had no family in attendance, except for a sister who possessed similar facial and physical beauty. The words from the pastor were moving. He dwelled endlessly about how the good and pure go first before all of the sinners. His strong passionate delivery, complete with choking tears and sniffles, left me with the clear impression that he really knew her, and she had really touched him in all the right places. Was this a budding Elmer Gantry at the pulpit or was I getting even more cynical?

The gathering after the funeral at the Wakonda Country Club was very somber. I saw several ladies in black who I recalled from my lustful brush with the Black Widow. I moved into their circle and with a few hugs and cheek kisses interjected myself into their conversations. They were very friendly and recalled me as the "old trophy" Rita had drug to the Black Widow lair on one of their first RAGBRAI trips. My ego was dealt a serious blow with that description, but I kept them engaged in conversations as I was very curious about the relevant circumstances of her death.

Ruth James introduced herself to me as the new organizer of the Black Widows for the next RAGBRAI trip.

Ruth said, "We've stopped going for a year because of the deaths of Mona Lee and Carol Pickett. Both had sudden heart attacks within six months of each other, and it really spooked us. They were in such great shape. Their deaths were so shocking as they were always working on improving their body's condition. Seeing them in their casket was really a downer for all of us for a long time."

I remembered the two demised Black Widows as being nearly as promiscuous as Rita during my few brief visits to the Black Widow lair.

"Ruth, what happened to Rita?"

"She was found dead in bed, apparently from a surprise heart attack. This third death of a member of the Black Widow's team has certainly dampened our thoughts about a return trip. Just last week we got together for a planning session and everyone, including Rita, had renewed interest. We had a wonderful time planning for this trip. We were planning on some new types of parties and costumes for our return, but today I don't feel much like trying to roll back the clock," whispered the Widows' new leader between large tears.

"That's too bad as you will be missed. I'm organizing Team Grey Geese for this year's trip. It is composed of six good looking, wealthy, fun loving, single guys who are in great shape and all are looking for serious female companionship. They are just a tad over their fifties."

Despite my exaggerations and outright deceit, I was pleased to see a sparkle in her eye.

Ruth gave me a wink, "Maybe we will be motivated to go after all. Not all of us favor the young boys, like Rita. You were clearly her oldest temporary trophy."

I keep getting these compliments which make me feel like a prize from the antique store. I was not sure if I had been complimented, seduced or insulted.

After a long talk about Rita with her friends, I moved to another group of grieving ladies who were clearly the Bittie Bitches. They also recalled me because of my friendship with their leader, Phyllis

Brokow.

Phyllis was a law school friend and she was now a district court judge. We had shared a platonic love of the law since our days in law school, even though we both understood how it usually fails to deliver justice when the parties ultimately arrived before the court. She had insinuated, on my first RAGBRAI trip, that I should stop by her chambers after hours, and help her get off that heavy robe. I had purposely failed to follow through.

Having a sexual relationship with a friend seems to be a great way to end a platonic friendship, not to mention having a jilted judge residing on the bench was not smart business. I also admit that her six foot well-developed frame, with muscular broad shoulders intimidated me.

"Lee Scott, how are you? You look fit and well for a man your age."

"I 'm not sure if you just complimented or insulted me, but thanks anyway, Your Honor. You look well yourself. Hell of a way to meet again."

"You are right on that, Lee. I have not seen Rita for some time. I missed a couple of RAGBRAI trips, and we really did not run in the same social circles. We seemed to only meet at funerals. I suppose that is part of this damn aging process. Our Team lost Denise Ray a few months ago from a sudden heart attack. Rita was at the funeral."

"I guess we'll not see you this year when my new team of old farts try the trip across our fair state?"

"You might be right, Lee. Our team has been trying to make up our mind and most of the Bitches are leaning towards going, but this type of occurrence provides a bitter taste of mortality. It has really shaken everyone's spirits."

After a few tears she continued. "We have merged with a new group and are now Team Cougar and not the Bittie Bitches. We found the new name far more accurate than the former name. If we do go, Lee, I am counting on an inspiring discussion of the latest new precedents in my tent the first night?"

I gave her a wink and a quick kiss on the cheek, as I moved away from that tricky question.

In the corner, I saw my friend, Matt Fielding, talking to the tall young blonde male massage therapist that I had recognized at the

Painted Woods Spa as being a participant on my first RAGBRAI trip.

The two of them noticed my stare and moved towards me. I had no escape route.

"Meet Roy Rose, Lee."

"Good to meet you, Roy. I saw you at the spa yesterday when I was on a tour. Did you know Rita well?"

"I knew her from the spa and a few gourmet dinners at her place. Matt was usually the head chef, I was always his main assistant and waiter. Rita, drunk or sober, was always the center of attention."

While we were talking, the tall, dark haired massage therapist from the spa and my earlier RAGBRAI experience walked up and shook Matt's hand.

"Lee, meet Steve Delong. Steve is Roy's half brother and was another friend of Rita's. He has also worked at The Painted Woods Spa for a couple of years. Steve says he can do wonders with a bad back. Rita was especially fond of his touch," Matt winked.

I decided not to comment and simply smiled. Steve flashed a smug smile at me.

Matt ended the silence. "These fine gentlemen are avid bikers. They have been filling me in on RAGBRAI and educating me on the best training methods. I told them about our new team, and how we are looking forward to their company on the trail. Their description of the ride, companionship and fun has me pumped-up to get on with training. I want to enjoy every minute."

The quick exchange of glances between Matt and Roy left me more than a little unsettled.

"You will find it quite an experience. A little of everything for every taste, including a lot of good people just out looking for a leisurely four hundred and fifty mile ride," I said, as I looked for a reason to move away.

I moved on to pay my regrets to Tina Knowlton, Rita's sister. She was younger, but possessed the same natural beauty. My experienced eye concluded she had not enjoyed all the extra enhancements as Rita. She was a very naturally pretty woman; dark skin, dark twinkling eyes, an up-turned button nose, a nicely shaped mouth and a well endowed curvy body.

Tina dabbed a tear away as I spoke my condolences.

"I am very glad that so many people were here and were touched by my sister. She was unique. She was very generous. All my children owe their education to her. I have driven several of her cars when she tired of them. I am the best dressed wife in Huxley, Iowa because of her hand-me-down wardrobe.

After a few more tears she continued. "We were very close. She on occasion could be quite a wild ass, but she was so very kind and caring. I think she was about to settle down after her latest fling."

After quite a few more tears from Tina, I told her I was a past acquaintance, and I had known her and enjoyed every minute with her. I thought that discrete summary was enough detail to politely describe our relationship.

"I wished I knew more about her new love as she was sure they were going to be a long term pair. She said he was younger so I know it's not you."

Again, I think I was just insulted.

"If I meet him, Tina, I will send him over as he was a lucky guy. He must have been quite a person to have captured her loving spirit."

As I was leaving the event, I met Tina's husband, Herb Knowlton. Herby, as he preferred to be called, farmed and ran the family trucking business in the small town of Huxley. He clearly loved his wife and family as that was his primary subject of discussion. His blonde crew cut hair fit perfectly with his red tone skin, and weather wrinkled round face. He was an enormous man.

Like many farm boys, his clothes were all too tight as he suffered from the dread Casey's Donut syndrome. Coffee and fresh glazed donuts every morning with "the boys" at the Casey's convenience store can have some serious fattening effect. He was very jovial and kind about everyone. He was clearly bothered by the loss and was very complimentary of his demised sister-in-law. While he was rather boring and predictable, he was the kind of guy you could not help but like and trust. The world never has enough Herbs to go around.

I walked out and headed home with a myriad of varied thoughts whirling in my mind. The death of so many healthy sixty year old wealthy women from sudden heart attacks puzzled me. At my age, I don't believe in coincidences. My lawyer's bull-shit meter was giving off a bad signal.

WARNING, THERE'S NO SUCH THING AS COINCI-DENCES WHEN IT COMES TO DEATH.

GOLF IS THE HARDEST GAME IN THE WORLD
TO PLAY, AND THE EASIEST TO CHEAT AT.

David Hill

Chapter Fourteen

****

WE FINISHED OUR GOLF GAME AS USUAL WITH BAD
SPORTSMENSHIP, OLD MACHO JOKES AND ERRATIC GOLF
SKILL. As we downed a post game icy beer, we bitched about our play,
how we hated the game and set the time for our next round.

I noted unusually somber attitudes. Doug looked exhausted. Matt
was distant. I was still bothered by the funeral and post funeral events.
Morgan was the only person who seemed to be upbeat.

I asked him, "What's with the unusually happy mood? You even
laughed after that four putt, which cost you the match."

Morgan swallowed a long sip and said, "You know me pretty
well. I am feeling really euphoric. I've gotten myself involved in a
fascinating new business venture. An old friend has engaged me to
develop programs to break into old computer systems and extract data
without being traceable. He won't identify the systems or why he wants
these programs, but he has written a handsome retainer. It's my own
stimulus program."

"It really has given me a new burst of energy and a nice paycheck. I
need an infusion of capital. The social security check just about covers
my club dues." We all laughed.

"Why so somber, Matt, you seem to be rather mellow or very hung
over?"

"Lee, I guess I am a little on the hung over side. I had a weekend interrupted by that rather emotional funeral. Afterwards, I imbibed a little too much. I am also frustrated. Sunday, I wound up testing the chemical for my new project and got the hell burned out of my arms."

"Matt, I figured you got burned cooking one of your special adult happy meals for your real friends," I chided.

"No, I was in no mood to act happy after that funeral. The unnaturally early demise of a beautiful, apparently healthy person forces me to examine what's left of my own life, and what I want to do with it."

Everyone went silent as he had hit a common exposed nerve.

Breaking the silence, Matt continued, "Actually, I have been engaged to develop a chemical composition to enable locomotives to drip it on railway tracks as they run over them. The idea is to eliminate all the junk that builds up on the rails and negatively impacts fuel efficiency. Unfortunately, my mixture is so strong it went through the metal barrels in my mixing room in a few hours."

Matt continued between sips, "I dumped the mixture into a Teflon-lined mixing vat that seems to now be holding up, but I splashed a few drops on myself in the process and was really burned. That shit is potent. It will clean the tracks alright. It may also destroy them. I need to go back to my calculations or find a different use for one hundred gallons of highly destructive toxic waste. This engagement is very lucrative. I could make back everything I lost last year in the economic meltdown. Right now it's a big failure."

Sensing Doug was unusually quiet, I commented about his scratched arms and knees.

"Doug, what did you do this weekend, fall down your stairs?"

"Oh, I spent a lot of time working outside, getting rid of some weeds and a noxious varmint with a little poison. I may have overdone it. This aging process sucks. I am so tired; I think I will let Mindy put more of her efforts into satisfying me for a change tonight. It's time she puts a little more effort into this relationship," he laughed the laugh of a dirty old man.

"What's up in your life, Lee?" Doug asked.

"I am in a shitty mood after Rita Keyes's funeral. I have also found out a couple other female friends have recently died. That funeral was a real emotional train wreck for me."

I continued after a cold sip, "On the positive side, my only client has summoned me for a drinking meeting tonight. Rod Faber is worth over two hundred and fifty million dollars, and he has an idea how to really make a killing in a new type of commodities fund. Tonight, he is going to discuss engaging me to put it together. Since he stopped smoking and chasing skirts, he has concentrated purely on his favorite game; making money. He is always fun to work with. "

"Besides, since our new President has amply punished the wealthy with a depression, increased insurance costs, decreased social security benefits and higher taxes, this injection of personal bailout money feels pretty good to me."

Morgan chimed in. "It's a damn good thing we have some skills to fall back on to try to replace everything that we have lost these last two years. I really feel sorry for those people who lived the American Dream, grew up in the ranks of their companies and then retired, only to find their nest egg cut in half and no way to recover."

Morgan said with an unusual level of anger, "Worse yet, those people are now vilified for being the rich and are lectured that in order to be patriotic they need to share their wealth."

Everyone shook their head with the reality of his angry and accurate summary of life in the era of President "The One." It was obvious that a bunch of aging liberal-minded independents were fast becoming republicans.

"Okay guys, enough whining on what we cannot change till next election. I will call the other two. We go to the spa Wednesday. Lunch at eleven -thirty sharp at Skips, and then we are off to a pampered day at the spa. Remember there are a lot of very proper, wealthy and nice ladies frequenting this place. No cussing, referring to sex, farting out loud or making a pass at the help. This is all about relaxing, getting in touch with our feminine side, and mellowing out."

"Tell me again, why are we really doing this, Lee?" shot Morgan.

"You guys need to expand your views in life. Some of you are getting on in years and judging from your diminished golf skills, it won't be long and a trip to the spa might be the highlight of your week. Besides, you are a bunch of classless old goats and I view it my mission to expand your social horizons."

The last beer ended with a chugging and in unison, "Fuck you, Lee."

It is hard to wean old guys away from habits. They can be so unappreciative of well intended efforts. Maybe, I should not have brought up the golf game since I had won every bet.

"A bunch of sore losers makes it hard to keep a positive outlook."

"Up yours, Lee," came echoing down the locker room halls from multiple sources. Old guys have such a poor sense of humor when they lose a couple of hundred bucks to a friend.

> ### WHAT IS A CROOK BUT A BUSINESSMAN WITHOUT AN OFFICE?
>
> **Brendan Behan**

Chapter Fifteen

****

IT WAS AFTER SIX BY THE TIME I ARRIVED AT RF'S OFFICE. We had maintained a very special relationship since he had lured me to Des Moines as a payback for getting his brother, Henry, out of the Viet Nam massacre mess he had created. He was a self-made person.

RF started life as a trucker for a small town company; Green Streak Line. In a few years, he saved all his earnings and bought the company. He had figured out that this traditional over the rode company was under-utilizing its equipment. The movement of food commodities from the food belt of the Midwest to the consumer-laden coasts was big business. The return loads of citrus and vegetable products made the round trips very profitable. He developed all the necessary contacts in the Midwest meat industries and the southeast and west coast citrus and vegetable industries through charm, wit, muscle and bribes.

He fought off repeated efforts by the Teamster Union to organize his company, as it was a great target for more union dues. After all, what are unions for except to generate dues? RF countered the union's efforts by making it clear to his employees that he hated unions and would fight to the end to avoid being dictated to by anyone.

It also helped that he paid them differently and better than union competition. Drivers' children got scholarships. Health insurance was designed and administered by the company. When insurance operated unfairly, he stepped in and wrote a check. Birthdays for the employees and spouses were always remembered by a gift. Bonuses for outstanding performances were generous. He also employed, I modestly recalled, a brilliant lawyer who helped him to stay legal, as well as non-union.

RF had a long term relationship with Chief Randall Walters, going back to the days when the Chief's investigative work pulled Henry Faber's nuts out of a fire and avoided twenty-five to life in a federal prison. RF regularly hired parolees recommended by the Chief. These people, for the most part, were like indentured servants to RF. He took very special care of them, but if they even hinted of a parole violation, they were gone. They were also so loyal that any hint of union organization efforts were voluntarily reported to RF.

I had warned RF many times that having a paid informant in the work force was an unfair labor practice and could land him before the NLRB. True to form, RF insisted these people were paid to do their job, not to be informants regarding union activity. I always understood that it was best to believe my client, even if he winked at me when he lied.

RF had turned this company into a cash cow by paying off the loans for equipment as soon as possible and thus not paying bank interest. He was always careful in his own spending and took a very reasonable salary. After a good ten year run, he sold the company to the employees through an ESOT. This process made the employees the owners.

The result of such a structure was that if an employee tried to bring a union into the company or sued the company, they were impacting their own net worth and year end dividends, as well as those of their peers who also owned part of the company. New, profitable efficiencies were welcomed. Creativity by employees was rewarded. Sharing the wealth blocked every union effort with ease. After a twenty-five year run, the truck company, packing plants, citrus fields and canning plants were sold. Many people became very wealthy because of their ownership; all were very loyal to RF. Money creates great friendships.

During his stint as a trucker, RF developed an incredible knowledge of the commodity business, especially about price fluctuations and their causes. The commodity trading process became his obsession. He studied everything that was available and with a little knowledge, a little luck and a lot of balls, he made a fortune again.

He was my long time friend. I had been by his side through many business challenges, three wives, two live-in girl friends, and a couple of palimony suits. He was always there for me whenever I needed a pillar when times were tough and not always fair. He was a best friend in every sense.

We knew each other like brothers, and we always respected our differences and enjoyed our similarities. He was ten years older than me, and we were reluctantly aging together. It beats the alternative.

He was, as usual, immaculately dressed in black slacks and a white linen shirt that showed off his deep tan, wrinkled face, gold necklace and snow white hair. His short thin frame was trim and his clothes fit perfectly.

"Are you ready to get to work for a change, or are you too busy fucking off to help me, Lee?"

"Your best interest and legal needs are always on my mind. This morning, I got up and I asked myself, what I can do today to enrich my friend, RF."

"Enough bull shit. How are you, Lee? I miss seeing you and listening to your sarcasm. We have a lot of catching up to do. This bike trip across Iowa that you are training for sounds crazy for someone of your now soft nature and increasing age."

"I am feeling fine. But you're right; this bike trip is likely to end with a few pulled muscles, a wrecked crotch and a sore ass. But, it's an adventure I want to try one more time. You have always said older doesn't necessarily mean smarter."

"What's on your money grubbing mind, my old friend? I'm bored and am looking forward to any new business challenge; if it's legal and you're not too greedy. Playing too much golf can make you ready to do anything that is satisfying and rewarding for ten consecutive minutes. That damn game is like senior citizens' cocaine."

"When are you going to give up that stupid, unsatisfying game and do what you do best; practice law? You are too smart to waste your time on that confidence wrecking, time sucking process you call a game."

"Anyway, skip my opinion on golf. Here is my idea. There are endless amounts of data regarding various grains and the how a multitude of factors impact their prices. This data is everywhere; in history, in consumer company reports, in weather reports and predictions, in consumption trends and production capacity. The government tries to gather this information and make its predictions. As usual, their systems are out-moded, they involve too many people, and they don't use the right people. The results are that the government predictions are usually wrong and the traders in Chicago rely on them, and people make and lose lots of money based on wrong information. It's the old Bull-Shit in Bull-Shit out system at work."

'Lee, I think I can access this same data, add some other data from interested companies, involve farmers' hands-on information and create a better prediction as to a year end outcome. I can make a fortune"

I thought a minute and said, "RF, this has been tried before and hasn't worked. The crazy gyrations during the year eat people up based on wrong information. How do you think you can avoid this?"

"Simple, my young scribe, I factor in the farmers' hands-on input by giving them a small yearend bonus if this plan succeeds. In addition, we don't trade any months except the ones when the crops are put in the ground and harvested. I have hired a friend of yours to create a computer system to allow the collection of specific key data and to assemble the results. With that data and the historical similarities of factors, I think the predictions are great bets."

I now knew the name of Morgan's new client. "This all might work, but you cannot try to access government collected data and predictions before they are public, if that crossed your mind."

"Oh, Lee, how could you even think I would ever have thought about such a possibility? I am crushed with your lack of trust."

"You are so full of shit, RF that the whites of your eyes are light brown, but I believe you."

My bull-shit meter went off as I lied to myself.

"I'll do a little research on what's in the public world that might be similar to this company and see how they are organized. We need to determine if this idea is infringing on someone else's protected concepts or patent rights to such programs. We also need to see how they have fared. Is this a public company or are you and your buddies the only investors?"

"I don't like gambling with other people's money so it's all mine. You get 10% for doing the work right, you over-priced scavenger of human wealth."

"Seems fair to me."

With business behind us, RF pulled out of his desk drawer two glasses and a new bottle of Crown Royal Special Reserve. We had a couple drinks and told a lot of lies about how much fun the retirement process provided to us every new day, and how many desirable ladies were chasing us.

RF took a deep shallow of the twenty year old, deep brown nectar, swirled it in his mouth, savoring the strong stinging flavor and leaned back in his chair.

"You know, everyone who is working tells me how lucky I am to enjoy no steady job and hours and the lack of pressure to climb the corporate ladder. I am living their dream. I always warn them to be careful about retiring too early. Retirement is a huge change."

After a long sip, he said, "After you retire your friends change, your goals change, and your self-image takes a big hit, as there is no more positive playback for a job well done. Most men spend the first thirty days of retirement hanging around home, doing projects they have ignored, and becoming incessantly badgered by their spouse to help her do more projects. Their spouse is also likely driven nuts by them after a few weeks. Most of them are soon totally stressed with what to do with the rest of their lives. No one ever thinks about that dilemma. Some, like you, fall into the golf paradigm, and think they will find joy in that time-wasting process."

With another deep sip, he philosophically continued. "The search for the next road of life to take is very hard to find when you are retired."

"That map is hard to read. It's difficult to move to something that is new and unfamiliar, where failure is likely. Failure is hard to contemplate when you are aging and were once successful. Aging egos are easily bruised. It's also frustrating to realize you have a limited number of years to follow those new roads.

"Like you, many people are financially well enough off to live out their lives comfortably. But that affluence can be a curse as these retirees spin their wheels, look around, become frustrated and never find a new road. They just sit in place and wither physically and emotionally. Their minds atrophy into a nonfunctional rock."

"You are really profound with a couple of shots of Crown under your belt, but you are giving good advice. We both know how easy it is for type "A" people to get bored. This aging process, to me, is very emotional, confusing and full of fears that are hard to identify."

"I am shocked every morning when I look into the mirror through what I feel are my forty year old eyes and see an old guy staring back at me. Every part of my body is going south despite my steady hard workouts. How fast will this process continue to accelerate? No matter how much male ego BS I dispense, I know my sexual attraction to good looking females is fast disappearing. I hate it when a young lady calls me distinguished or well-preserved for my age. "

"I hear you, Lee. This process of going to bed and waking up with fewer friends on earth isn't fun. I know I don't have any need for money as two hundred-fifty million dollars should hold me, but the fascination of getting a venture up and running profitably still gets me energized every day. It's my hobby. It's my passion. I also love the feeling of making a deal, making a profit, and giving good employees a big bonus for their efforts. Their smiles are worth the risk."

I'm not sure I bought that last bit of self laudatory BS on loving giving big bonuses, but I nodded in silent agreement.

We had one more drink and parted with a hug. It was clear this was not about money. It was about RF needing a challenge to keep his mind fresh and growing and to keep his self image intact. If I was really honest with myself, my own fears about aging and the need to demonstrate my self-worth also kept me coming back to be involved in each new project. With drinking, chasing skirts and screwing less, you need something to fill in the abundance of leisure time. Golf won't do it; trust me.

Chapter Sixteen

✱✱

THE EERIE SOUND OF THE LATE NIGHT FLOATED THROUGH THE WINDOW ON THE GENTLE MAY BREEZE. The cry of the Whippoorwill looking for a mate, the howl of coyotes finishing a feast of an unlucky rabbit, and the rush of bat wings as they darted about catching their fill of flying insects, all blended together.

The smell of settling dew, and the sweet odor from budding trees, bushes, and lilacs all combined in the fresh night air. It was invigorating.

Roy Rose was wide awake, sipping coffee while watching the faint hint of a sunrise through the east window of the seventy year old bungalow located in the dense forest of the South of Grand area. He was more than wide awake. His heart was racing. Every logical part of him said it was time to move on to another city.

They had been in Des Moines a few years earlier after they had first left their home in Dallas. Then, like vagabonds, they moved to Minneapolis, then Omaha, before returning two years ago. They had found excitement, intrigue and trophies in all of these towns. This one had been their best hunting ground. The female game in this area was very easy to fool.

As he sipped his coffee and smelled the night's aroma, his mind drifted back to the first kill. Linda Lou Rounds was a neighbor to his Grandmother in a budding country development in North Dallas, which is now Plano. He had been left with his single grandmother, Mandy, by his mother, Susan, when she ran away with her latest lover and sugar daddy. Susan never returned.

At eighteen, his hormones were raging. The Linda Lou era all started so innocently when she asked him to trim her hedge and grass. This led to a fresh mint tea after a hot afternoon's work and accelerated to a few beers. Linda Lou talked loud and nonstop about how it was such a shame the way he was left alone to be raised without proper guidance and worldly advice.

After a few weeks, Linda invited him in as usual. This time she was dressed in sweaty tight spandex pants and overly-filled bra. She had obviously just ended a long workout. At fifty-five, she was fighting the slow metabolism of menopause, and was trying desperately to get twenty-five pounds off her six foot, broad-shouldered body. Her bleached blond long hair hung in strings fully laden with her sweat. As she wiped her pale forehead and dabbed at her deep blue eyes, she handed him a beer, took his hand and they headed up the stairs. She had decided a couple's shower was a good way to help develop his education about women.

The shower was exhilarating for the teenager. Linda did indeed enjoy every minute of the educational process, and taught a full semester's course in sex education in a single afternoon. After a few hours, she looked at her watch and announced it was time to leave as her husband, Clark, would soon be home from his insurance business.

These encounters continued for most of the summer. Unfortunately, the relationship ended badly. Roy was getting increasingly repulsed by Linda's demands and age. He felt like a stud horse performing for stud fees. He suggested that it needed to end, and she became enraged. She swore that if he ever told anyone, she would tell his grandmother it was rape, and he would go to jail. Then she ridiculed his sexual performances as amateur efforts by a fumbling oversized young boy.

The emotions from that event were confusing; shame, fear, uncertainty, and most of all anger at being rejected by an older, out of shape, lusty woman. His anger had built for months until one day he saw Linda Lou at a spa, where he was working at learning to be a masseuse. She was more aggressive and louder than he remembered. As she brushed by him, she squeezed his rear and whispered and order to report at five to her house to give her a massage. Her smile repulsed him, but he nodded and gave her a forced grin and nod.

As he was about to knock on the door, it flew open and Linda Lou shed her pink robe and displayed her naked body. The diet she had followed for six months had been a complete success. Her powerful body was now trim and firm. She took his hand and led him upstairs to her all too familiar bedroom where she had her massage oils heated and waiting.

His hands were new to massage techniques, but as he probed deep into her back muscles, she moaned with pleasure. She demanded deeper and harder movements and more effort. His anger built. His disgust for her aggressive attitude, constant criticisms and orders caused bile to flow into his mouth as he held back the retching sensation. He knew then that he simply could not stand older women.

He ended it all by simply using his strong arms and snapping her neck backwards with a violent jerk. She never flinched. To his surprise, he was calm and, in fact, enjoyed both the process and the results. He thought calmly; put her robe back on her, put away the oils, straightened the bed and carried her to the base of the stairs. Several ounces of gin in her dead mouth, on her robe and the floor around her body and a broken glass near the gin bottle strewn next to her body made a perfectly believable scene. Old, drunk people can obviously trip and fall.

He left with a smile and a strangely pleasant feeling of satisfaction and power. He would remember the surprised look in her eyes as her neck snapped.

As he sipped his second coffee, he opened the container to count the trophies and smell their scent. There had been many more since Linda Lou. He had been an avid reader. As a result, he had discovered better and less obvious killing methods. The relationship with Hanna Manning, his grandmother's health club instructor, and access to her husband's drug store, had given him several new ideas. She was his first experiment with potassium chloride into a vein behind the ear, preferably in the scar left from a facelift. Such a location was not detectable.

The more he thought about Linda Lou, Hanna and others, the more he was beginning to obsess for another kill. He could almost feel the surge of adrenaline as the night for the final conquest approached, and the feeling of dominating power while he fooled the rich, horny old gals into believing young love would last forever.

Watching their eyes explode with fear as their hearts began to race towards a massive blowup made his own heart accelerate and his body turn warm with lust. He actually could feel himself becoming aroused with the recollections of the memory of the last minutes of these old, now departed lovers.

He again opened the chest by his side and fondled the trophies collected from each of them.

The bedroom next to his was silent. He needed to decide if he would move on alone or keep up the teamwork with his long time special friend and hunting partner. He had become increasingly weird over this last kill. He actually believed there was a real romantic connection and that he could change his predatory nature. How naive to think that either of them could change, or that either of them knew what love with a female really involved. This last kill was like the others. She needed to join them. However, it was clear that this kill had created some tension; it hadn't been planned in unison like the others.

As he nibbled at a bran muffin, he began to think about starting a new life. He had accidently found someone who was smart, rich, charming, a great cook, and a razor sharp sense of humor. Obviously, rich was the main attraction. He could see himself dumping this current life, his jealous partner and starting to enjoy a rich stable existence. Maybe he could start his own business where he did not need to kiss the ass of every old patron to encourage tips and referrals. He hated every second he had to be kind and gentle to these old relics.

Leaving would not be easy. The two of them had moved around the country from their original home in Texas. They had enjoyed many well planned charades that involved pure animal lust, and always terminating with the thrill of taking someone's life.

His partner was both a partner and a lover. They had shared much together while growing up, maybe too much. He knew his partner was a very sexually motivated predator who was very controlling. He would not be easy to leave.

After counting the trophies one more time and smelling them while recalling each owner's names, and their last gasping looks, he poured more coffee in a to-go cup and quietly left. He needed to get to the spa early as he was booked for a busy day.

> THE BIG DIFFERENCE BETWEEN SEX FOR
> MONEY AND SEX FOR FREE IS THAT SEX FOR
> MONEY USUALLY COSTS A LOT LESS.
>
> Brendan Behan

Chapter Seventeen

****

ROY ROSE AND STEVE DELONG WERE THE ACCIDENTAL RESULTS OF TWO TORRID INDISCRETIONS BY THEIR MOTHER. Both of them were conceived while their amorous mother was married to other men. Despite these two bumps in the road of life, she used her brains, charm and body to keep moving on to even more wealthy men and amassing her fortune. She totally ignored her two mistakes, but her example deeply impacted them. One hated older women and one just hated women. They knew little about the way she died; that event also had a long-term impact on them.

ON APRIL 4, 2000, SUSAN JOHNSON-ROSE-STANTON-MCCOLLUM AWAKENED WITH A SHARP FLASH OF PAIN. It was shooting violently through her brain. Her eyes were starring at a kaleidoscope of colors. All her muscles contracted violently and froze in unison. Her breathing process ceased to function. She had looked up in frozen terror into the dark piercing eyes of a small man dressed totally in black; including a mask covering his face, except for slots exposing dark, unblinking eyes and a slight smile.

As she attempted to scream, her body again contorted in extreme pain, and her words froze in her throat. Her movements were paralyzed.

Her vision quickly darkened, and her heart accelerated as if it was trying to burst out of her trim fifty year old body. Suddenly and mercifully, the racing heart stopped and the darkness increased as her heart's chamber's arteries burst in multiple locations.

The last words she heard were when the small man leaned over her and whispered, "Say hello in hell to Big Ed from his family."

The man moved with catlike grace to the drunken body of Marty McCollum and injected him with Accupon. This new experimental tranquilizing drug quickly placed his already drunken brain into a six to eight hour deep sleep. He would awaken tomorrow with a start, and without any memory of the events of the previous night.

In a drug and alcohol-induced stupor, he would awaken and find his beloved, but not so faithful wife, dead on the bed of their large suite in The Royal Tower on Paradise Island near Nassau, Bahamas. Her six foot tall body was resting peacefully on the bed, fully dressed in a skimpy blue negligee; her shoulder length, blonde hair lying perfectly draped across her shoulders. Her wide open blue eyes would be staring straight ahead, reflecting her last look of uncontrolled fear. Her body would be starting the rigor state of death, and the paralyzing and lethal injection of poison from the skin of the purple dart frog would be dissipated to a negligible level.

Susan Johnson was born in the west Texas town of Odessa in 1949. Her mother, Mandy, was a local cheerleader who unfortunately fell in love with Tyrone T. Johnson, a local rodeo hero. They quickly had their one and only child, Susan. Not surprisingly, T.T, like most rodeo heroes, led a hard drinking and equally hard woman-chasing life, equaled only by the professional golfers of that era. When his knees and back gave out from too many falls, he was forced to do the unthinkable; trying to earn a normal living. He and Mandy packed up Susan and moved to the budding North Dallas equestrian area.

In North Dallas, during the late 1960's, huge rolling ranches owned by old name Texas families spread for miles. Their perfectly kept pastures were filled with cows, horses, buffalo and beefalo grazing next to track home developments. Local ranches sold for multiples of their value as new, young, rich people of the area started to live out their Urban Cowboy image.

T.T. became employed at the Bar Two Rose Ranch to care for the horses. Susan grew up in one of the small homes on the ranch, watching the uninhibited display of wealth arrive every Friday and stagger away every Sunday.

By eighteen years of age, she had the tall blonde looks of a twenty-five year old and knew it. She was smart and took immaculate steps to appear well groomed and sexy on a low budget. She soon learned quickly, by OTJ training, every possible way to flirt with and control a man. While control of a man by flirtation, sex and charm is common to the female gender, Susan had taken it to a lofty level at a pace far in excess of her age.

T.T. used his charm and endless tales of his rodeo days to captivate and befriend the ranch owner, Rick Rose. With his new found friend, Rick, leaving town on numerous trips to check on his drilling company, T.T. found a new hobby. Satisfying thirty year old Rebecca Rose consumed untold hours.

T.T. approached the challenges of servicing Rebecca's needs with the unbridled efforts he always threw into riding a bucking wild-horse in the finals of a rodeo. After being caught in a compromising position in the main house's bedroom by Mandy, T.T. and Rebecca ran away, hopelessly in love.

Rick, quietly and quickly, paid Rebecca the amount called for in their prenuptial agreement. Susan never saw T.T. again. After the money ran out, he was divorced. Rebecca quickly learned it's hard to love an older, poor man.

Susan and Mandy stayed on at the Rose Ranch. Mandy did the books for the ranch operations. She also made periodic overnight trips to the main house to help heal Rick's broken heart, when he wasn't off starting another drilling operation. Mandy renewed her services as a real care giver in every way.

By the time she was twenty, Susan was a six foot blonde, blue eyed Texas beauty who had won several beauty contests. With a limited income, college was never an option, but a receptionist job at Rose Industries offered far more opportunities for advancement.

By the time she was twenty-one, Mandy was still a bookkeeper, and Susan was now Mrs. Susan Rose. Her marriage to a rich man twenty-five years her senior surprised no one, except Mandy. The mother-daughter relationship was virtually destroyed.

Roy Rose was born two years later, much to Rich's surprise, as he had a vasectomy 10 years earlier. Young Roy ironically had the near white hair look of Klaus Mueller, the head of finance for Rose Industries, and none of the freckled red hair features of Rick Rose's Irish heritage. Even with a limited knowledge of genetics, Rick concluded that Roy was not a mutant.

Susan received the million, five hundred thousand dollar settlement that the prenuptial called for, plus a lump sum pay off of child support. Klaus got the ax, and because he was broke and unemployed, he also got the cold shoulder from Susan. Mandy dusted off her negligees and went about helping heal Rick's broken heart and wounded ego. A good care giver does not hold a grudge.

Big Ed Stanton, an early wildcat operator in the oil fields, had spent his life developing the Stanton Refineries into a local power-house. In his golden years, he backed off his break-neck work schedule and divorced his wife of forty years, who unfortunately, had failed to understand her pre-nuptial agreement.

Big Ed started the process of becoming part of the Dallas elite, by buying one of the largest homes in the University Park area. Very soon, he was part of the old, rich oil wealth elite, despite his low class manners and cowboy vocabulary.

At nearby SMU, Big Ed's oversized bronzed bust, complete with a Stetson hat and piercing black eyes looking powerfully from his weathered cowboy face, stood at the entrance to several buildings bearing his name.

Unfortunately, his uncontrolled drinking and eating had caused his huge frame to become increasingly flabby over the years. His bulk, bad drinking habits and hobbling knees no longer allowed him to walk his vast land holdings. He sorely missed gazing at the many operating pumps which, with every stroke, increased his wealth. Luckily, he found a caring, loving secretary who would usher him around and help him adjust the oxygen on his walker or motorized cart.

Susan had struck oil herself. Very little deep drilling was involved in bringing in this gusher.

When the marriage of the beautiful twenty-six year old secretary, turned nurse, to the legendary eighty year old Big Ed was announced, his family attacked like Santa Anna at the Alamo. But Big Ed prevailed when a prenuptial was signed. Another immaculate conception occurred within six months and Steven was born. His nearly black hair, deep bronzed complexion and raw-boned frame gave off the appearance he might have been sired by Big Ed, but Susan knew better. The family's chauffer, Garret Delong, was always fond of the soon to be widow. She was also fond of occasional drives in the country to check on Big Ed's pumping wells.

Big Ed had the heart of a Texas long horn steer, and he lived another eight years. An unfortunate fall from his handicapped equipped golf cart into a deep ravine near the ranch, plus the eight hour delay in locating him, accelerated his demise.

Susan played the role of a grieving widow with an Oscar winning performance. One day after the funeral, Susan's litigation to nullify the prenuptial started. After three years of emotional court proceedings, Susan, Roy and Steve moved on with five million dollars in the bank. Garret Delong was left to finish his career behind the wheel of the Stanton's fleet of vehicles.

Susan's two boys, Roy and Steve, out of necessity, were close to each other and spent the bulk of their early years with Grandma Mandy. Susan was void of the mother gene, and she seldom was involved in their nurturing. In fact, Susan could care less about them. When they graduated from high school, she gave them each a small amount of cash, a hug and kisses and a boot in the ass into the cruel world. Susan had decided marrying for money was behind her, and marrying for true love was ahead for her.

Marty McCollum was a local singing cowboy who owned a country style bar in Plano that catered to the rich, urban cowboy image. Each night, young executives put on their jeans and embroidered cowboy shirts and galloped in their Mercedes, BMW or Jaguar down to Marty's Dallas Stud's Bar and Grill. Within a few months, his new female singing sensation, Susie Boone, was filling his place nightly. The price of booze, pot and coke went up. Susan had changed her image and name to Susie Boone. She mesmerized the urban cowboys with her whispering whiskey voice, tall sultry body, blonde blue eyes and shameless jokes and charm.

Marty could still strum his guitar and belt out all the Texas favorites with the best performers around. Not surprisingly, after a few years of playing second fiddle to Susie, Marty was fast consuming the bulk of the liquor inventory. Susie was absorbing the loose cash and young bartenders at an ever increasing pace.

The banks finally ended the process with foreclosure proceedings. Marty, with Susan's guidance, had stripped the company of all cash, and they simply handed it over to the bank with a good luck wish. A few days after handing the bank the keys, Marty and Susan decided to renew their love and try their luck at the Atlantis Casino in Nassau. Unfortunately, they arrived on a Trans-Eastern plane at the same time as a small, dark complexioned, bearded passenger who quietly watched them throughout the night as they lost at every game they attempted, and as Marty became increasingly drunk.

The stranger entered the Royal Towers, blending in with the other guests. With ease, he quickly stole a pass key from a janitor while he asked for directions. He watched with some pathos at the unlucky couple's continuous bad luck and lack of skill.

It was extraordinarily easy to obtain their room number as they frequently sought more credit and loudly gave out that number. They were on the top floor where the penthouses occupied three thousand feet. It was filled with every known electronic device, extremely gaudy decorations and unlimited liquor. With ease, the small stranger ascended to the roof overlooking the ninth floor balcony of their penthouse. He simply had to be patient and wait for his prey to arrive.

The predator in black was amused as he watched the unhappy couple return from the casino. Susan and too much wine produced one horny big blonde. Dancing like a striptease queen, she peeled off her clothes on the balcony and demanded satisfaction from a very drunk Marty.

The stranger silently chuckled as he had a front-row seat at a comedy. He now understood the phrase "trying to fuck a wildcat with a noodle." After half an hour of feeble sex, a very frustrated Susan and a staggering Marty crashed. He passed out on a white couch, which he quickly stained with whiskey soaked vomit, filled with half chewed shrimp and an abundant amount of cocktail sauce. Susan went to her bed, tired, drunk and unsatisfied.

With ease, the amused stranger rappelled from the roof and entered their bedroom through the balcony. With cat-like movements, he picked the lock, injected Marty and then with another syringe ended the saga of Susan Johnson-Rose-Stanton-McCollum.

With a good feeling from his prompt delivery of vigilante justice, he left Marty behind to justify his alibi to the authorities when her rigid body was found the next day.

He wondered if Marty could find a way to compose a new western song from his jail cell; "Today I Went Broke, Lost My Ass at Cards, Got Drunk, Almost Got Laid and Found My Wife Dead Blues."

LIFE BEGINS AT FORTY-BUT SO DO FALLEN ARCHES,
RHEUMATISM, FAULTY EYESIGHT AND THE TENDENCY
TO TELL A STORY TO THE SAME PERSON THREE TIMES.

Helen Rowland

Chapter Eighteen

****

I ARRIVED EARLY FOR LUNCH AT SKIP'S. The food was predictably good, promptly delivered with a Cheer's type of smile and greeting. Most of the crowd knew each other and exchanged a lot of barbs and good natured personal attacks.

"Good to see one more lawyer isn't out there chasing ambulances," came the boom from retired police Chief Randall Walker.

Despite having helped RF deceive me in order to get dumb Henry off for his crimes in Viet Nam, I still trusted and loved him. He had always been a friend to me through some challenging times.

"Randy, it's good to see the food economy of the town is being subsidized by you. Your gravy-decorated tie seems right out of GQ. You spill enough to feed a tribe in Somalia," I replied.

With a big bear hug from the giant, we started to ask about each other's lives since our paths had last crossed.

He had retired from the city police force with a full pension because of the side effects of a gunshot wound. He simply was breaking up a domestic spat when the woman unloaded a Glock in every direction. Bad timing.

He hated golf, which I understood. He was overweight and hated exercise. He still had a passion for the good things in life, so he regularly consulted with RF on employment issues and occasionally did some PI work. He made more in retirement than when he worked full time. His kids had all grown up and moved away, and his ex-wives had all remarried so he was free of child support and alimony. I noted, from all the ladies that stopped by his table, that he had not broken all of his old habits.

"Chief, do you stay very close to anyone in the homicide department?"

"I have a few friends, but they are pretty overweight and tired. They are just riding along till they can retire. Giving them a case is like throwing an old dog a bone. You see a lot of chewing and not much results."

"I'm not sure I am anything but a goofy old lawyer, but there have been a series of sudden deaths among wealthy, single females over the past couple of years. I just went to a funeral and heard about four of them. There doesn't seem to be any suspicious aspects as they are all in their sixties and die of sudden heart failure. The only thing that bothers me is they all were in great physical shape, and I knew them from my only trip on RAGBRAI."

"The facts do have a little odor to them. Coincidences at our age are like bratwurst and sauerkraut: a little hard to digest. I can do a little checking with a few cronies after I ply them with ample after work drinks. A few beers to keep their beer bellies from shrinking should be enough motivation to see if they are working any files. Give me the names."

I picked up a napkin and wrote down the names and approximate times of death and folded it into two hundred dollar bills. "Make sure they have plenty of good beer and give me a call when you're ready."

The five spa-bound guys entered the door, and I gave my friend a big pat on his powerful back and left.

"Well guys, are you ready to be poked, squeezed, powdered, oiled and pampered? Hope you brought your credit cards as this is not as cheap as a day of golf?"

"Let me get this straight, Lee. We can't pinch, feel or even be suggestive with the help?"

"Morgan, if you try anything, the owner said they would super glue your pecker to your thigh during the massage. Is that clear enough?"

"I think I get the picture, but it's asking a lot to change sixty-four years of training. Couldn't they make just one little exception for a gray haired old man?"

After a quick lunch, consisting of two Bloody Marys and half a sandwich, we entered The Painted Woods Spa with a surprising amount of interest. We were greeted by the owner, Dr. Shelley Keene who looked as gorgeous as ever. We promptly were shuttled off by two very petite guides to the changing room where we received our fluffy warmed robes and wine. Then we were off to the massage rooms.

The room was quiet except for the faint sounds of soothing elevator music and bubbling water. It was decorated in natural colors; woven bamboo textured walls and dark brown covered floors. The lighting was muted without a single glare and lots of soft feeling shadows. The temperature was warm and the atmosphere humid from the warm rocks already placed under the blankets on the massage tables. The smell of various oils and herbs floated throughout.

I was beginning to doze off when, enter stage left, masseuse Steve. His six foot five, two hundred pound frame of young muscle, topped by long wavy, unkempt shoulder length black hair filled the doorway. I visibly gulped.

"Do you feel bashful or apprehensive about enjoying the hot rock treatment semi-nude, which means a towel draped in one key area when you're on your back?"

"At my age, bashfulness is more of a memory than a reality son, so let's get going."

His hands worked oil over my back and probed deep into some muscles, that I didn't recall owning. The warm rocks under the mat irradiated a relaxing heat that made my body turn to Jell-O. After thirty minutes of this process, I was smothered in warm towels and left to soak in the heat and music.

I was awakened by a pat on the shoulder by my new friend, Steve, and escorted to a shower. As I entered, the spray hit me with water pressure that felt like my skin was being removed. When the jets automatically moved to a cool setting, the invigorating feeling was like a massive B-12 intravenous shot. My penis, to my embarrassment, disappeared deep into its shell, escaping from the cold blast.

Steve and I shared some herbal tea as we waited to move to the facial stage of our stay.

"I recall you and another young man from my first RAGBRAI trip. I believe you knew Rita pretty well during that trip. I saw you when I had a few visits to the Spidermobile."

"Yah, Roy and I were just moving back to Des Moines from Minneapolis, and we were still job hunting. Rita seemed to like me a lot and helped land this job. She was a great client and big tipper. I am going to miss her. Awfully surprising, how she went. I guess a bad heart can surprise anyone."

My bull-shit meter went off. I knew there was a lot more he was going to miss than the tips and her charm.

"Your friend, Roy, seems to know Matt Fielding pretty well. They were carrying on some long conversations at Rita's funeral. Matt mentioned all of you being acquainted with Rita through some dinner events at her place."

"Yep, I've been to a few of those fancy dinners at Rita's insistence, but I was a little uncomfortable. Rita would hang on me like she was showing me off to her old friends. Roy didn't have that problem as he and Matt were always very involved in the food preparation, wine selection and cooking. I guess gay guys really get into that sort of stuff."

I pretended like I wasn't surprised by what I had just heard. "Yes, I have noticed that they tend to have those shared interests myself."

After my time with Steve, all of us reconvened in the relaxation area, had another wine and were ushered off for a facial, manicure and pedicure with a great deal of good humor from the technicians and each other. Everyone seemed as relaxed as napping babies. I was quiet. I was bothered about my new found knowledge about Matt's sexual preferences.

After paying a hefty bill and tip, we left to reconvene at Doug's house for a quick beer. Mindy greeted us with a quick kiss and a plate of cheese, veggies and salami. We all melted into our chairs.

"Personally, I'm glad I did this, but it won't be on my every week agenda. I guess the macho side of me needs the sweat and pain of a run and hard workouts to be happy," Doug mumbled in between sips of an ice cold beer.

"I don't know. This is as mellowed out as I have been since my first date after my last divorce."

"Morgan, you have been divorced so many times how would you recall that feeling?" I quickly pointed out. "How was the massage for the rest of you?"

Luke, Tim, Morgan and Doug had raves about the young ladies that had such great hands and were too discrete in their work.

"I was rather proud that I did not give them just a little feel or get just a little woody," Luke noted in between bites of salami and cheese.

Doug choked on that statement. "Luke, any woody on you would be little. But it was a great experience. I think I will take Mindy the next time for a couple's treatment."

Mindy was in earshot, "I am ready when you say the word. I bet I could add a few items to the menu while we are in the couple's room alone. I think I could make your old Willy stand up and salute."

Matt was strangely quiet and by simple math I knew Roy had worked his magic on his chubby little body. I knew he was struggling with revealing a lifetime issue, but I left it alone. He would find the right time.

I broke off the evening and announced that I was ready for bed. Steve had left every muscle in my back and shoulders screaming. We slowly got our exhausted bodies moving and dragged ourselves to our cars. I think we all were in bed by nine. There might be something to this pampering that could become a long term habit.

Women always find the great things in life before men even realize they are available. No wonder they directly or indirectly have most of the world's wealth and power.

We men are pawns in the hands of higher beings.

A STUDY SHOWS THAT 90% OF MEN INFLATE THE NUMBER OF THEIR SEX PARTNERS, WHILE THE OTHER 10% INFLATE THEIR SEX PARTNERS.

Craig Kilborn

Chapter Nineteen

✳✳

THE STUPID IRRITATING GAME OF GOLF WAS FORGOTTEN. I had scheduled a training ride every other day over the numerous bike trails in the area. The Great Western trail to the south of Des Moines ran through wave-like rolling hills which are common to Iowa. The Saylorville Trail from the Botanical Center on the banks of the Des Moines River provided work on good gear transitioning because of the severe valleys and hills. The seventy mile trip from 63rd Street in Des Moines to Yale, Iowa on the Great Midwest Bike Trail provided the endurance aspect.

The Great Midwest Bike Trail was the venue for today's training session. It was built on an abandoned rail lines track bed. Its paved roads ran through small towns, dead towns, farm fields, and many areas totally canopied by the old, untrimmed native trees. The sight of riding for miles through a tunnel covered totally by tree limbs over head was unique. The smells of the crops, trees, berry bushes, wildflowers and wild grasses were heavy in the air. Allergy victims were extremely troubled in this environment.

It was a typical late June day and the heat from the summer was steadily increasing, and the humidity was constantly high. Because of these elements, the crops were growing to immense size and emitting even more humidity.

"The photosynthesis process, when plants combine water, minerals and sun light into their cellular growth, emits moisture into the environment; it's part of the reason a natural hot house environment exists in this region. This process, when combined with frequent rain falls and summer heat, creates immense levels of humidity. This is a significant reason why Iowa has such huge crop production. But, this environment makes for uncomfortable, sweaty, sticky days for human life."

"We have to get acclimated to this environment. RAGBRAI occurs at the peak of such hot and humid weather."

I noticed no one was listening and everyone was shaking their head. I was boring them with my scientific pontification.

"Thanks for that helpful information, Mr. George Washington Carver," mumbled Matt as he put his helmet over his always messed up hair and totally saturated sweat band.

We were getting used to the fundamentals of a long bike ride: make sure your bike seat is properly adjusted to avoid a very sore anus, use plenty of Butt Balm to avoid chapped inner thighs, check tire air pressure and apply mucho Cutter's insect repellant to ward away the numerous little pests that emerge in swarms during this season.

Everyone also was accustomed to drinking significant quantities of water before it felt necessary in order to avoid dehydration, eating enough fiber to satisfy a buffalo, taking ibuprofens like candy to avoid aching muscles and joints and using athletic drinks to keep the electrolytes balanced in our old bodies.

No longer could train like young pups on beer, chips and burgers. Boy, was this fun?

We continued the long ride at a pace of fifteen miles an hour. We stopped frequently for water breaks and stretching old muscles. Doug was always far ahead and ready to start after a brief rest before anyone else mentioned starting. His small body clearly was up to this challenge.

I was getting into this process and was feeling younger by the day. The steady exercise, proper eating and limited alcohol consumption combined with a hand full of vitamins, acai berry juice by the quarts and plenty of B-12 was, much to my surprise, having a positive impact. I had also lost interest in my latest best new female friend, so I was getting good rest every night uninterrupted by someone else's needs. My selfish male side was showing.

As I rode along with a lot of time for thought, I was increasingly convinced that the deaths of Rita, Mona and Carole from the Black Widows, and Denise Ray from the Bitty Bitches in an eighteen month time frame were not just nature's way of telling me I was growing old. I also kept trying to fit Scott Norris's unanticipated flight off the cliff into the equation.

THE CHIEF AND I HAD A QUICK BEER AT PAL JUANS AFTER MY TRAINING SESSION. His report, assembled entirely from his investigations conducted at the Pal Juan's Bar, concluded that there were no ongoing investigations and that there were no autopsies on any of the victims. However, the veteran cops all found the repeated and identical events a little hard to accept as "just one of those things."

I did not want to upset families by taking steps to turn up the pace of the police investigation, so Chief and I decided to be something unique to both of us; subtle. We planned a RAGBRAI kick-off party at my house with a real motive of finding out more about these deaths and to identify any suspects.

I invited the Black Widows, the Bitty Bitches, the Slow Pokes and the Grey Geese for a "Let's Get Ready for RAGBRAI Party." Matt had asked to invite his friends, Roy and Steve as well as their Spa from Hell team. I had reluctantly agreed. Their presence would give us more people to question in order to see if any clue emerged as to the cause of these "four coincidences."

We decided the Chief would be my bartender. This also served as a venue for some investigation on his part. He had recently agreed to drive the team bus. The idea of roughing it for seven days while driving across Iowa behind the wheel of a forty-five foot Winnebago with air-conditioning, fine food, unlimited beer and booze, and with the chance of getting laid every night quickly sold him into volunteering.

The party came off very well. Everyone came dressed in team outfits. The Black Widows all looked well groomed, in shape, well endowed and covered with jewels. The Bitty Bitches, now Cougars, were also well dressed in clothes that displayed their plus size bodies as strong and in shape.

The Grey Geese team members milled around and quickly made some friendships that would have benefits on the pending trip. I think the jersey I created of a very buff, well endowed goose in biking shorts and motto of "Want to see my beak?" was a good ice breaker.

The Spa from Hell boys were all wearing matching tight, black jeans and white shirts with ruffles up the front with the top three buttons open, displaying their hairless chests. Chief may not do a good job interviewing them. Matt was quickly involved with Roy and Steve by having them sampling a couple of expensive new wines and cheeses that he had brought. Steve left this group and was soon mingling with the various women like a beagle sniffing the floor for dropped morsels.

I was surprised to see Rita's sister, Tina. She was beautifully attired in a Black Widow jersey. I gave her a little hug and cheek kiss and again expressed how sorry I was for her loss. My real motive was to size up how she felt next to me; she felt very firm and in shape. Old guys are still not to be trusted as they are always prone to cop a little feel.

"I decided to get on with living. Rita often told me that she had great times and memories from this trip, so the Black Widows were nice enough to invite me. Besides, Herb has been gone a lot. He has been getting advice from a lot of sources on the best investment for the money from Rita's estate. He's also consulting with an older businessman who Rita knew very well. He is setting up some kind of commodity company, and he needs to involve farmers as barometers for crop production."

This sounded like RF's project. How intimately had my lecherous old friend, RF, known Rita? RF's favors usually had an ulterior motive.

To my surprise, Doug brought Mindy along. Could he be slipping into a steady relationship? She seemed mesmerized by this happy, festive, energetic group of people thirty-five years older than her. She was obviously like many young people who think of sixty year plus aged people as one step out of a nursing home and wearing oxygen support system in lieu of jewelry.

I watched Morgan turning on his charm. He had developed a list of three prospects for budding up. The poor ladies would soon find out that the true Morgan would likely get derailed from his journey to their tent by younger ladies. He may not be spending much time on

RF's project next week.

Chief worked the crowd, getting to know everyone as he served drinks. He always made sure to remember their drink preference and nick named the recipient as he quickly developed a life history on each of them. The big teddy bear was smooth. His full head of grey white hair, ruddy complexion and Irish smile were infectious. He had developed a chemistry with Judge Phyllis, and I could see that the judicial system would likely be well served in the week ahead as the law enforcement and judicial representatives on the trip got better acquainted under the stars.

The party went on well past midnight, which is forever for people my age. Anything beyond the ten o'clock news is nearly an overnight party.

When everyone left, Chief and I had a glass of Crown Royal and reviewed the night.

Chief started. "Your friend, Matt, has very little female interest. He seemed to be awfully chummy with the Spa fags. Hope it is only because he likes back rubs."

"Your friend, Morgan, is horny enough for both of them. He was all over the crowd, flirting with half the beautiful women, most of who were near his age. I hope they know that he is like a buck rabbit in heat. As soon as he sees another young female bunny, he will hop away for a new mate. By the way, does he ever get tired of telling the same lame jokes three times a night? Guess that's an old man trait."

"Luke and Tim will get laid a few times because of their constant effort. They both are charmers. Luke's military consulting jobs are kept awfully close to his vest, but he lets out enough information to keep listeners very intrigued. Have you ever watched his hypnotizing routine? Is that for real? He had three Cougars singing like a choir, and when he touched their shoulder, they stopped and denied doing it."

"I am not sure if I believe his version of his self-developed hypnotic powers. He claims that he can make golfers good putters, but he is one of the worst. He has told me it only works with receptive people or people under severe stress. We will see if he tries it on the trip after he suffers severe stress when he gets rejected by a few ladies."

"Doug is a mystery. I think he has lost his interest in the lady-chasing process. His young friend has him hooked. I am jealous that a twenty-five year old beauty doesn't find me attractive, even for a night. I have no idea what he did in the past. He drops zero hints on that subject. He's certainly well versed on a lot of subjects, but that government agricultural employee story is hard to believe. He is too aggressive and smart to be in government for a lifetime. He appears to have considerable wealth, even though he is careful not to display it. He still travels a lot according to Mindy, but the purpose of the consulting is extremely vague."

"The two big spa guys are half brothers, even though they have different hair color and complexions. Apparently Mommy got around a little. They grew up in the Dallas area. They were on several of these RAGBRAI trips and seem to deal with a lot of the ladies through their spa jobs. Obviously, they know a lot of the ladies who were here tonight."

"What about the deaths, big guy? I wasn't interested in what I already know."

"Be cool, little feller, or I will squash you like a bug. Quick, fill up this glass, I worked awfully hard tonight. The deaths were like you said; all sudden heart attacks to seemingly healthy, well cared for ladies. They had a couple things in common. They all died within the last eighteen months. They all went on RAGBRAI. They all like young men, good food, good times and spas. They all had met you. Maybe you're a suspect?"

"Seriously, we need more hard evidence in order to connect the dots. Why would someone kill them? Money is always a possibility, but there were no hints of robbery. Jealous lovers don't appear in the picture. So why? How could they do it so cleanly?"

"Sometimes such questions have no real answers, my inquisitive little friend. Death can occur for no good or logical reason other than being in the wrong place with the wrong person at the wrong time. The answers to how it happened are impossible to find when there are no autopsies or crime scene work-ups. But if we can get a suspect to focus on, then there are ways both inside and outside the system to get answers."

We ended the night without any answers and a lot of questions. We both knew we had a situation that did not make sense.

I kicked back and looked up thoughtfully at the full June moon. "Time and patience will be required to figure out this puzzle. Let's just wait calmly and see what develops."

We both were silent for a minute when Chief said what I also thought about my last idea. "You are so full of shit. That's the worst idea I have ever heard."

I could not argue.

THE NEXT DAY, CHIEF AND I ARRIVED AT PAL JUANS HAPPY HOUR. After my awful idea of resorting to being patient, Chief had called the best investigator in the area, John "Jock" Tenny. He had agreed to meet us to discuss using his unusual talents.

Jock had been in the area for thirty years. He had moved from St. Louis after a four year military stint as an MP. His career had followed several paths; policeman, teacher, broker, pyramid marketing guru, and thespian in local playhouse productions. His love of disguises had led him to become a PI.

"He uses his disguises to get involved with people and charms unlimited information from them. He may act weird, but he is smooth." Chief insisted he had used him on various occasions with great success.

As we sipped a drink, I asked, "Tell me about him. I know you are high on him, but I am not sure."

"The most distinct thing about him is he has almost nothing distinct about him. He is of average height and weight. His brown hair, hazel eyes, and tan complexion make him like a thousand other males. He easily blends in and can change his appearance with a few subtle changes that aren't obvious. The only give-away is his ear-to ear-smile with a big gap between his front teeth."

Next to me sat a man with a four day old beard, a long scar on his cheek, sunglasses, a filthy work hat and a dirty jean coat with a Kenworth truck line logo on the front pocket over the name Ken. In between slurs of beer, he leaned over towards me.

"I heard the name Jock Tenny. If that low life comes in here I intend to kick his ass from one end of this bar to the next. He had an affair with my old lady and I want him." He was so upset he slopped his beer into my lap.

I jumped back from a second beer slop. "If you two are his friends, I may just kick your ass around a little for a warm-up. You're first Shorty. Your big, gray haired, fat, old friend might be too tough. You look soft enough to me."

My German-Indian temper was about to erupt, when Chief grabbed the lout by the neck and swung him in front of my face.

"Jock, I want you to meet your new client. Lee Scott, meet Jock Tenny."

We all erupted. He was good. All I had focused on was his scar and filthy appearance.

We adjourned to Nick's Steakhouse after a few drinks.

"The job is very ill-defined. I've stumbled onto this situation where four healthy, sixty year old, wealthy ladies have died of sudden heart attacks in the last eighteen months. They all appeared to be in good condition and were working very diligently to stay in shape. I met them all on this bike trip across Iowa three years ago."

"You mean RAGBRAI? I went on it about five years ago. I had a blast and promised myself I would try it again."

"Good, you are familiar with this event and all the teams and parties?"

He gave me his big gap-tooth grin. "I had heard all about the parties and wanted to participate. I started alone, but ended up with Team Skunk. It's a big group from all over the Midwest. I may still have my black jersey with the white strip down the back. I tried my best to get laid, but struck out every night. I need to locate a new team with fewer morals or take some refresher courses in seduction. I was a real failure. Maybe this job will help me find a dream team of nymphomaniacs with an acquired taste for middle-aged men."

"Jock, what I want is for you to move around among the different teams, ask questions about these four ladies and see if there are others. Generally just nose around. I have no idea what to tell you to look for and will leave that up to you. For two thousand dollars a week and all the food and booze you can consume, I hope I can get some facts, even if you conclude I am nuts."

"Keep your cell phone on you, boss. I will get in touch every evening. It's best we not hang around together. I do have one request. If you find a lady who needs my really special service call, don't hesitate to call me. I am available day or night. Have disguise, will travel. I have a very injured self-image that needs repaired."

As we were leaving Nick's, I had a fleeting suggestion. I told Jock and Chief about the Scott Norris death flight story. Chief, why don't you check into any available records to see if anything was concluded about his death? Keep it in mind. I don't see how it's connected, but who knows?

BEFORE YOU JUDGE A MAN, WALK A MILE IN HIS SHOES. AFTER THAT WHO CARES? HE'S A MILE AWAY AND YOU HAVE HIS SHOES.

Billy Connolly

Chapter Twenty

****

SHE MOVED AROUND THE KITCHEN IN HER SKIMPY RED BRA AND THONG PANTIES. Mindy was totally uninhibited as she finished preparing a turkey burger, fresh vegetables and salad while Doug showered. He was a fascinating man, even if he was her father's age. His weathered face, graying black hair, and piercing brown eyes were attractive, in an animal sense. His passion for staying in shape was challenging to be around, even for a twenty-five year old former athlete. He talked of news events with a prospective and passion befitting a CNBC news personality covering a Republican rally. He was a constant user of a complex computer system, which she could not use without him opening it up for her. All of this fascinated her. She knew very little about his past. It was a subject he avoided.

She knew her future with him was doubtful, but her mystery man was fascinating; he treated her with more respect and manners than the younger men she had dated. Besides, he was talented in bed, unlike the self-satisfying younger men she had known.

Doug entered the kitchen, fresh from a long shower, wearing black shorts and a tight black sleeveless Under-Armour shirt. His strong legs and arms seemed even more sinewy than ever, as a result of the recent bike training. His attitude of late was consistently light; his humor was constantly present. He laughed a lot at life's twists. They talked and enjoyed a relaxed dinner with a good bottle of a Mexican wine that Doug had brought home from a resent consulting trip.

After discussing his day's golf game, hole by hole, which is a common malady with golfers, they talked about the upcoming bike trip across Iowa and what to expect in the Iowa countryside. Doug had been in Iowa over ten years, but he had never really explored the area. He flew in and out on consulting trips. When he was home, he simply disappeared into this town filled with many hard-working, fun loving people.

As she got up to get him another glass of wine, he slowly moved behind her and slowly, softly massaged her back and neck. His strong hands softly glided over her young nearly nude buns with deep caressing squeezes. His lips nibbled at her neck's nap and her shoulder.

"I often wonder how long I can keep you interested in me. While you are still interested in me, why don't you go with us across Iowa? I know it's a guy trip, but we can throw your bike on board; ride when you want, and act as the Chief's driving assistant when you want. Just don't fuck the charming, horny old teddy bear."

"Whatever your motive, keep doing what you're doing. That massage feels wonderful. With that talent, I will be here forever. I could never replace those touches. If the invitation is open, I will think about going. Won't the others feel intimidated with a female along?"

"That's a point. I will talk to them, but I'll need to assure them if they do anything that they want to stay on the trip and you tell, I will need to kill you. Okay?" He laughed.

"If you do have to kill me, why don't you do it by screwing me to death?"

With that invitation, they moved hand in hand to his bedroom. The lights were already dim, a couple's porn show was showing on the fifty-inch plasma TV and a bottle of champagne was cooling.

"It looks to me like you planned to seduce this tired little body all along, young lady." With a wink, a cute flip of her hips and a lick of her lips, the lights went out.

The next morning, Doug was up early, sipping his usual freshly prepared carrot and apple mix, with a slight smile permanently affixed on his face. He fixed two omelets filled with freshly cooked vegetables from the farmers market, topped with sour cream and a home-made mild salsa sauce. He put them into the stoves warmer along with the white corn tortilla wraps. He knew Mindy would not stir for a while after having quite a busy night, and since it was a week-end, she had the day off. It continued to amaze him how loving and caring she was, and how her touches could stimulate his libido after over six months of being together. He had seldom remained interested in any female for six months.

He then moved to his salt-water aquarium, tested the water and sprinkled the day's food supply on the surface. As the bright light in the tank came on, the occupants started to move about in frenzy, sensing breakfast was floating above them. Doug called them by their nicknames; Sid the Sand Shark, Yancy the Yellow Fin, Bart the Bottom Feeder and Teresa the Tiger Mollie. All were darting rapidly around, driven by hunger.

With a quick dip of the net, Perry the Puff-Fish was netted. Doug quickly thumped Perry a few times with the blunt handle of his knife. As a response, he blew up to three times his size preparing to defend himself against his unknown opponent. After a minute of puffing, he was laid on the counter, decapitated, and gutted. The poison emitted into the exterior skin, but his defense mechanism had not saved Perry.

Perry was purged of his prickly barbs and quickly cooked. He was then chopped into small bits, placed into brine and stored in a small jar in Doug's travel case.

Mindy came into the kitchen wearing only his sweat-soiled Under-Armour shirt and sleepily hugged him. He patted her bare bottom and presented her breakfast. As they slowly enjoyed his handiwork, Doug reached for her and touched her hand.

"I appreciate your house sitting and taking me to the airport. I'll be back in two or three days. I may need to cut back on these trips, if you keep screwing me all night. I'm exhausted. You seem to keep learning new tricks. Are you watching porn flicks without me and shopping on line with Porn-R-Us again?"

"My horny old friend, I spend the whole day, every day, figuring out how I can surprise you. Buy that?"

"No, but it's good to hear from a lovely little tart like you," he replied in his best pirate voice.

The flight to Los Angeles was uneventful. It took the whole day, as he used three one way tickets that took him to Chicago, Denver and then LA. He arrived with his typical nondescript appearance: a pair of jeans, old running shoes, untucked dark blue golf shirt, and nondescript Ray-Ban sun glasses. A cab ride to the small Francis Hotel on Wilshire took an hour, as it slowly wandered through the endless traffic. The day was hot, smog hung in the air, and the smell of new pollution set the foul mood for the day.

After checking in, a walk along the Miracle Mile ended at the newly erected Beverly Heights. It was thirty floors tall and was enclosed by a silver metal surface. The first ten were filled with offices and upper eighteen floors contained eighteen full floor condos. The last two floors were the location for the "Movers," the most exclusive restaurant in a town, where wealthy patron's appetites for culinary adventures were always satisfied.

He made a quick trip to the top floor using the counterfeit pass key. A freshly added large scar on his left check and a white contact lens on his left eye assured him that the people at the front desk would only remember those features. He quickly checked that a table for Mr. Perry Fisher and two guests at 8 pm was reserved as scheduled. With a fifty dollar bill for encouragement, the reservation for Reverend Wallace Winston at 7:30 pm was also confirmed. He quietly slipped back to his hotel to don the server's uniform for the evening.

The next day, the LA Times, in the entertainment section, announced the death of the famous Reverend Winston during dinner at the Movers. It reported he was there with three media advisors when he complained of an increased tingling of his lips and tightness in his chest before he began to violently shake and vomit. The news said the death was under investigation.

Beware of chopped Puff-Fish in hollandaise cream sauce over a broiled grouper filet. The combination can be lethal. In fact, it caused an abrupt end to the Reverend's evening. The combination is also extremely hard to detect, especially when the waiter has removed the serving plate and silverware, before the emergency response unit arrived.

What the LA Times could not report was the fact that two CDs were delivered to its editor after press time. The CDs contained documents about the improper use of millions of dollars donated by true believers to the Winston Foundation for World Wide Health. They contained documented proof of investments in off-shore gambling, prostitution operations in Cambodia, groups known to run opium from Afghanistan, and of course, generous travel allowances to the right Reverend Winston. The content and pictures would be enough to fill weeks of news print.

The second CD would make the first one seem boring. It detailed the path of Wally Wallace from small town Mississippi. It detailed a suspicious acquittal of a charge of raping a fifteen year old girl, a trip to a juvenile school for his sexually-aggressive nature, and eventually to prison for a year for defrauding the life savings of a seventy year old foster mother.

Three years after release from jail, he re-emerged in Missouri with a traveling gospel group and the new name of Wallace Winston. His booming bass voice and fire and brimstone closing sermons filled the offering plates with ever-increasing levels of cash donations. His life continued to spiral upward when he connected mentally and physically with the widow Ester Black. She was overweight, overly-cosmetically enhanced, talkative, under educated and very wealthy, thanks to the chain of small town radio and television stations inherited from her husband, the late Ben Black.

In a few years, Winston had used this media empire to build his image and cash flow. As an aside, it helped expand his message of caring for the poor, uneducated and under fed to a national level. When Ester died by falling down three flights of stairs in a drunken haze, his half of the media stock was quickly redeemed at a premium by Ben Black II. Winston then moved to LA in order to go international with his message of hope and caring. His unusual taste for young girls on his international trips was documented by pictures, films, and tapes in the two CD's.

Someone had methodically performed their homework in a very professional manner and provided explicit, documented and extensive detail. The Reverend would be long remembered as the CD's contents became public. His foundation would collapse and be distributed for its intended purpose. His life would be vividly documented in an X-rated film that would set radio and TV evangelists back twenty years. Perry the Puff-Fish had died for a greater good.

FRIENDS ARE LIKE CONDOMS: THEY PROTECT
YOU WHEN THINGS GET HARD.

The Mammoth Book of One-Liners

Chapter Twenty-one

****

FOR THE LAST SIX WEEKS, WE HAD TRAINED LIKE EXTRAS
AUDITIONING FOR THE "300 SPARTANS" MOVIE. Our muscles
were now strong and hard. We had even developed six-pack abs.
Unfortunately they were not obvious as they were covered by a layer
of fat.

Before leaving on the RAGBRAI adventure I needed to visit with
RF. All the necessary paperwork for his new venture was complete.

"Your new commodities fund concept doesn't violate anyone else's
intellectual property as all of the data used in your analysis is in the
public domain. If you want to try it, let's go for it. Here is an outline
of the organizational steps and the formation documents. When you
say go, I will see that they are sequentially filed, and then you are the
sole owner of Fleeting Star Enterprises. I thought about Flaming Star
Enterprises, but that implies a quick burnout."

I handed him another 2 inch pile of documents. "Here are the
contractual documents you need signed by the farmer advisors. Under
these contracts, the consultants have considerable commitments to
you, especially promptly reporting their findings and maintaining
necessary security of the information. They are also restricted on future
employment by a tightly drafted non-competition provision. If you
have a key supervisor such as Herb Knowlton, he also will need to sign
the enclosed contract with some expanded provisions on his duties and

139

non-competition obligations."

"Lee, how did you know about Herby? You are a snoopy little shit. That's why I love you. I have only known Herb for a year. I met him through a young lady with whom I used to enjoy a few evenings. He is not the brightest bulb in the lamp, but he makes up for it by hard work and honesty."

"Herb and I had a common friend at Rita's recent funeral. His wife, Tina, told me about his new venture in the commodities business. I still can put two and two together."

"Lee, I missed the Rita Keyes funeral on purpose. Rita was a wonderful lady. She was witty, classy, sassy and perpetually horny. She had it all, from this seventy-five year old man's point of view. I really have a hard time believing she is gone."

"Besides, funerals leave me depressed for weeks anymore. I always dream of myself looking up from the casket at the mourners. She was so healthy and alive. I saw her a couple weeks before her death. I tried to get her to come over for a few drinks and to rekindle my love for her. I used every bit of charm left in me. I got rejected."

She said she was through with her old ways; she was in love for the first time in a long while."

I paused as a small tear formed in his eyes.

"Look, enough about your decaying love life. I suspect you have Morgan Snyder doing the computer program work, so tell him to get in high gear if you are going to go forward with this project. But remember, no trying to steal government reports before they go to the public, and no trying to access government data before the reports are assembled and issued. Understood, amigo?"

"Of course, my overly cautious scribe, I would never try to beat the public to information for my own profit and their detriment. Thanks again for the stern reminder."

"I know you too well, and that's why the reminder is necessary, Mr. Boss-Man."

"I'll have my cell on while I pedal my old bones across the state next week. Let me know if there are any questions."

"In the meantime, I am hoping to see if Team Nude is still involved in the ride, and if they have aged any over the last three years. Odds are that gravity may also have also taken its toll on them. I have learned with age, all good things eventually go south."

RF pulled out his bottle of Crown Royal Reserve and poured us each a three finger deep drink.

He rocked back in his chair and said, "Lee, I was so spooked about Rita's death I called the Chief and hired him to do a little snooping. Chief told me of your suspicions about these four women's coincidental deaths. "

"I have asked him to dig a little deeper. I smelled something very wrong with all these alleged coincidences. He will do some investigating while he is your driver on that ridiculous bike trip."

As he finished another deep sip, he surmised, "The commonality is obvious. The victims are all middle-aged, wealthy women, in apparently good health, who once or more rode on RAGBRAI, suffered unforeseen heart failure and all of them knew you. Seems to me you are the best suspect, barrister."

RF laughed at his own wit. "I always knew you had a black heart. But, if we assume you are innocent, isn't the obvious common factors health clubs, spas, fitness centers, and beauty shops?"

"Chief can use his cell phone and see if these ladies were common customers at an establishment."

I said, "Sounds like good use of his extra time. Otherwise, he will drink too much and try to pick up every young lady that gives him a second glance."

"Enjoy your trip. Don't get drunk, fall off your bike and break one of your brittle bones. You know more people your age die from the side-effects of broken bones than any other cause? I need you in one piece to help me get this new venture off the ground."

"With that piece of medically inspiring information, I am leaving. I will ride carefully. If I get lucky, I will warn the women to be gentle because of my brittle bones. We will be in touch. Don't steal any private government data when my back is turned."

He winked.

**THE BEST TIME TO MAKE A FRIEND
IS BEFORE YOU NEED THEM.**

Ethel Barrymore

Chapter Twenty-two

****

THE RIDE TO MISSOURI VALLEY COMMENCED WITH THE
ROUSING SOUNDS OF WILLY NELSON'S "WE'RE ON THE ROAD
AGAIN" BLASTING FROM THE CD DECK. Chief was breaking
every speed law and gruffly cussing at all the slow driving idiots that
got in his way.

Everyone was eager to get started; the air was filled with light-
hearted banter, jabs and badinage. We were acting more akin to a
fraternity of college students than a bunch of long term AARP card
carriers. Some of the BS may have been alcohol stimulated as we were
well into the second batch of Luke's Bloody Mary's, which he blended
the night before from a closely guarded recipe.

Chief and Mindy were in the Winnebago's driver bay, planning
the exact location of their daily stops at mid morning, mid afternoon
and day's end. This process required considerable planning in order to
locate routes that intersected the rider's routes.

No motorized vehicles are allowed on the biker's route, although
an occasional pissed off farmer does pull out of their farm lane only
to find themselves surrounded by hundreds of vocal and pissed off
bikers. Typically, the unfortunate farmers failed to read the local news
regarding the hordes of bikes on the road, and the farmers' tolerance for
abuse is seldom high. More than one middle finger gesture occurred at
such stressful encounters.

With Chief's heavy foot on the gas pedal, we quickly passed team vehicles of every shape and color: Team Skunk in its black bus with a white strip, Team Nude in a pink van with a cute butt painted on the rear, Team Black Widow in their black renovated bus, covered on each side by a big spider, and the new entry, Team Cougar. The Cougar's tan colored RV displayed a large plastic female cougar head on the hood, complete with ear-rings and lipstick; their motto "We will eat your young," was boldly painted on the rear.

Tim was intrigued with Team Cougar. As we passed, he held up to the window his cell phone number on a quickly created sign. He had three calls in the next five minutes. The flirtatious process was starting.

Matt was unusually quiet, so I moved to the captain's chair beside him. "What's wrong old friend, scared of a little four hundred and fifty mile ride?"

With a long pause, Matt raised his head. His big blue eyes were tearing. "I think my friend Roy's half -brother, Steve, may have let my personal secret slip after Rita's funeral. I have been getting quite involved with Roy over the last few weeks. Unlike Steve, who is very straight, Roy is openly gay and is not a control freak."

"I have been wrestling with my feelings for a long time with, and I think my conclusions are clear to me."

With a slight sniffle Matt continued. "There is a reason I have never established or maintained a sexual relationship with a female. It has profoundly bothered me for a long time. It has been very frustrating. I have tried to live this false image with you guys for years."

"I love our friendship as well as all aspects of our relationship. I don't want to lose that, but I have to become honest with myself." He ended with a slight sniffle.

I put my arm around his shoulder and patted his back, I felt sorry for the pain he had been keeping inside him.

"Matt, you are always a friend. We have known each other too long to let this revelation get in the way."

"This isn't a shock, you know. I suspect all the others will feel the same and won't be blown away. We all have our secrets and differences. We are too old to be hung up on what makes us different. We need to focus on what makes us the same."

"Do you want to talk to everyone, keep it quiet, or just let it play out? Just be ready for some good- natured kidding."

"Thanks, Lee. I will talk to them over the next few days. You're right. Let's get on with the trip, and have a week of butt-busting fun. Excuse the choice of words."

I got us both a beer. "Not to change the subject, but I notice you keep watching the railway that parallels Interstate 80. What's your big obsession with railroads?"

"I can make a fortune, if I can figure out the glitches in my railroad track cleaning solution. The Union Pacific has offered me a big number for the license to my patent rights, as the fuel efficiency factor is huge. That chemical is the one that burned my arms a few weeks ago. It was eating up every container I used to store it in. I now have that damn powerful crap stored in Teflon-lined steel barrels in my lab in a cave in the limestone cliffs near Winterset."

Matt became increasingly animated as he talked about his new and troubling invention.

"Those caves are so big you can put all the bridges in Madison County in them and have extra room. I have a state-of-the-art lab set up in one. The climate can be perfectly maintained for any project. The cool atmosphere, in the deep cave, seems to have slowed this one's aggressive chemical process."

"The damn stuff will clean the tracks all right. I am afraid it will eat them up, and if it runs off, I guarantee it will destroy the wood railroad ties like butter in a microwave. I am close to a fortune if I can just solve these problems."

"When we get back, I want you to look at the contracts the UP sent over, while I try to get this stuff under control. I will try a couple more ideas to solve these potency problems. What about 10% of the profits for you handling the legal aspects?"

"Sounds like a deal to me, my little fairy friend." We both hugged and laughed so loud the others turned to see what was up.

Doug was watching the farm scenery that was flying by us. He had Mindy by his side, as she and Chief had completed all their planning for interim stops. The two of them were talking mindlessly about the landscape. On each side, hundreds of white, three-hundred foot tall wind power plants arose in the clear, blue sky. Iowa was quickly harnessing wind energy, thanks to Warren Buffet's owning the biggest power company in the area.

Huge weed free farms of soybeans, alfalfa, and corn filled the rolling hills on each side. This weed-free status was thanks to Pioneer and Monsanto Round-Up Ready genetics which had modified this crop's cellular structure to tolerate the strong, killing effect of Round-Up weed spray. All these sites were a blur, as they flew by for endless miles, at Chiefs customary ninety miles an hour.

Doug was taking in all of Mindy's stories and history of each town in an unusually calm fashion. His long, piercing gazes at Mindy were uncharacteristic. She looked like an excited beautiful farm girl, as she talked endlessly, with the enthusiasm and freedom of spirit of a young person who had not seen or felt some of the cruelties of life.

AT LAST, MISSOURI VALLEY APPEARED ON THE HORIZON AS WE HEADED NORTH ON I-29. We had made record time, thanks to Chief and his conveniently placed calls to several old friends on the Highway Patrol.

This kick-off town of six thousand people was located five miles from the Missouri River on the intersecting banks of two of its tributaries, the Willow and Boyer Rivers. For the pure biker, a five mile ride to dip the bike tire in the Missouri River was a "must do" event. For the less ambitious, a one hundred yard stroll to the Willow or Boyer River for a tire dip was available. For the biggest share of us, we just lied, and said we, of course, participated in the customary tire dipping ceremony.

The Winnebago door opened, and the hot air resulting from eighty percent humidity and ninety degree temperature combined hitting us with a blast furnace impact. Everyone had the same thought: what have we committed to do?

The campground, at the local fair ground, was filled with dozens of two hundred year old oaks. The scene was buzzing, like a hive of bees, from the sounds of thousands of camping bikers having a party.

The smell of barbeque ribs, sizzling pork chops, frying donuts and funnel cakes and beer filled our nostrils. The sounds of Johnny Cash and the Tennessee Two boomed across the campground from the beer garden's huge sound system. Everywhere, friends from different teams were hugging, and talking as the sweat poured down their bodies.

RAGBRAI was about to commence.

Team Grey Geese's members disappeared like leaves in a November wind. I wandered around by myself doing some people watching. The crowd had definitely aged, but the enthusiasm had not been reduced. There appeared to be considerably more family teams utilizing the week for a reunion time. The exercise, camaraderie, and daily trail events would become family lore for generations.

I noticed a lot of younger riders listening to their own age of music in a far corner of the park. The sound of the Black-Eyed Peas combined with the overriding tones of Johnny Cash to form a strange background reverberation for the festivities. I actually stopped and listened to this younger sound. To my surprise, I think I could like the Black-Eyed Peas, despite my generations predetermined conclusion that all new music sucked. I recall my parents making that comment regarding rock and roll. Some things never change.

The younger set were all drinking sports drinks, eating pasta and talking about leaving at sunrise. W.C. Fields was right; youth is wasted on the young. They were clearly, letting their testosterone get in the way of taking their time to breathe in the aromas of the country-side, let the sights of the summer beauty take over their mind and to feel the rejuvenation of their bodies' as they moved across the miles. God, we old guys can be profound with our wisdom.

When I arrived at the beer garden, the Village People's recording of YMCA had replaced Johnny Cash and was blaring at eardrum-breaking levels. I found Morgan and Tim in the middle of one hundred people singing and acting out the song. Both were performing like cheer leaders encouraging louder responses each time the YMCA name came up in the lyrics.

I located Luke leaning on the beer garden fence watching the sweat pour from the crowd of dancers. He was quietly talking with three very well endowed fifty to fifty five year old women proudly wearing their Cougar jersey. The victims did not understand, they were dealing with a world class shrink, and self-proclaimed hypnotists, who specialized in profiling people at a very rapid pace. Little did they suspect, they were being sized up for his seduction, or for rejection as too much trouble.

The sweet ladies had no reason to know that beneath that tall military look, blue eyes, soft voice and huge body was a mind calculating just one thing; how, when and if he wanted to attempt to get into their biking shorts. Watching an old but accomplished lecher at work is worthy of the time. Unfortunately, we men all know that despite all the male cunning and planning, females have total control over sex. No one ever seduced a woman; they just let males think they have.

The Chief was bellied up to the bar in the beer garden with the Honorable Judge Ruth. Her six foot large frame looked far less intimidating out of her robe. The tight black biking shorts and sleeveless blouse showed off an attractive plus size shape. In fact she was well proportioned and had arms and shoulders that were amazingly buff. Her long brown hair was no longer in a bun but in a ponytail. Her glasses were gone and her green eyes sparkled. She had a round rosy cheeked face, with a cute pointed nose and some very well applied makeup, that made her look far younger than her years.

"Lee, get your mangy old body over here, before I impose a bench warrant and sanctions. Great to see you! We decided to give this happening, one last try. How do you like our new name and jerseys? Off course none of us are really Cougars," she winked.

I cautiously said, "I love the jerseys and the new name. I would always assume the best of motives from someone of your stature, Your Honor. Do I call you Your Honor, Judge, Her Excellency or what this trip?"

"Take your choice Ruth, Ruthie, Ruthie Baby or hey you bitch," she laughed like a twenty year old at a sorority party.

"I think I'll stick with Ruthie Baby and be semi-safe. By the way, be careful you are hanging around with a pretty unsavory ex-member of law enforcement. One false move and he will frisk you under the pretense of looking for hidden weapons."

Judge Ruth looked long at the Chief. "You know, I was hoping he would get around to the frisking stage one of these days and cut out his war stories and lame sexist jokes."

He gave a sly smile, as she grabbed his big hand and led him into the darkness. The power of the judiciary strikes again.

Matt was nowhere to be found. I had my suspicions that he and Roy were having a clandestine gathering planning the rest of their week, while they sampled the goose pâté and expensive French wine that I had seen carefully packed in Matt's back pack. Nosey lawyers never can control that instinct to poke their nose into someone else's business; in this case, a carefully packed back pack. I suspect that Matt will never figure out where the cans of caviar went.

While, I felt quite alone, I was having fun and was feeling invigorated. I was looking forward to this return trip. I remember how this event had been like a fountain of youth years before when Rita and Mona had made me feel like a teenage stud. My attitude had already changed as I realized you will age, but you don't have to get old in mind and spirit. It is your choice. I elected the "stay young" route as it is a lot more fun.

My cell phone went off. An unidentified number showed on the cell's face. I answered.

"Hello, this is Pepe Le Pew with Team Skunk; I assume this is Mr. Scott the self-proclaimed famous barrister. Meet me by the Methodist Church food stand on the west side of the campground in five minutes for an update." Jock Tenny was on duty,

As I arrived, I had trouble not laughing as I saw a Team Skunk member with a handle-bar mustache talking in a very bad French accent to a young female server at the Methodist food stand.

With a big grin I whispered, "I see you are using bad costumes and a worse accent to try to get to first base with someone a third your age, Pepe."

"Guess I'm busted. You can't blame me for trying. I struck out every day last time I was on this trip, and my ego is very fragile," he laughed.

"As you can tell, I am, for today, a Team Skunk member. A few of their elder statesmen remembered me from five years ago. I hope a couple of their female members don't remember me, as I did not make a good impression. This Pepe Le Pew gig gets the relationship off to a humorous start; it opens people up quickly and allows me to ask a lot of questions."

"One point of interest, besides going on RAGBRAI part of this team goes on another long bike ride in late September called the Nebraska Plains Ride. The more interesting fact is that about three years ago they had three members of their team die over a short period from sudden heart attacks; all were financially well off women, over fifty, in supposedly good health. Sound rather familiar?"

"Great first day, try to get some victims names and see if they had any connections within their team or other riders that might be suspects. Maybe we can help narrow this search."

"You may be as good as Chief says, Pepe! Be careful."

MAY THE FORCES OF EVIL BECOME CONFUSED
ON THE WAY TO YOUR HOUSE.

George Carlins

Chapter Twenty-three

****

THE EVENINGS TEMPERATURE WAS AT LAST COOLING. The breeze slowly filtered into the tent through its screen sides and cooled the two sweaty male bodies. The smell of all the foods from the evening party floated about and was mixed with the other smells of the night: the humidity-laden dew, the fully-filled wild flowers surrounding the fair grounds and the fresh cut grass of the camp site preparation.

The sound of the Black-Eyed Peas was gone as their listeners rested for tomorrow's early morning challenges. The beer garden sounds had shifted from a steady blast of rock and roll classics to the love songs of the sixties. The Lettermen, the Righteous Brothers, Pat Boone and Del Shannon crooned endlessly as the fading number of dancers hugged and groped in rhythm with what they thought was ageless music.

Roy Rose tossed restlessly.

"God, that music is driving me nuts. I'm exhausted and the trip hasn't even started. But, we had a good night. We have both identified targets for the trip and after the trip. We need to be very cautious. We've had a lot of success so far. Why risk it by moving too quickly."

"I agree," came the sleepy voice of Steve Delong.

Between yawn Delong said, "I think we should move to another town. We've been here too long. In fact, I may be moving whether you want to or not. I am still pissed about the way you ended my last golden oldie without my okay. We should have talked. She was getting to be rather special; maybe even a long termer. She had lots of money and could have changed my life, but no, you ended that potential without so much as asking."

Roy became agitated, his face contorted as the veins on his neck bulged.

"Steve, I am getting sick and tired of your hassling me. I've explained over and over that you were getting too close to the old broad; I thought you were ready for the relationship to end. I probably should have asked, but it never occurred to me that you had the ability to develop some romantic feelings."

After a pause, Roy said, "But, you have a point about going our separate ways. I've found a new friend. There are a lot of things about him I really enjoy. Mainly, he is loaded. This might be my ticket to a new life without the need of dealing with the rich, old people who want me to help them feel young."

"You're right Roy. I think this might be our last hunt together. We've had a lot of thrills and some laughs, but we have been lucky. Maybe, we need to settle down."

"Besides, my newest trophy-friend, Tina, might be my ticket to the easy life. She is as good looking as her sister and is not nearly as manipulative and controlling. I hope she is just as good in the sack as her sister. She seems a little reserved, but I have a week to soften her up. That should be enough time to convince her to be a nymphomaniac like her sister."

ELSEWHERE IN THE CAMP AREA, the members of Team Grey Geese were finishing up the night with a sip of fifty year old port and Matt's caviar; mysteriously removed from his back-pack.

Tim was soaked in sweat and wore a frozen smile. "Tonight, made me feel like a kid again. I have three names from the Cougars and Spiders, all suggesting a night cap tomorrow evening. How do I handle this predicament?"

"Tim, has it ever occurred to you that you aren't up to three nocturnal visits in a night? You will be lucky to satisfy the expectations of one of them."

"I know you're right. But Lee, it sure is good for my ego to dream about trying. I'll figure out a way to space them out so I can recover and perform up to each of their expectations."

"I hope the expectations of number three are very low, as she is likely to get awfully disappointed," came a soft female voice from the rear bed room, where Doug and Mindy had spent most of the night.

"Just what I need; a smart-ass, twenty-five year old map reader, poking holes in my dreams. Mindy you can go back to sleep with that old fart you're fucking, and keep your young opinions to yourself." Tim laughed.

A giggle came from the rear bed room. The love of life and the enthusiasm for new experiences bubbling from a young woman can be extremely seductive.

As the evening ended, I did a nose check and everyone was back except for the Chief and Morgan. Matt reported seeing Morgan surrounded by four members of Team Nude. He reportedly was discussing the best methods of avoiding sun burns and bike seat rash while riding nude. I had last seen him dancing with two of his new best friends to the beat of the Righteous Brother's, "You've Lost that Loving Feeling." He was wearing a Team Nude Auxiliary tee shirt decorated with a very well endowed male figure silhouetted on the front.

The Chief arrived just as we were bedding down. He had a devilish smile on this ruddy face and his white hair was filled with grass.

"Have you ever noticed, how clear you can see the stars if you lie on your back and look up long enough? I'm beat. I think I put too much effort into star watching. Good night my little bunch of losers." The Chief fell into his tent and was snoring in a record one minute. Booze and sex mixed with age is a great sleeping remedy.

THE BEST WAY I COULD FIGURE TO IMPROVE UPON COCA-COLA, ONE OF LIFE'S MOST DELIGHTFUL ELIXERS, WHICH STUDIES PROVE CAN HEAL THE SICK AND OCCASSIONALLY RAISE THE DEAD, IS TO PUT RUM OR BOURBON IN IT.

Lewis Grizzard

Chapter Twenty-four

****

THE SMELL OF COFFEE, BACON AND EGGS WERE LIKE AN ALARM CLOCK. The sounds of the Village People belting out "Macho Man" started my day like a bugle. Chief was leaning in the bus door turning up the stereo. An apron, with a Julia Child face on it, was draped over his blue sweat suit. His rumpled curly white hair was still filled with blades of grass.

Chief and Mindy had been busy. They had coffee, egg and bacon sandwiches plus fresh juice set out for each of us. They also had our water containers chilled and filled for the start of the voyage across Iowa.

Doug was up, dressed and sipping coffee. His nervous energy showed that he was obviously anxious to get on the trail.

Because I had not gotten drunk, screwed or even over eaten at the kick-off night, I felt great and was ready to get started.

Luke stoically ignored his sore and very stiff right leg, which had been irritated by too much dancing.

Tim showed resilience, despite all his enthusiastic efforts with the Cougars. He was tenaciously shaking Morgan, who was barely moving.

Matt was not around. But he arrived as we were checking our

bike's tires for correct pressure, adjusting our seats and inventorying our bike pouches for essentials; spare tire tube, first aid kit, butt balms, muscle cream and Aleve. His wispy, graying hair was askew; his round cheeks were growing red, his pear-shaped body held his clothes in a rumpled manner. He had a sheepish smile on his face; he winked at me and proceeded to get ready.

Morgan was starting to get enthused, as he downed an extra strength power drink and tried to remember the names of the three Team Nude friends who he had formed a conga line with the night before. He was like an old Jimmie Buffet getting ready for one more gig. Aleve, ice water, combined with a vitamin B and ginkgo drink can work magic, for a while.

The westerly breeze was at our back, and the sun was in our faces, as we headed up the casual slope from Missouri Valley. The slope grew increasingly steep as we entered the Loess Hills. The old elm and cotton wood trees formed a canopy over the narrow, old black-topped road to BeeBeeTown; our first town on the route-map.

This nearly dead town consisted of ten rundown houses, a long ago closed and collapsing school and a tavern where fifteen Harley's rested. The hairy bare-chested, vest draped, long haired riders sat on the bar's step sipping beer; watching the spectacle of gaudily clad bikers passing through their town. Their disdain for the passing health-nuts was obvious. Their admiration for the many beautiful ladies in tight biking wear was expressed in macho crude gestures and comments.

Doug whispered, "Let's go kick over a couple of their hogs and see what happens."

"Just keep pedaling and shut up, feisty little man. They maybe look dumb, but I can smell testosterone oozing from them from here."

The portion of the ride was extremely strenuous for a starting day as it wound through the Loess Hills as we headed to Red Oak. Numerous severe elevation changes were a steady part of the process.

The food stops were essentially the same as on my first trip. The Pancake Man, the Mutton Man and the Pork Chop Man were all at similar stages of each day's trip. The crowds swarmed to these old reliable providers. At five dollars a pop, they were having a good day. I am sure the IRS was getting its fair share!!!

The banter, humor and good nature of the crowd was entertaining and completely spontaneous. Some of the food stands created by local groups were innovative; frozen pineapple soaked in gin or vodka, health drinks charged with deep green wheat grass juice, fried snickers, honey coated dill pickles and oversized frozen chocolate-chip cookies. We estimated that for every 2000 calories burned, 2500 calories were consumed.

The farm folks lined their small town's street agog, cheering and waving as we entered the town they called home. Small boy's squirted water from hoses as bikers arrived with sweat pouring off them. Each location had a refreshment stop featuring local specialties and local entertainers. The best of the day was the near-naked singing cowboy at Oakland, and the pickled pig's feet at Macedonia. The Dolly Parton look-alike at Avoca and the deep fried pickles at Emerson were close seconds. Everyone was getting into the mood and had a grin frozen on their faces despite the long and arduous first day.

Doug had shot ahead and had not been seen for hours. Matt had last been seen riding and talking with Roy and the other members of The Spa from Hell team. Larry, Tim and I were staying together and soaking in the entire festive atmosphere.

As we stopped for a water break, the sounds of Abba's "Dancing Queen" roared by with twenty Team Drag Queen members singing in their best or at least loudest bass and baritone voices. Jock was the last one to pass. He had changed teams. He gave me a toothy grin and wink.

Not far behind the Drag Queens came Team Nude. They all had their tops off. They were all as good, firm and upright, as I remembered. In the middle of the sea of bouncing boobs, was Morgan, with a smile on his face and sweat streaming down his naked upper body. The residual effect of the booze from the night before was clearly torturing him. But, being a macho male, he would not show the pain to his new team of friends.

We finally arrived in Red Oak after eight hours of riding and two hours of assorted breaks. Chief had parked the RV in a heavily tree-filled area in the local park. As we all sipped, or in some cases, gulped nearly frozen beer, Chief gave us a history lesson about the town. He pointed out the statute of the wounded soldier holding a fallen comrade featured in the park. It honored the National Guard Unit from Montgomery County that stood firm when Rommel's Africa Korp roared over them at their break out from Tunisia through the Kasserine Pass. In 1942, they were fresh-off the farms of Iowa, when the biggest loss by a National Guard unit was suffered.

The thought of the fear and courage of those young farm boys in the middle of the Tunisian desert was sobering. Life can be very unfair: wrong place at the wrong time.

After a cool refreshing shower, a long stretch on the recently mowed grass and a second bottle of ice cold Miller High Life, we all quietly, looked at each other and started to laugh. We had made an eighty-five mile trek, and despite the signals of pain from some old body parts, we were ready for more. The fear of failure was gone, moods were light hearted and night fall was near.

One cell phone call inviting us to visit the Spiders lair was enough. We all pulled ourselves together and left, except Matt, who proclaimed the need for a nap, and Doug who had grabbed a cold bottle of LaCrema chardonnay and Mindy as he headed into the air-conditioned bus.

The Spiders were getting into high gear when we arrived. Chief was pleased to see the Cougars bus was parked next to the Spidermobile and had joined the party. He quickly moved to the Judge to discuss the latest in judicial news. He was as obvious as a horny male beagle in heat.

Morgan was just getting deep into a conversation with a small, short-haired, cute Spider when his cell phone buzzed. He answered, smiled and quickly left. Team Nude's twenty-five year old leader had trumped his new fifty-five year old acquaintance. Surprised? Morgan's lower brain had taken control of his body.

Tina saw me, waved and came over and delivered me a glass of Crown Royal on the rocks. She gave me a hug. She talked about how she was using this trip to recover from the deep loss she could not understand. From out of the crowd came Steve Delong; with his long black hair, tall, well muscled body and hugged Tina and shook hands with me.

I noticed, she was flushed and both embarrassed and happy. The two of them slowly moved away, and I caught the hint that they might have more in mind than idle chatter on politics, the stock market or the economy. I wasn't sure if my reactions were an old man's jealousy or a fleeting fear that nearly caused me to stop them and blurt out; careful, Rita had also been a tent mate with good old Stevie.

I concluded, that telling Tina that her sister was a slut on my last trip was merely the over reaction of a jealous old man. Young guys can be very irritating, especially when they are good looking, well built, overly cocky and are swooping in and taking away an old man's female prospect.

As I stood watching Tina move away into the dark of the night, I noticed the small, well muscled, dark complexioned lady who Morgan had just abandoned. She had brown, Bambi-like oval eyes appropriately featured by her pixy cut dark brunette hair with a few gray streaks.

"First time rider?"

"You're right. It must be obvious? My name is Millie Clark from Des Moines."

"You just made a long, tough ride. No need for any fear about not making the whole trip now. Just kick back, eat too much, drink too much and let your attitude float. My name's Lee Scott, also from Des Moines."

Millie was interesting and very easy to talk with. She was a recent transferee to the area; she worked with Microsoft. Her three boys were grown and out of college. She was renewing her career in software development as a way of renewing the useful exercise of her mind. I detected she was single, very choosey, and emitted a deeply lonesome overtone to much of our idle conversation.

We laughed about the crazy sights that are found on the trail. The Team Road Kill labeled smashed skunk was the clear winner. It was at least two feet wide, covered with tire marks and was sporting broken sunglasses and a tobacco pipe. Although, Millie's dance with the near Naked Cowboy in Oakland was her personal favorite.

She sighed, "I kept hoping that what was poking me was his guitar."

We ended the night with a casual kiss on the cheek, a hand squeeze and a polite. "See you on the trail, Millie."

I decided to move very slowly with Millie. She was most captivating, funny, smart and attractive. The smell and chemistry might be there.

My cell phone rang and no name appeared in the screen. Jock answered in a falsetto voice.

"Honey, I am hanging out with the boys to night, so no need to meet. I have the three names of the deceased Team Skunk ladies."

I took down their names so Chief could make a few calls tomorrow in an attempt to find out more about their deaths.

"These guys are far from Drag Queens. They are some really macho tough guys. Most of them have wives or girl-friends with them. They have awards for best outfit every night. My pink tights and red bra with the propellers was second. I think the propellers were too over the top for their taste. See you on the trail, sweetheart."

As I walked to the Grey Geese RV, the sweet smells on the gentle breeze made me feel very alive. I thought sadly about Rita, Carole, Denise and Mona and the three ladies from Omaha who were very dead. How they would like to be here on this night or any night. It was becoming clear that their deaths were not a fluky coincident of life.

YOU CAN STILL CHASE WOMEN, BUT ONLY DOWNHILL.

Bob Hope (on his 70th birthday.)

Chapter Twenty-five

****

AFTER SURVIVING THE ROLLING HILLS INTO RED OAK, THE NEXT TWO DAYS WERE RELATIVELY EASY. We all developed mechanical riding routines and rhythms; lean forward with the back properly aligned to deliver power to the legs, relax arms to repel bumps, keep soft hands to quickly shift gears and keep up a steady pedal pace. The fresh air, exercise and constant changing scenes, terrain and people left us agog for the next day's events.

The southern part of Iowa resembles the bordering state of Missouri. Its land is rock infested, mildly rolling, and ravine filled. The area is far less fertile and valuable than the land in the northern part of the state.

Many man-made terraces contoured across the hills, evidencing an effort to avoid the creation of more ravines from water runoff during frequent hard rains. Large deep, gaping crevices left from pre-terrace days crossed the rolling land. The ravines were filled with huge one hundred foot tall cottonwoods and elms grown from seeds blown there by the winds years before. Most homes were very run down and had yards filled with old cars, old farm equipment and old dogs. Farming here is a tough way to try to make a living. I expected to see Henry Fonda standing by a rundown truck giving his speech from Grapes of Wrath at any moment.

We spent the night at Creston in the Southwest Iowa Community College Campus. The campus was extremely well-manicured, and the red brick buildings were perfectly maintained. A few summer students milled around, trying to join in the festivities. The handsome, polite and pleasant boys did not have a chance. The female students, on the other hand, were quickly integrated into the evening's events. There is no equal opportunity law involved in partying.

I was relaxing with the Grey Geese members after a great dinner of chicken and noodles over mashed potatoes at the Baptist Church stand. We were all very relaxed, sipping water to hydrate our bodies and talking about the day, when my phone rang. No caller ID appeared.

"Meet me at the water-tower. You may not recognize me. The pass word is blow-me."

"Jock, are you going nuts? You sound like Maxwell Smart from Get Smart days. I will find you in ten minutes."

I located Jock by the only water tower in the area. The sight made me double over with laughter. He was dressed in farmers' bib overalls, a plaid shirt and straw hat. "You look right out of a Grant Wood picture."

"Laugh as you will, it worked. I left the Drag Queens and picked up with a yappy, long winded lady from Team Slow-Poke who told me all about the history and background of every stop on the way. Did you know Creston has a population of seventy-five hundred people? It is an Am-trak stop. It started as a camp for survey crews for the early Burlington–Northern Railroad. Frank Phillips of Phillips Petroleum was born here. Do you want to know the history of how Stanton, Villisca and Corning were formed? Did you know Johnnie Carson was born in Corning?"

"Let me guess. Her name was Helga Harmon?"

"Great guess, boss! I really thought I had hit the mother-lode, when I discovered that there was an older guy on the trip three years ago who thought he was a Viagra injected stud horse. Helga, said he tried to do every lady he looked at, including two of the names on the death list. I thought I was on to something till she described him. Are you sure you aren't guilty?"

"Stop with giving me a little shit, Jock, and tell me why am I here listening to all of this?"

"Helga did tell me about Scott Norris. She felt awful and always thought something was askew as he was very athletic and a good rider. He was not a candidate to take a header off a turn. She recalled that on the morning of the last day, he had a heated exchange with a big guy as they left the campground."

"Was he tall with white hair and a splint on his right hand?"

"I don't know about the splint, but she said he was young, dark haired and in very great shape. That eliminates you."

"Good work, I will have Chief call the Dubuque County Sheriff's office and check if they found anything unusual about Scott's death."

"I've had enough of the Iowa history, so I am leaving Team Slow-Poke. I will catch you in Winterset. I'm going to check out the Killer-Bees. They are a big group and have been involved in this trip for years. Look for a bee with a very big stinger; it will be me."

The rest of the night in Creston was uneventful. The parties were subdued. Everyone was tired and a soft pillow felt better than anything we could imagine. The next morning everyone was up and ready by 7:30. We were rested and ready to party. The time between parties was getting longer. Winterset was the next stop.

The city event organizers had planned town square ceremonies; not surprisingly focused around a Bridges of Madison County theme. The town still markets the movie, the historical bridges and the era when Merle Streep and Clint Eastwood spent a summer in their town.

This well-preserved town of five thousand citizens was filled with many old, stately brick homes and offices. It's the county seat for Madison County and proudly proclaims itself to be the birthplace of John Wayne. Its greeting signs touted numerous tours to see the local historical sites related to the Duke's brief time in the town. His parents had moved to Los Angeles when Marion Morrison was very young, but he still was a local hero.

The progressive town leaders had planned well for the lucrative invasion. They had bands, skits, food and memorabilia in mass. The food stands were erected, stocked and staffed. They had missed control of one factor; the weather. The afternoon environment went from cloudy, to blustery and then to rainy with a twenty mile an hour head-wind by mid day. We all donned our yellow rain capes and forged on with a valiant effort to ignore how bad we felt; especially how grating the damn seat was on our crotches while pedaling in soaked biking pants.

By four in the afternoon, the sight of Chief and the RV at a cross road was a welcome sight. One by one we pulled in, toweled off and loaded our bikes. Even Doug called it quits.

"Let's get to the party. I have a standing promise, from a twenty-one year old natural blonde from Team Nude, to warm my cold old bones when I get to town," shouted Morgan.

"I doubt that, but the Cougars are having a "midway there party" at their bus and said I could bring my older friends, if they were up to it. They even promised to bring little blue pills for the old guys I hang around with," shouted Luke.

We were just getting our positive moods re-engaged with our usual verbal attacks on each other and overly macho bragging, when Matt stopped us.

"We are going to have a unique evening, my wrinkled, old friends. Chief, drive to where I said and when we are there, I will explain. Meanwhile, I have a few calls to make in order to get this event all pulled together. It's tough to be a shepherd for such a bunch of old degenerate prunes, like you, and keep a sense of humor." Matt's light blue eyes twinkled and his chubby cheeks looked like a chipmunk who had just garnered his favorite food for the winter.

As the RV climbed a steep hill two miles south of Winterset, Chief abruptly turned the RV left and headed up a narrow road built on a deep bed of huge limestone boulders, topped with a fine coat of crushed limestone. It appeared we were heading up the steep narrow road headlong into a wall of limestone. With a quick turn to the right, we passed through a slot in a twenty foot high wall of mammoth limestone boulders.

As we entered through the narrow passage, a solid steel, rust-colored guard gate over twelve feet in height slid open, triggered by a signal from Matt's opener. The slot was of just sufficient width to allow the RV to enter. The internal area consisted of a paved parking area the size of a football field. In the center of the five hundred foot shear wall of limestone sat two massive twenty foot tall, rusting lance topped doors, with the name "Fort Madison Prison" welded into the metal top. Matt pushed another button, and the huge doors slid open.

"This looks like an entrance right out of Batman," I said with a growing astonishment.

As we entered the cave, my level of awe for Matt's skill and taste increased. The cave's interior had a thirty foot tall ceiling supported by one foot thick I-beams; painted red. The yellow painted HVAC duct-work ran in numerous directions like an octopus's tentacles, providing a perfectly controlled environment in all parts of the interior.

Across the north wall was located a gourmet kitchen. The recessed lighting illuminated all stainless steel appliances. Numerous utensils and pans hung in perfect symmetry over twin Viking eight burner gas stoves. On each side of the stoves, stood solid wood preparation tables and spotless stainless steel preparation sinks. The shelves behind the stoves were stocked with hundreds of spices, varied types of cooking oils, vinegars, and untold other ingredients. Erma Bombeck would have an orgasm seeing this sight.

Next to the stoves stood a large oak table surrounded by twenty heavy, wood carved chairs. Several vases of fresh cut tiger-lilies and a very white linen table cloth covered the candle-illuminated table. To the right of the dining area was a conversation area, featuring a three inch thick glass slab resting as a table on a single ten ton block of limestone. Ten smaller blocks of limestone topped with red, blue and yellow cushions served as chairs and surrounded the table in a semi-circle.

Behind the conversation area carved into the limestone wall was a forty foot square wine cooler with two clear walk-in doors. Matt had not filled it with Two Buck Chuck. It held at least two thousand bottles of inventory, all immaculately placed by type and age. It also had a series of slots carved into the limestone wall where different cheeses were resting in wrappers of various colors.

In a small seating area in the cooler resided a case of Templeton Rye and a story about its bootlegging era origin in the small town of Templeton, Iowa. Beside it was a note, "Save for Lee."

On his proud tour, Matt pointed out the steel walls at the south end of the cave.

"Behind that wall is my lab and mixing room. It's soundproof and explosion proof. It houses all of the mixing vats and storage containers, for whatever project I am working on. Right now it's storing a hundred gallons of high potency metal cleaner for my railway project. If I don't figure out how to dilute it to not eat up steel, it will be a real disposal problem."

Just as we were looking at the library and record storage area on the south side of the cavern now titled, "The Matt Cave," the massive steel door entrance opened and was filled with the Cougars, the Spiders, Team Nude, Steve and Roy and the other eight members of the Spa from Hell team.

Matt took control, and two lovely girls, dressed in cut off bib overalls and tee-shirts, appeared carrying tubs of iced down Corona beer. The overalls, showed off their very muscular tanned legs in a way that made us old men ashamed to get caught staring. Next came ten opened bottles of Rombauer 2007 Chardonnay and 2004 Merlot, presented by two handsome black-haired, brown eyed well tanned men in overalls with no shirts. I think a few ladies were also staring at the extremely well muscled farm boys.

Everyone buzzed with excitement as they sipped great wine, munched on palate-tingling snacks and watched three inches of rain fall in one hour. So much for the Bridges of Madison County skits in Winterset.

After about an hour, our chubby slightly drunk host mounted a three foot high rock in the middle of the complex.

"Friends, I am glad you could all stop and see my project. It has been a labor of love for me. I have put a lot of my flair into this venture, not to mention a couple of million dollars. If my next project pays off, I intend to expand it and provide a series of incubator locations for starving young inventors to get started. I will mentor them and my dear friend Lee will provide legal guidance."

"The "Caves at Madison County" can be a place for creativity to flourish with little pressure to meet corporate or economic deadlines."

Everyone applauded our host, his wine-induced gusto for life and his high flying ideals. I was curious, when I had agreed to my role in Matt's venture. Oh well, what are friends for if not to take advantage of.

"I have one more item to mention before we adjourn to a home-cooked chicken dinner with fresh sweet corn and mashed potatoes. I have lived my first 62 years trying to understand myself, and some feelings that were struggling inside me. I know now, I'm gay, and I'm tired of trying to live a lie. I hope you will all keep being my friends as I treasure our relationship like life itself."

After thirty seconds of deafening silence, "I love you, you cute little fag" came a cheer from Morgan. In unison all of us moved in to hug our friend. Who cares? We are too old to lose friends over bigoted ideas. Not surprisingly, the ladies all moved in rapidly to congratulate Matt on his courage and sensitivity.

Morgan, noticing all the feminine attention given to Matt and pondered to me, "Suppose it's too late for me to become a switch hitter?"

Before I could answer Morgan, my cell phone buzzed and no callers name appeared.

"Jock I hope your tent is on a side hill and not in a valley, oh great master of disguises."

"You dry smart-ass, I'm setting under what was to intended to be a food pavilion for the Winterset Jaycees. It is now a mass of soaked hamburger buns, cold weenies and water-soaked spaghetti. There are a lot of great prices, if you don't have any concern for quality. Seriously, that rain was a disaster for them. I suspect you are in a warm bus all cuddled up with a nineteen year old female."

"You are half right. I am dry and cuddled up. But, it's in a cave with a bunch of old people getting drunk. About half are horny and the other half are looking for a big fluffy pillow for the night. Sorry about your situation."

"My Killer Bee outfit fell apart, the first half hour of the rain. The rain did give me an excuse to move around through the group and get to know them. The Bees are a bunch of zany characters out for a week of sun and exercise. Their Killer Bee attacks are just part of their process to meet people and give a lot of laughs. They are great people. Unfortunately, my brilliant efforts did not find anything of value on our case."

"That's unfortunate, but I have a lead. I am looking at Steve Delong, who is tall, young, dark haired and in great shape. Sounds like Helga's description of the person Scott had his tussle with? He is riding with Team Spa from Hell. They are here with us tonight. I don't know much about them, other than they are involved in spas. Some are dressed in very gay looking outfits, some are in very macho outfits and a couple of them are in normal biking clothes."

"Steve seems to have a very over-developed testosterone system. I know he had something going with Rita and Carole on my last trip. His brother, Roy, ignores ladies, but seems locked onto Matt. He was the one whose fingers Scott wrecked at the start of the last trip."

"Sounds like we've focused on a real prospect. I will try to connect up with them tomorrow. Call me if Chief hears anything on Scott's records." The phone went silent.

The evening wound down with a twenty year old port from Travis Peak, a Texas winery that Matt had discovered. Little groups disappeared into the shadows where the warming impact of the wine and food acted as an aphrodisiac. For most however, including me, it acted more like a sedative.

Larry, Morgan and Tim were among the missing from the cave and our RV. What a surprise. I noted Matt and the Spa from Hell team were still celebrating around the wine cellar. Steve was missing. Tina was also absent. Being a quick-witted barrister, I put two and two together. Herb Knowlton would be one mad six foot five farm boy, if he ever suspected his petite little wife and mother of three was sampling young dicks on this otherwise healthy venture across our fair state.

I saw Millie, sitting alone, at the big oak table by the kitchen stove area. It was obvious she was tired. I took a bottle of Matt's port and sat beside her. As we sipped and watched the light fog develop beyond the open cave entrance, she began to talk about her past, and how it had led her to Des Moines.

After her children were raised and in college, she had pursued a long known talent at computer system designs at UCLA. She had graduated and received her Master's degree in record time. She had taken a job, with a small startup company, trying to create a system allowing the many AOL users to instantly switch to another provider and abandon this dinosaur system with its many problems. Unfortunately, her husband of twenty-five years became terminally ill. Thirty years of smoking and jogging in Los Angele's smog had taken a severe toll on his lungs. She spent six months being a caretaker and watching him deteriorate till the end.

During this period of unusually bad luck, she also had some good luck. Her new employer had been acquired by Microsoft. She received a small fortune for her stock, and was enticed into a contract to open a new site in West Des Moines.

As she talked about her loss, it was clear she was filled with both grief and relief about the end to her husband's long battle with cancer.

"I just can't shake those feelings of guilt; I am here and he is gone. I can't believe I am relieved that I don't have to watch him suffer."

I looked for a long time into her tearing brown eyes. I knew those feelings from my past.

"You need to try to forget feeling guilty over feeling relieved. The guilt of not being able to do enough, of feeling relief when it ends and feeling immoral by moving on with your life, are all deep feelings. They are normal feelings for a survivor. Don't fight them. Accept them as normal and move forward."

This piece of heartfelt advice was given with a little tearing of my own and provoked a long kiss and hug. As we continued to talk about the process of recovery and being alone, I knew this was a relationship to move slowly in developing.

As we ended the evening, I concluded, suggesting a quickie or the even a harmless little blow-job could ruin what looks like a real friendship. I marveled at the romantic instincts, I had developed. Maybe this new found sensitivity for female emotional needs was a side effect of the spa outing?

The next day, we were mid-way to Centerville when an ambulance worked its way through the crowd. When we got to the ambulance's destination, Matt was laying near a bridge over a three hundred foot deep gorge. He was scraped about his right cheek, his helmet was cracked, and he was clutching his collarbone. The grimace of his gnashing teeth showed the efforts he was enduring while holding back the tears of pain. After the shoulder was relocated by the EMT, I asked what had happened.

"I was just cruising along thinking about what a great night we had, when something hit me; rather I think pushed me. If I hadn't caught that rail with my feet, I would be at the bottom of that ravine looking like a rag doll."

Mindy went with Matt in the ambulance, with instructions to report when he was at a hospital in Des Moines and had a thorough check-up. My bull-shit meter went off with its highest warning level. This was no accident. Matt's proud announcement of his gay status, and his involuntary flight off his bike into a bridge rail, without a witness, had to be connected. Was it connected to Scott's premature flight to heaven?

THE LESS PEOPLE KNOW ABOUT HOW SAUSAGES AND LAWS ARE MADE, THE BETTER THEY WILL SLEEP AT NIGHT.

Otto Von Bismarck

Chapter Twenty six

****

WE WERE NEARING THE END. The trip to our next to the last stop, Ottumwa, was non-eventful. Our bodies were showing the wear of many miles up and down the slopes of southern Iowa. We were quiet.

The idea of going to party and visit the ladies was not even mentioned. A warm shower, cold beer, quick dinner, Aleve and muscle cream, followed by a long deep sleep was all that anyone wanted scheduled for the night. As I looked around half of the Grey Geese were snoring by seven. I wonder if age had anything to do with it.

I did receive a free tour of the town on the back of a motor scooter driven by Jock. He called as usual and said to look to my left and wave. I followed the instructions and saw a Peewee Herman look alike straddling a motor scooter. The big gap-tooth smile signaled that Jock had arrived.

As I hopped on, we sped away. "What is this Peewee look?"

"I needed a way to hook up with the Spa from Hell team so this unusual character seemed like a good way to get their attention. I represented, with a few sniffles, that I was a broken down actor from LA trying to get a job in the budding Iowa movie industry. They bought right in to my story."

"You are as good as Chief said."

"That team is unusual. It changes in makeup every day depending what spa related person could take the day off. I found out most of these guys are straight and take the spa business very seriously. They are truly trying to perfect their skills by exchanging information and ideas in order to find new ways to deliver their product. One is even a surgeon with two spas and four kids; he is working on entering a body building contest."

With a toothy smile, Jock pretended to whisper, "If you haven't noticed, Roy is a flamer and never follows the ladies. He and your buddy Matt were the focus of some gossip, but he seemed genuinely concerned about his condition. It seems unlikely he helped Matt prematurely exit his bike."

"On the other hand, Steve is a real hound dog. He chases every older lady, about your age, in sight. Older and rich is his focus. Could be an Oedipus thing? He has a semi-steady thing going with a dark haired lady from the Black Widows."

"Lee, what I can't figure is how these two big boys survive each other. They are constantly bickering. Their verbal jabs are vicious not good natured. The other riders reported a real shoving match a couple days ago."

I interrupted Jock. "Add to our facts, the Chief talked to the Dubuque Sheriff's Office today. Scott's case is still open. They concluded the rear brake-wire broke, but it could have been cut. The multi-strand rear brake wire had clean cuts at the edges. The real killing event was when a plastic garbage bag flew into his front tires spokes. The possibility that he hit a wayward garbage bag in a precise way to allow it to enter his wheels spokes is just to incredible to believe. But the fact is that the bag had several small rocks in it, so it could have been thrown. That makes the matter murder."

We were both quiet, as we realized the true.

"You know Helga caught me on the trail again. Despite my Peewee costume she recognized me. For half an hour, I heard about Ottumwa; home of Tom Arnold, fictional home of Radar O'Reilly from Mash fame, birthplace of Indian activist and movie star Russell Means, naval training base where President Nixon obtained his flight training and home of an alleged rare book thief named Steve Blumberg. Do you want more detail?"

"I'll pass on additional details about Ottumwa. It looks pretty tired and worn out. The closing of the packinghouses and railroads really damaged this town. It's a shame as there are a lot of nice people here."

"Well, time to get off, boss. I will keep snooping around, but it seems to me we have Roy and Steve as likely suspects. The only thing we lack is evidence. See you at Fort Madison.

DAY SEVEN, WE HAD AT LAST FINISHED. The ride over the tree covered bluffs and down to the valley below on roads carved out of the steep limestone hills was beautiful. The local people and early-bird finishers were cheering. We were cheering. We had done it.

At the locks of Fort Madison, we dipped our tires ceremoniously into the mighty Mississippi, and chugged a couple of cold Dubuque Star beers directly from a tub filled with ice compliments of the Chief.

The day was blast furnace hot, the breeze was nonexistent. We were drained and looked at each other asking, "Wasn't this fun?" We all roared with a cheer and hugged each other.

The ride home in the air-conditioned comfort of a plush RV was almost regal in feeling. Mindy presented a fresh salad filled with excellent local products; cucumbers, onions, bib lettuce and tomatoes. Chief's home-made lasagna was aggressively attacked and washed down with more ice cold beer. The food, relaxation, beer and cool temperature put us all into deep nap.

It was very satisfying to have accomplished this feat, especially for a bunch of pre-baby boomer vintage bikers. I wondered if we would do it again. The event will likely get better, more lustful and more exaggerated, the farther we got away from it. Like child-birth, it sounds better a year or two after it's over.

After an hour of napping, everyone was awakening. I moved to the front of the RV.

"It's time we have a long talk. This has been an extremely satisfying experience. We all have become even closer friends, if that is possible. But, I need to fill you in on what I think is either a life-threatening problem or my over-developed, constantly suspicious lawyers mind working overtime."

They all looked at me like I was about to announce a terminal illness.

"For weeks, I haven't been able to get it out of my head that the death of four very healthy and wealthy women from heart failure in a short period of time wasn't a coincidence. The fact that I had met them all on my previous RAGBRAI trip and screwed fifty-per cent of them also made it less likely a coincidence. I know my short fling with them did not weaken their hearts. So, I had Chief check with the local police; there are no open cases and there were no autopsies. Chief has been doing more snooping. It is likely all four deceased ladies frequented The Painted Woods Spa and enjoyed the massage work of Rose and Delong."

"There's a lot of evidence that point at Delong, but not much at Rose. Both were on several RAGBRAI trips. Steve was very involved in more than a flirtation with Rita, Mona and Carole three years ago when I was participating in their Spidermobile parties. I am sure that Rita was sleeping with Steve right before her death based on some comments made by Tina. Affairs with older, beautiful wealthy ladies is a consistent MO"

"I hired a PI for this trip in an effort to unearth some concrete evidence. He was unique in his approach, but by the end of the week, he was focused on the two spa boys. He is not sure how Roy fits as the victims are all women, and he is very gay. Steve was the one who was always involved with the victims. This bizarre PI thinks Steve may have argued with Scott Norris right before his death. I know Roy also had a losing fight with Scott on the opening day of that trip. The Chief confirms with the local Sheriff that Scott's death was likely intentional."

The guys all looked up and gathered closer.

"What really scares me is that I am sure Steve is focused on Tina Knowlton. I don't doubt they enjoyed a little afternoon delight on a few days of the trip. Roy is also very focused on our chubby, little buddy, Matt. That fall of his, after announcing he was leaping from the closet, doesn't make sense."

"The PI reported that Roy and Steve had been arguing frequently and violently, since Matt's announcement of his gay status in the Winterset cave. Matt has become a good rider. The way he left the road and almost feel three hundred feet into that rocky ravine suggest a push to me, not a clumsy hung over little old man's error. Roy appears to care about Matt. So, he seems unlikely to have been the culprit."

Chief yelled back, "What now Dick Tracy? You have some great guesses and no evidence."

"You're right; we need to get some concrete evidence before we make a big leap in judgment. With the evidence we have the police would conclude we are pre-Alzheimer victims. We need real evidence, and I know how to get it. It will involve committing a few crimes in the name of Truth, Justice and the American way. My fear is if we do nothing Tina, and maybe Matt are at risk."

"A little fudging on the law has never been a problem for me, as long as it's for a good cause," Luke quickly said. "What do you need?"

"I need someone to break into the Painted Woods Spa with me and check some of the crucial records. Chief believes all four ladies were customers at the spa, we need to confirm that. Accessing their personal files will provide a lot of valuable background on both of them. We need to get their tax returns and find where they have worked, so we need their social security numbers. With their past work locations, we can determine if they have police records. Their addresses will help us in case we need to do a visit to their home."

After a lot of suggestions on what to do, we decided, if we were going to be criminals, we would be good ones. The first step was to do some careful planning for our felonious act of breaking and entering The Painted Woods Spa.

Morgan volunteered to get a massage and check the security systems.

"This should be kid's stuff to shut down their system by remote for a few minutes. No one will ever know there was an interruption of the security."

Doug volunteered to get a massage and facial, and while he was being pampered, to check the locks and file locations. I undertook the task of finding the least used route to the spa after closing hours. A late day massage would be my excuse for being there. I warned everyone of the risk of breaking the law; they were incorrigible and laughed at my over-cautious comments. They wanted to accelerate this new adventure.

The next day, we took the last three available 7 pm spots on the spa calendar and placed our very worn bodies, in the hands of three very sweet twenty-five year old, well groomed, smiling lady masseuses. They performed magic on very stiff and sore old muscles and joints. The combination of the music, herbal scents, soft flowing water and nimble female hands, left us all weak kneed and as mellow as joint smoking teenagers.

We reconvened at eight-thirty pm at my house and poured a glass of our favorite adult beverage. I sipped my Templeton Rye with a growing confidence. "What did you find Morgan?

"They have the simple security system used in most strip malls. They have a sensor pad on the main door and windows. They have a camera sweeping the entrances. They don't have internal motion detectors. If the sensors by the door or windows sense something moving, they send a silent signal to the monitoring station. The station then calls the designated phone, and if no one answers with the pass word, they dispatch a rent-a-cop. I could very easily get the password, but their records will show the system went off at a certain time. The better route is for me to enter the monitoring stations system, by way of their own computer, and place the system on standby for a few minutes while the insertion of our team occurs."

"What's this insertion of the team shit? It's just Doug and I sneaking into the spa acting like two guys imitating Rambo while committing a few white collar crimes? Skip this military shit, I am scared enough."

Doug looked very confident and almost smug. "Lee, relax, let's move. If the system is down, we can sneak in and out in ten minutes. I checked the records location. The spa closed at eight tonight. The front lock is easy to pick. The records are in the doctor's office. I have a camera that can scan the records as fast as you can turn them even with just the minimal parking lot lights. We can be in, have everything we need, and be back here for the ten o'clock news. Morgan, can you get on line and control the monitoring system, ASAP?"

"I can have it handled in thirty minutes, with time to spare."

With a deep gulp of Rye, I saw the next fifteen years of my life in a 10x10 cell. "Let's go." We were off on a new career; geriatric criminals.

Doug and I arrived at 9:15 pm and parked in the shadowed part of the parking area a block from the spa. I felt like a kid playing Rambo. With black mask, jeans, gloves and windbreaker, we exited the car and scurried, as fast as two sixty year old very stiff men can scurry. A quick call to Morgan confirmed the monitoring system was under his control. He was confident that if the tapes were ever reviewed, they would never see anyone enter, as the system would be on standby.

Doug pulled out a small set of tools in a worn black case, and we were instantly inside.

"Did you learn that trick at the Agricultural Department?"

He winked. His eyes were piercing and darker than ever. He moved cat -like and efficiently around the spa. I tried to copy his behavior, all the while feeling like a fool playing burglar. Doug again pulled his magic tool kit and was into the file cabinets in thirty seconds. We laid the Delong and Rose files out on a table near the window, where the street lights could reflect on them.

As fast as I could turn pages, Doug's magic Pentex camera captured the image. "This sure beats the Brownie that I still used."

We were gone in five minutes. After we exited into the shadows, a quick call to Morgan released the monitor from their standby mode.

"Doug, that was incredible work, but I am so scared, think I am about to shit my pants. Let's keep moving."

As soon as we arrived at my home, we printed the results of our first excursion into the life of crime. I looked at Doug with an all together different prospective. This sinewy little guy has very unique and well-trained skills for a government employee.

"Okay, the records show the spa boys grew up in Dallas. They list no living parents. They trained as masseuses in Dallas and worked in University Park at the Texas Angels Spa till 2003. They then went to Minneapolis to the Warm Touch Spa for a year. Their next stop was Des Moines at the Painted Woods Spa for most of 2005. Then they moved to Omaha to the Pampered Heifer Spa for one year and then it was back to Des Moines in the summer of 2007."

Chief held up his note pad, "Rita died in May of 2009, Mona died in October of 2008, Carol Picket died in April of 2008 and Denise Ray died in November of 2007. The spa boys were here during all four of these sudden heart attacks."

Chief looked at me, "Counselor, your evidence doesn't prove shit. Some smart ass, self centered, know it all attorney would have them out in a day. But, I think you're right. I grew to dislike Steve on the trip. He was always beating me out, every time I was on the trail of some young pussy, even while he was servicing Mrs. Tina's tired, little horny body."

"Chief, I suspect you didn't like Roy either because he likes dicks better than pussy, right?" I laughed.

"Good guess Sherlock. I am a little old fashioned that way."

I silently looked at my friends and sized up our evidence. With a sigh, I reluctantly concluded it was short of the mark.

"We need more proof. Doug are you up to a little more breaking and entering tomorrow? We need to visit their home while the spa boys are at work."

"Morgan could you use your over paid computer techy mind to illegally access the police records in Dallas, Minneapolis and Omaha and see if they have any records of similar deaths of wealthy middle aged women during the time the spa boys were in each of those towns? While you're at it Morgan can you get into the IRS records, and verify they were in those towns at the times their resumes say?"

"Chief, can you go get Matt from the hospital? He is being released tomorrow. While you're at it, pump our recovering friend to see if he can recall anything about how he jumped off his bike into a retainer wall of a bridge at fifteen miles an hour?"

Everyone looked at me and gave me a salute and a middle finger. "Yes Sir, General Scott."

Men get more sarcastic the older they get.

> **I HAVE COME TO REGARD THE LAWS COURTS NOT AS A CATHEDRAL, BUT RATHER AS A CASINO.**
>
> **Richard Ingrams**

Chapter Twenty-seven

****

THE LIFE OF AN AMATEUR CRIMINAL WAS GETTING QUITE EXHILERATING, EVEN FOR AN AGING SPIRIT. In fact, life was extremely exhilarating, even with the haunting thoughts regarding possibly spending the rest of my life in jail. These forays into a life of petty crime beats making an ass out of myself trying to play golf at a level of perfection that exceeds my abilities.

Early the next the morning, Tim and I, dressed as meter readers, scouted the spa boys' home on twenty-eight street in the South of Grand area. The area was on a large hill-side which was heavily carpeted with old majestic oaks and ash trees.   It was still considered by many to be very exclusive, despite its age. The homes featured many turn of the century brick structures with classic southern mansion designs. Scattered among these ageless mansions were some very tired, old structures that were nearly ready to collapse.

The spa boys' seventy year old bungalow was fast falling into a sad state of disrepair. Green mold covered its shake wood roof, which had a sag in the middle where it supported a black-streaked brick chimney which was leaning at an odd angle.

The brown brick siding of the two floors displayed numerous stress cracks. The deep brown trimmed window frames and double doors sadly needed fresh paint as the extremely old lead paint was severely cracking; in places falling off. The five towering oaks surrounding the cottage created a canopy over the house, and assured that the nearly dead grass lawn would seldom need mowed.

The realtors for the South of Grand area would refer to this shack as a Hansel and Gretel Home that needs some loving care. Move it thirty blocks east, and it would be called a tear down or slum property.

My cell phone vibrated. Morgan reported the house was free of any security systems. He also point out a traffic surveillance camera was in place to watch movement on the street, so entry into the spa boys' house might be detected, if anyone knew how to enhance the images. He assured me the security camera would be in his control by noon; he could enter the cities system and put it on standby at will. He warned not to linger since the place was a dump and likely was home to several unknown forms of fungus.

Luke had insisted on joining us during the break-in. Doug arrived at my house with three very loose fitting pest control company uniforms and a white rental van. Its license plates were covered with mud which is unusual on a dry day. The uniforms all had a logo on the back displaying a dying roach gripping its throat with the caption "Death to Pests."

I continued to be apprehensive concerning Doug's weird sense of humor. We drove to the house in silence. Upon arrival, we quickly exited the van and carried our pest spray cans to the house, trying our best to act-out our pest killers' role. With a quick flick of his hands, Doug opened the front door lock; the three of us entered the Hansel and Gretel House.

The house was a contradiction. It was a pit on one side and immaculate on the other. Luke moved quietly into each bedroom, placing a tracking chip provided by Tim into each cell phone charger, athletic duffle bag, toiletry kit and jacket that was lying around.

Doug took the messy bedroom and I took the clean bed room. We completed our search and merged in the kitchen area which was clean, well organized and well stocked. It featured old well maintained all wood floors; light blue colored plaster walls and a kitchen with immaculately cleaned expensive silver Viking appliances. One unclean bowl lay in the sink with oatmeal caked on the sides. One neat freak and one slob lived here.

I looked around for details we may have missed. "Well, let's check this living area out."

The central living area had a couch with a very flowery design that was right out of the sixties, surrounded by a huge sound system. In the middle of the room was a relatively small TV located on an old trunk. So far, we looked like foolish old clowns on a trip to the circus. I spotted an ancient trunk that had the Sony flat screen TV setting on it. I carefully moved the TV and popped open the trunk lid.

"Shit." I held up an armful of biking jerseys.

We counted twenty-nine biking jerseys. The top eight were from the RAGBRI trips over the last six years; each year the jersey is numbered and has a unique design and color. There were five from the Austin Hill Country ride, three from the Nebraska Plains ride and two from the Minnesota Great Northern ride. The rest of the multi-colored jerseys were unidentifiable as to any specific event.

We took pictures with Doug's spy camera, replaced the jerseys and got the hell out of there.

Doug and Luke moved calmly to the van talking as if they were relaxed workers who had just completed a job. I tried to swagger with the confident walk of a teenager cruising a mall. Inside, I felt more like an old guy with an enlarged prostate looking desperately for the nearest bathroom. After we drove away, a quick call to Morgan switched the street security cameras from their hibernation mode.

We called Chief and scheduled a late lunch at my place. Chief said to make his lunch half-size as he had just finished lunch with Matt. He also said to get braced for some surprises. He refused to be more specific. Stubborn, secretive old guys can be a real pain in the ass.

When everyone arrived at my house, I put some deli products, bread and condiments on the polished brown granite counter opposite my refrigerator.

"Help yourselves. There is water and beer in the cooler. Feel free to fix yourself a stiff one, as you may need it."

I summarized our findings. "What we have are one or two very sick boys. One or both of them keep biking jerseys as trophies. I doubt they are just gifts from lovers. But, we cannot be sure which of them or if both of them killed the former owners of the jerseys. There are no blood stains or any similar physical evidence on the jerseys that suggest a killing occurred. I did see Rita's name embroidered on the collar of one and Mona's name ink printed in the label as part of the drycleaners route delivery process."

"I saw other names on a few jerseys. Maybe, we can pick off the names from the pictures I shot", noted Doug.

Chief blurted out. "Well guys we have a little complication involving Matt. He was quite chipper when we had lunch. He talked about Roy moving in with him. Two little lovebirds about to build a nest; how sweet. I almost hurled on that note. But, being the good detective that I am, I just smiled and kept him talking."

"Before the move-in celebration occurs, they are going on a cruise to the Caymans to do a little scuba diving, eating and sun bathing. Can you imagine little chubby Matt in a thong? Matt feels he needs to get Roy away from Steve's domination so it's a secret quick trip to let Steve's temper settle down. They plan to leave Friday. Matt even talked about backing Roy in business or making him part of his new caves venture.

"Matt is convinced Steve pushed him off the bike because of his relationship with Roy. Matt said Roy and Steve had a few very angry words before his fall."

With quick analysis from my aging legal wit, I commented the obvious. "Guys, we haven't got enough to convict either of these guys of anything let alone being serial murders. I'm scared for Matt and for Tina."

"Morgan, I know you did a quick search to identify deaths of wealthy middle age women in the towns where the spa boys lived. Any luck?"

"The search parameters are too wide to find much. The police and county death records were a snap to get into, but they weren't very helpful. They use extremely old systems. The people in charge of these systems will never know I was into them. Unfortunately, I have over two hundred and eighty three possible names of people in the right age bracket, at the right time with similar causes of death."

"If you can blow up those pictures of the jerseys and find some first or last names, maybe we can get closer to identifying potential victims."

Within half an hour Doug had loaded the pictures to my computer. Morgan had enhanced the pictures to reveal names on the fronts or the labels: Sammie, Bobby and Irene from Dallas: Rita, Mona, Sharon, Vicky and Denise, from RABGRAI, Helen and Sherrie from the Nebraska Plains ride and Sonya from Great Northern ride in Minnesota. We knew there were other names, but in our rush, we had failed to look closely for other names. We had looked at only a few of the jerseys.

"One more trip to Hansel and Gretel's little cottage, Doug," I sighed.

We waited till the next morning, checked the boys work schedule and again donned our exterminator uniforms. Morgan had the traffic light under control, and we made a quick entry and exit. To our surprise we found five more names. Two were from the Austin ride, and three more were from RAGBRAI. We also found the kitchen was a mess. Food and dishes had been thrown all about and pieces of mashed potatoes and vegetables were growing old and solid on the floor. A spot of blood was on the counter near the stove. A rag in the neat room had blood on it, as if someone was trying to control a nose bleed or cut.

"Looks like a brotherly spat turned extremely aggressive," I noted.

As I left I saw two duffle bags, neatly packed with clothes, lying by the bed in the neat bedroom.

"Looks like Matt's friend is packing for a romp in the sun and waves of the Caribbean. Think I should check to see if they have matching thongs?"

Just as I was about to leave, I saw a note crumpled on the kitchen table. I picked it up. It read, "I am sorry for the slap. I cannot let this happen. I need you to stay with me. We are more than brothers."

"What are these two? Brothers? Lovers? Or, oh shit both?"

IT'S NOT THAT I AM AFRAID TO DIE; I JUST DON'T WANT TO BE THERE WHEN IT HAPPENS.

Woody Allen

Chapter Twenty-eight

****

WE QUICKLY EXITED THE HANSEL AND GRETEL HOUSE WITH MORE INADMISSIBLE EVIDENCE. As we hurriedly ran to the van, I called Morgan to tell him to put the surveillance system back on line, and that we had new names from other jerseys. I gave him the names and the jersey's event name.

"Without being detected, can you quickly access the coroner's records in the respective towns during the time frame these two lived in each such town? See if any of the deaths on your lists coincide with the first names that we've found."

"By the time you get back to your house, I will be there with what's available and have a cold drink waiting for your shaky old hands. These coroners systems are old, easy to enter and nearly impossible to secure. That's why guys like me make a fortune telling them how to upgrade their systems and make them secured. Unfortunately, most places don't have the funds or skills to do it right. Maybe they should have called President O and applied for stimulus money? With all of the mold on that house, it should qualify for some type of "green" stimulus grant."

When Doug and I arrived at my home, we saw Morgan approaching in his white Cadillac Escalade, moving at twice the legal speed limit. He jumped out with a tortured look on his normally smiling face. A pale white blemish from tension appeared around his eyes and mouth.

"Shit, those names fit someone in each town where the spa boys lived, and at the time they lived there. The victims all are in the fifty-five to sixty-five year old age bracket. They all died suddenly of apparent heart attacks according to the coroner's reports."

"In addition to the four RAGBRAI riders we know about, Vicki was likely Victoria Hanson, and Sharon was likely Sharon Liu. In Dallas, Sammie coincides with Samantha Braun, Bobby with Robin Robertson and Irene with Irene Wesley. The Omaha names fit with Helena Hunter and Sherri Horn. Sonya from Minnesota was likely Sonya Harlan. We have twelve names that fit with the names on the jerseys."

I thought for a moment. The conclusion was obvious and the solution obscure.

"To me, this new evidence is convincing that one or both of the spa boys are killers. They identify their female victims on the long bike rides and later eliminate them."

"Unfortunately, we obtained all this great circumstantial evidence by breaking the law. So far, we have twice engaged in breaking and entering the spa, breaking and entering their home. In addition, we illegally accessed the IRS computer database for their income records, illegally accessed the records of coroner's offices of four counties in four states and illegally entered and controlled the county's street surveillance systems. I assume we have violated a few federal laws along the way by doing all of this across state lines. We have all this wonderful proof, and it isn't worth shit. This case will never see the inside of a court house. We, on the other hand, are now multiple felons."

The debate as to how to turn this evidence over to appropriate authorities to secure a proper outcome went on for hours. We had ideas ranging from anonymous calls, secret delivery of packets of evidence and a CD with masked narrators. We finally all silently concluded we were screwed. They would walk free and likely, we would be in jail. American Justice in action!

We were just kicking back for evening cocktails watching the deer emerge from the valley south of my home when my cell phone rang.

"Matt, what's up? No shit? How did that happen?"

After a long, rambling, near hysterical two minutes, I told Matt in a firm commanding voice, "You stay put. Don't call him. A couple of us will be over. Trust me. We can handle this."

I said with a grim look, "Well, our newly announced romantic buddy has added a new twist to this mess. Matt went to Roy's home to pick him up. They were going to run away for a romantic weekend after Roy told Steve about his long-term plans with Matt. When Matt knocked at the door, it was open. He stepped in, and there was Steve, cut to shreds with a twelve inch long butcher's knife stuck in his chest. Then our little friend really fucked up. He grabbed the knife, panicked, dropped it and ran, leaving his prints behind on the knife. Can you believe he left without the knife? Roy is still around. He just called Matt and said that he would swing over about 10:00 so they could get ready to leave. Matt was cool and just said okay."

"Get your "Men in Black" outfit on again, Lee," Doug whispered.

"We need to retrieve that knife before the police arrive. Morgan, can you commit another crime and tap into the police communications systems? See if there is a dispatch to the Hansel and Gretel house and be ready to shut off that damn street surveillance camera in fifteen minutes. In fact, can you copy today's data from the camera and then erase it, just in case Matt was caught on camera entering the house?

"Doug, it can all be quickly handled from Lee's computer. Call me when you arrive to verify the camera is on standby mode."

Calmly, Doug looked sternly at me. "Let's get over to my house and on your way out, grab a few towels, alcohol and plastic bags."

I changed quickly, and we cautiously drove the speed limit to Doug's house. He was in and out in two minutes, wearing his black garb with a lump in his rear pocket about the size of a small pistol. He strapped a stiletto around his ankle as he entered the car.

"Is this all normal equipment for agricultural consulting?"

"No, this is part of my hobby of pest extermination, but don't ask me anymore about it. If I told you, I'd have to kill you." Doug half smiled and winked.

I think he was kidding.

It was dark when we arrived. We scanned the street. It was free of any cars or joggers. We parked directly beneath the street camera as we had verified the camera was out of commission, and ran quickly. Our strides were spurred on by an ever-increasing adrenaline rush.

We quickly moved through the darkening shadows. I tried to mimic Doug's grace and speed with increasing success. Maybe I had a long term future in his hobby. The door to the Hansel and Gretel house was half open. The scene inside was a mess, with everything strewn about in every direction. A grand scale fight had inflicted significant damage; all the furniture, lamps and pictures were broken, dishes were shattered, legs of chairs were twisted off and curtains were lying on the floor.

Steve lay in a pool of blood. His head was nearly severed, he was gutted and a butcher knife was lying by his side. The twelve inch long blade was covered with blood to its hilt from the stab wound to his heart. We bagged the knife. We were both shocked to see the initials MF on it. We quickly placed bags on our shoes and started to look around.

There were several bloody foot prints. The tennis shoe type prints were the larger ones, so we left them. There were three small flat sole shoe prints which Doug promptly wiped away with an alcohol soaked rag.

The old trunk was gone, and there was no sign of the jerseys. Roy's duffle bags were gone. We moved quickly out the door and to the car.

I started to wonder, where was Roy? What had happened to him? I called Tim.

"Can you determine if any of the tracking devices Luke planted are moving about? We need to find out Roy's possible location?"

We headed to Matt's house. It was still an hour before Roy was scheduled to arrive for his romantic overnight stay with Matt.

On our way, Tim called.

"Since Steve isn't moving around a lot these days, Roy must be on the move as three bugs are active and show movement. He is headed north on the road to Huxley."

"Doug, Tina lives on a farm just south of Huxley. Let's move it, I screamed." I was in a state of panic.

Doug's reached under his seat and placed a fuzz buster and radar jammer on the dash and sped north. What's a little speeding ticket added to our other crimes? I had Herb Knowlton's address in my cell phone system and quickly put it into Doug's car's navigation system. Old guys with new toys can still be effective.

We were racing down the country road at one hundred mph. The harvest moon was bright. The elm tree-lined country road was well paved. The trees, tall corn and fence posts sped by in a blur. We finally saw the lights of Herb's house.

With Doug's car' lights shut off, we navigated by moonlight into the Knowlton's driveway. I had become surprisingly calm. This rush of fear and panic wasn't all bad when you have finally calmed down. I liked the feeling.

The traditional two story white and green trimmed farm house was immaculately maintained. The thirty year old spruce trees surrounding it were perfectly trimmed. All the farm buildings around it had the same color and perfection of appearance. All lights were off, except the ones upstairs.

We carefully exited the car, like aging lions stalking prey, and entered the front door, which was ajar. We heard a female yelling upstairs followed by a crash and the tell-tale pop of a shot. Roy came tumbling down the stairs into our arms. A slight trickle of blood was oozing from his shoulder. Tina was still upstairs, screaming obscenities and challenging Roy to come on back for more. No need to check on Tina. She sounded fit and angry as a she-devil.

In a flash, Doug wrapped one arm around Roy's neck and used the other as leverage. He pushed with all his strength on Roy's carotid artery. With a surprising small amount of struggle, Roy's large body went limp. Doug quickly reached into his jacket pocket and produced duct tape, which he immediately used to bind Roy's arms, ankles and cover his mouth.

It took both of our power to move the dead weight. We quietly exited the house, threw Roy into the back seat and backed out of the driveway to the Knowlton farm. Suddenly, Roy started to kick and jerk with adrenaline-induced strength.

Doug stopped the car, leaned over the front seat and wrapped a length of duct tape over Roy's nose. His eyes went wide. His face went red. He began to kick and flail violently when the reality of suffocating set into his already agitated mind.

"Roy, your only chance to live is to stop moving and listen to me."

He stopped. "I'm going to remove this tape, but if you act up again, it will go on for a much longer time. Do we understand each other?"

Roy nodded and the tape came off. His eyes were wild with fear. He had wet his pants during the process.

"Where did you learn that sleeper hold and how to use that duct tape to control someone?"

"They are just a few tricks I picked up on one of my consulting trips to Asia. Maybe I will use one of them on you next time you fuck up a putt and cost me money," Doug winked.

I think he was kidding!

"YOU HAVE A LITTLE EXPLAINING TO DO MATT. What was your carving knife doing in Steve's chest?"

Matt's usually red face was totally white. He bit violently at his lower lip. Tears were welling up in his blue eyes and were about to spill over the lower eye bags that emerge involuntarily on most sixty year olds. He was a nervous wreck.

"Lee, I knew that knife was missing for a couple of weeks. Last time I saw it was when I had a gourmet dinner for Roy and the rest of his bike team before the RAGBRAI trip. I had a beautiful beef brisket with fresh Iowa veggies and a great wine. I used that knife as its razor sharp. I like to carve against the grain to give the meat added tenderness."

"Skip the galloping gourmet's review, what was up with you and Roy?"

"No need to be so terse, Lee. Roy and I had agreed he was going to stop living with Steve. Steve was a half brother. He had severe control complex and an incurable womanizing fetish. He loved to find them, service them, use their money and then move on to the next true love of his life. He found middle-aged women who were working hard at retaining their youth particularly attractive and gullible. "

"Steve was strange as he could not stop his sex addiction, but he had a problem ending any relationship. He always had Roy break the news. It went back to their common mother, who had a lot of men in her life and who always moved on to the next love of her life, just as the boys got attached."

Matt continued, "Roy had agreed this weekend he would tell Steve he was leaving and move out. We were going to the Caves for a weekend. Then we were off to a week in the Grand Cayman for sun, food and snorkeling in the reefs around the island. I had agreed to loan him twenty-five thousand dollars to give him a little time to decide his future. I have it here in cash to give to him over dinner in the Cave. I suggested he work for me, but Roy was unsure as to his direction. He was tired of Steve and his never-ending appetite for new lovers in his life. I don't know if we had a future, but he made me feel young."

In a few minutes of graphic details, I burst Matt's romantic bubble. I explained the trunk of jerseys, the names, the names aligning with the untimely deaths and the spa boys being employed coincidentally in each town at the time of each of the deaths. Matt's complexion turned deathly white.

The clincher was the details of Roy rolling down the stairs of Tina Knowlton's house with a bullet in his shoulder. Matt was now turning beet red with rage.

"I was being set up for Steve's death. Roy was going to kill Steve's latest old tart. He probably was going to rob or kill me during our little romantic stay in the Caves."

Matt's anger was on the verge of a stroke.

"Calm down. You may be right, but there is a lot we don't know. Roy is in the back of my car. Let's go to the Caves. They are in a remote area so we won't be disturbed while we sort this out and have some serious conversation with Roy. Luke claims he has an uncanny talent for extracting information from reluctant people. Let's see how good he is. He can demonstrate on Roy."

"Let's go. We might as well add kidnapping to our resume," said Matt as he slowly reclaimed his composure. Revenge for being played as fool was now Matt's focus.

"Before we go to the next stop on this merry-go-round, Matt, could I have a stiff belt of Templeton Rye? It's been a long night. This life as a criminal is exciting, but it has left my aging nervous system in a frazzled state."

> **A JAIL IS LIKE A NUT WITH A WORM IN IT.**
> **THE WORM CAN ALWAYS GET OUT.**
>
> **John Dillinger**

Chapter Twenty-nine

****

WE ARRIVED AT MATT'S LABORATORY CAVE WITHIN TEN MINUTES OF EACH OTHER. Everyone was confused by my quick and nervous calls to them at such a late hour. Anything after the ten o'clock news is considered late.

"Guys, Doug and I will bring you up to date about the mess we've uncovered, and the one we've created. Based on Morgan's illegal computer work, we know where these two guys were living for the last several years. We accessed their tax returns, through the IRS computer system, and they leave a fool-proof map of their locations."

"We have matched the names of twelve people who died early deaths from apparent heart attacks to the names on the jerseys from the trunk. We have matched Rose and Delong's presence in the towns when the twelve deaths occurred."

"When we went back to their house to retrieve the knife with Matt's finger prints on it, the place was like a war-zone. Steve was very dead, and the place was very bloody. Someone was out of control; the knife nearly cut him apart. The trunk with all the jerseys was gone. Thanks to Tim's tracking bugs, we headed off Tina being a new victim. Roy was at her house. She must have been mad. She shot him and was yelling for him to come on back for more when we grabbed him."

"Our latest problem is that we have Roy tied up in my car's trunk. He is fine, except for a small caliber wound to his shoulder. Looks like the bullet went through some muscle and exited without touching an artery or bone. Two bandages and the big SOB is fine. We are in a real quandary; one dead masseuse, a wounded murderer, and a massive amount of illegally obtained circumstantial evidence. We have developed one gigantic brouhaha. Where do we go from here?"

Matt was quick to suggest we turn Roy over to the police and lay out all the evidence we had assembled.

"Look, I am a lawyer and I have always believed in honoring the law. So, normally, I would agree to follow the law. The problem is we have broken several state and federal laws, and all our evidence, while it is convincing, is likely inadmissible. Then there is a little issue about all our own criminal activities. Spending most of my remaining golden years in Leavenworth Prison is not on my agenda."

In an extremely calm and confident voice, Luke stood ramrod straight and firmly declared, "Lee, we know they are guilty and are truly disgusting humans, but we don't know the details or the extent of their action. Part of my military studies related to developing methodology for using kinetic interrogation. By watching people's subtle reactions, using certain other motivational influences, plus a few drugs, I can have a lot of answers in a very few hours. I would feel a lot better knowing more about them and their antics. Give me a crack at him."

From behind us, Doug whispered, "Why wait? Let's just kill him and get on with it."

The room went silent. We went white. Five wealthy semi-retired men in good health simultaneously gulped as they rapidly sucked in gasps of air. Doug's stoic face emitted a slight smile on one corner of his mouth. His eyes sent chills through all of us.

"Doug, you may have the only real solution, but I want to know more. I'm not sure I am up to it… yet," came a whispering voice from Matt.

Tim, Morgan, Chief and I nodded in silent agreement.

"Luke, the show is yours; what do we do first?"

"We do nothing for about four hours. Let him cool in the darkness of that mixing room. The whirl of the motors on the vats cooling and mixing system will create some serious disorientation. In the meantime, I need to run home for a few items that once injected will encourage an honest response."

Doug and I dragged Roy's very agitated body into the cave. He was using every ounce of his two-hundred pound body to resist us.

Doug got tired of the struggle, dropped his end and whispered, "Remember big boy, one more little over-reaction on your part and that duct tape goes over your nose. It will remain there until you learn how to behave. It may stay there permanently, as you are really pissing me off. I'm old, sore, tired and ornery tonight. Don't press your luck."

The struggling stopped as Doug reached for a strip of tape. As we sat Roy on the floor of the cave, Doug again bent over and whispered into his ear; he smiled as he walked away. Roy's eyes became oversized and flitted rapidly.

"Doug, what was that all about?"

Doug gave a small mean grin, "Nothing much, I needed to establish the rules for lying and the penalties for getting caught."

I asked, "Have you done this before?"

"I've had some similar experience. Every time is different, but in many ways they are all the same. They all talk," Doug hissed.

Matt was still red-faced and his blue eyes were jumping with emotion.

"I cannot believe how stupid I was not seeing through him. His stories about being without parents, being dominated by Steve and wanting a fresh start were so persuasive. I guess, in my process of coming out of the closet, I forgot that people are the same gay or straight, young or old. There are very few people who won't lie to you and tell you what you want to hear if they can use you for their own purposes."

Matt wrung his hands. "I am too old and experienced to get sucked into believing that there is true love out there for guys our age. I let my cynical instincts guard down, and got fooled; probably nearly killed."

"Matt, we all do that same thing on occasion. It's hard to live out the last part of your life doubting whether you will ever find love again. Why do you think Morgan and Doug have that never-ending appetite for younger ladies? It's not about sex, but the need to keep looking for that one person who, when the initial lust is gone, still means something to you."

I patted his shoulder. "Our wealth, success and good health allow us to participate in some very enjoyable but superficial activities and relationships. We are very lucky. But, let's face it, it's very easy to get emotionally frozen, depressed and feel very alone. We all find ourselves, at various times, hoping there is one more soul mate out there just waiting to spend these alleged golden years enjoying our fabulous wit and insight. No one wants to exit this world alone and unloved."

"So much for my AARP philosophy on aging people's emotional rollercoaster. We can't dwell on that deep subject now. We have a big hunk of a murderer to deal with."

Matt nodded and walked across the cave to the kitchen area. His shoulders were slouched. His hair was more disheveled than usual. He downed a straight shot of icy Belvedere vodka.

"What the hell! This is just another little adventure. We'll figure out this whole mess and deal with that piece of shit. In the meantime, let's kick back and be patient. I always wanted to see Luke in action."

Matt opened his refrigerator and threw out some homemade pasta sauce, a bag of frozen meat balls, onions, peppers and mushrooms. He threw in my direction three garlic bulbs, a roll of frozen Italian bread and a stick of butter.

"We have a lot of time to kill, among other things. Lee, you make the garlic bread. Tim opened up a couple of bottles of Chianti from level 3A of the wine cellar. Morgan, can you and Doug help me cut up the onions and peppers? I can never make big decisions on an empty stomach." Matt, doffing his apron, took out the necessary pans for our late evening Italian dinner.

We all stared at each other for a several seconds, not believing the surreal situation that had evolved. We were multiple felons and enjoying it.

"What the hell. Great idea! This scene looks like something right out of "The God Father" when James Caan got out all the Italian foods and announced, "We are going to the mattresses boys," laughed Morgan as he headed to the bar for a straight vodka before dinner.

In the pitch black storage room, with the vat grinding and buzzing endlessly, Roy's mind grew increasingly petrified. He heard the whirling electrical motor, smelled the scent of industrial oil from the gear box and felt the moisture of the cave accumulate on his skin. His body shivered with fear and the cool condensing moisture. Why were those old goats laughing? What did they intend to do with him? What had they done to Steve? He vomited into his duct tape gag and was forced to swallow or choke.

> TRUTH'S LIKE THE SUN, YOU CAN SHUT
> IT OUT, BUT IT AIN'T GOIN' AWAY.
>
> **Elvis Presley**

Chapter Thirty

****

WE WERE ALL GROWING IMPATIENT WAITING FOR LUKE'S RETURN. Not even Matt's gourmet meal and mellow Chianti could take away the edginess we all felt. Time was moving at a glacial pace.

Doug finally asked what was on everyone's mind. "We all know a lot about each other, and yet there is a lot we don't know about each other's past. That's always been good for me, but this is an unusual situation. What is this secret power to quickly interrogate someone you and Luke are referring to, and what's he after?"

I thought for a minute and decided to open up. "I am going to break a few ethical rules and give you some insight into our big friend, Luke."

"He grew up in Des Moines as part of a very rich founding family. They were early settlers from Germany. With hard work and smart moves, they amassed a fortune. In those early times around 1848 when Iowa joined the union, they developed land, built streets, and the early buildings that formed the town. They were involved in every form of venture possible in those early days; river-boats, hotels, trading posts, tanning operations, meat packing, you name it. They always came back to their true roots as builders."

"Luke was a 4th generation Walz. He grew up in a world without concerns for money. Because of their zealous ambition and self demands, his family raised him with a high level of expectation about attaining the highest goals possible in every venture. His family always displayed an incredibly high patriotic attitude. The family always understood how a free capitalistic system functioning in a democracy let them use their skills and sweat to make a fortune. They were always huge givers to local charities and civic ventures."

"Luke was a giant when he was eighteen years old, with a six foot five inch heavily- muscled frame. He was a terror on the gridiron, and went to the University of Iowa to play football after being All-State three years in a row. He played two years in those crazy mid-sixties. Iowa's team under its new coach, Ray Nagle, stunk. The campus was a center of growing rebellion over Viet Nam. Luke was a patriot through and through, and had a couple of bad fights with a few long-haired, pot-smoking fellow students."

"When he tied two male students' ponytails together and applied super-glue to the knot, he was given an ultimatum to keep his opinions to himself or get off the team. He quit. He went into ROTC and graduated as the student commander."

"He went through every program the Army had in record time. In 1967, he was assigned as a second lieutenant to a Ranger platoon that specialized in being inserted as the "anvil team" as part of the" anvil and hammer" sweeping techniques used at that time. The larger groups of Rangers would sweep an area and drive Charlie into the anvil group which was composed of the most prolific dispensers of hell and mayhem. The big risk was that the anvil team could get run over and wiped out."

"His first insertion was executed by the text book, until the captain in charge panicked. He ordered a retreat by the anvil team when Charlie showed a little piss and vinegar as they hit the anvil team. That captain was a second generation West Pointer. He had kissed ass up the ranks and possessed no real leadership skills or combat experience. Retreating was the exactly wrong move. The anvil team held the high ground, and if Charlie occupied it as the Rangers scrambled downhill, the team would get wiped out by the firepower of Charlie from the top of the Hill."

"Luke refused the order, and the remaining half of the team held the high ground and stopped Charlie's last charge. The captain looked like a fool to his men, but a hero to the brass back in Saigon. He and

Luke never spoke again."

"The next insertion, a week later, was a disaster. The same captain read the coordinates wrong, or something, but the results were they started to place the entire anvil team right in the middle of a retreating horde of angry Charlie's."

"The first three choppers were wiped out. The captain was on the third chopper and died a hero's death. Luke was in the fourth chopper. He saw the disaster developing and called for a quick withdrawal. While he was one hundred feet off the deck, a rocket turned his chopper into a six-ton mass of molten metal. Fortunately, Luke was near the door when it was hit. He flew out of the door and fell at least a hundred feet onto a fallen tree trunk breaking his right hip socket and knee. Despite his injuries, he pulled three of his guys from the wreckage."

"The rest of the choppers saw their fallen brothers about to be captured so their gunners and everyone who could get an M-16 pointed at the ground, put down a torrent of fire that allowed a chopper piloted by a Sergeant McGee to extract the four survivors."

"McGee received a Medal of Honor, but unfortunately tried the same maneuver a few months later and took a bullet to the head."

"Luke was shipped to Walter Reed where he received a new hip and knee. His limp is the result of at least eight different surgeries to solve the problem. While he was recovering, his mind was driven wild by the first-hand evidence of disasters caused by incompetent leadership decisions under stress. He knew this type of result did not necessarily have to happen. He decided that there needed to be a testing system to eliminate these faulty leaders from the system."

"So, while still recovering, Luke earned a master's degree from Georgetown in psychology. He had started working towards his Ph.D., when he met an injured army colonel named Pike. They spent a lot of time discussing this common frustration and drank a lot of Jack Daniels to help clear their minds in order to find a solution."

"After a year, it was clear, Luke would never be physically fit to be in the army, but he refused a discharge and cut an interesting deal. He re-upped for two more years as a trade off for access to military records of failed leaders. This information allowed him to earn a PhD with a thesis on "Testing Techniques to Determine Leadership Skills under Severe Stress." The thesis focused on the failings of traditional methods based on physiological testing as he added several variations where the candidates where actually subjected to various forms of stress after sleep deprivation and drugs. He also suggested several concepts of kinetic testing."

"Kinetic testing is more an art than a science. It's a process whereby the physical reactions of the candidate under stress are examined by a person trained in interpreting the meaning of such reactions; a twitch of the eye, a change of voice pitch, a defensive reaction, an offensive response, a change in word patterns, etc. I don't know if I understand all the nuances, but Luke claims to be a human lie detector. Long story short, his thesis was viewed as ground breaking thinking, and he and the colonel were off to the pentagon."

"Luke and Pike designed numerous testing methods to determine the aptitudes of candidates for certain roles, like snipers, scouts, Green Beret leaders, and so forth. Luke got tired of this process, after the fall of Saigon. He left the Army with a chip on his shoulder toward those who ran the war and those who mistreated the hero's of a crazy era."

"He took his concepts and returned home with his new wife Nancy Kay. They had met at Georgetown. She was getting a master's degree in statistical financial analysis. He and his family had a couple of great years together until his father, Fredrick, developed Alzheimer's. Luke spent a year being a great son in a miserable situation."

"After Frederick's death, Luke met with his two brothers and proposed a very attractive method for them to buy their mother and him out of the business over five years. The entire process went quickly and everyone severed their business relationships on very honorable and healthy terms."

"Luke was bored and started to utilize his testing methods in the corporate world. He charged very healthy fee's to help corporations qualify or disqualify employees for key leadership roles. In the meantime, Nancy was managing the family's money. She was incredible in her judgments. She applied several self-developed statistically driven systems and was uncanny in her stock trades."

"I met them at this stage of their life. I reviewed his consulting contracts, and helped him set up and fund a foundation to help educate injured veterans. He also set up an educational foundation for the two children of his savior, Sergeant McGee."

"I was fortunate enough to know him and his wife socially. They were an incredibly happy couple. Their two children were progressing through school with high marks, numerous achievements and only a few typical teenage problems, despite having their father's aggressive nature."

"They were a striking couple. He still stood ramrod straight, despite a bad leg, even though he was now carrying two hundred and seventy pounds. His short cut blond hair and piercing blue eyes presented an imposing sight. Nancy was 5'4", thin with dark hued skin, compliments of the genes of her Sioux great grandfather. Her shoulder length black hair beautifully accented her nearly black eyes, and a petite high cheek boned chiseled face."

"This Shangri-La situation all went to hell on 9/11; Nancy was in the World Trade Center selling a new customer on buying her trading systems."

"Luke spent three months in isolation. I stopped by twice a week to check on him and his very dark moods. He slowly pulled himself together. Then one day, he was totally engaged. He had reconnected with now General Pike. They began collaborating on testing techniques to interrogate prisoners. He would go away for weeks at a time, and come back with a near euphoric attitude."

"He never talked much about what his techniques were being used for, but clearly he felt like he was making a difference in the battle against terrorists."

"He would only tell me that several 9/11 events were avoided, and our country never really understood how a few dedicated people had saved a number of lives. He started to ease back after a couple of years. The Iraq invasion by Baby Bush significantly blunted his edge. He didn't think the Army could change a religious war that had been waged for years, without any resolution. He was more of the mind that our resources were best spent protecting our citizens in this country, not trying to solve some other countries long standing secular mess."

"He completely pulled out of military consulting this past year when the Democratic leaders in congress and their President piously condemned prisoner treatment tactics that had saved thousands of lives. He saw good people being condemned, just like Viet Nam veterans, for serving their country diligently and with great passion. Unfortunately for them, the political standards had changed to a kinder gentler standard from one of reality."

Luke has often remarked that when the next terrorist strike occurs, these same people will be eating their pious words. Jimmie Carter's methods for acquiring world peace through constant talk, love and understanding will soon be forgotten."

Just as I finished, Luke entered with a spot light, a medicine bag, a stethoscope and a video cam recorder.

"Well guys, let's find out the truth."

At this point, I took the floor. "All right guys. This is the time to walk or man up. I don't think Luke plans on giving Roy a manicure and pedicure. This might get a little weird. Don't feel embarrassed to leave or not participate."

In a second, Doug's quiet almost evil voice whispered, "How can I help handle this monster?"

No one left. Luke led us into the mixing room where Roy was waiting in the darkness. We heard a child-like whimper coming through duct tape as Luke grabbed Roy's equally big body by the throat and placed him into one of Matt's huge wooden dinner chairs which he had positioned under a spotlight.

"Roy, we are going to learn a new game. It's called Truth or Consequences. You tell the truth or you suffer the consequences." With a quick flick of his hand, Lucas dislocated Roy's right hand small finger. Roy passed out.

"That, my big white-haired friend, is your introduction to this game."

Doug laughed, "Good move. I think he will remember it when he wakes up. Remind me to stay four feet away from you, the next time I snicker at one of your yip-induced four putt exhibitions."

MEN KNOW NOTHING OF PAIN. THEY HAVE NEVER EXPERIENCED LABOR, CRAMPS OR A BIKINI WAX.

Joan Rivers

Chapter Thirty-one

****

BEFORE ROY'S MIND BECAME FUNCTIONAL AND RETURNED BACK TO THIS WORLD, WE STRAPPED HIM TO THE HIGH-BACK WOODEN CHAIR WITH HIS HEAD HELD FIRMLY BY DUCT TAPE. He was placed just outside of the mixing room door so the whirling of the vats was ever so slightly discernable. The spotlight was set on high and placed three feet over his stationary head. The DVD recorder was focused and started. The room was otherwise totally black.

Four of us sat in chairs in a position that Roy could only make out our silhouettes, not our faces. Doug stood behind Roy. He placed a six inch strip of duct tape down one side of Roy's nostrils. Luke administered a shot of Truvan, a hypnotic drug left over from his post 9/11 activities.

I handed Luke a hand written outline of the subjects I wanted addressed. I had the questions organized like a deposition that could convince any judge of his guilt. Luke and I reviewed them and made a few changes. We decided I would ask the questions from the darkness in order that Luke could watch his reactions and test his pulse in varied locations.

"We are going to commit a few more crimes, but we'll get the truth," Luke grinned.

With a few slaps on the face, Roy came to life. His eyes adjusted to the dim light. His face was white with fear. His eyes were wide and moved with the wild look of stark terror.

In my deepest commanding voice, I announced, "Roy, this is your chance to tell the truth. The big guy beside you will be holding your neck and arms to check variations in your pulse. He can tell if you are lying. The smaller man behind you will place that duct tape over your nose every time you lie. If I or anyone sitting out there gets tired of your lying, he will not remove it. Show our big brave friend how it works."

With a quick move, Doug pulled the duct tape over both nostrils. He whispered into Roy's ear, "Ever try breathing through your ears, smart guy?"

After a minute of watching him grow red, with eyes bulging and body quivering and straining to break free, I signaled and Doug ripped off the duct tape. "Nod if you understand and the tape over your mouth will be removed. Act up and the duct tape comes out again, understand?"

"Where am I? Who are you? What are you after? Why me?"

"Roy, you are a killer. You don't deserve answers. Your only hope is to tell the truth and hope that the jury sitting just beyond the light feels in a good mood."

His eyes again grew wide with fear.

"We are going to start with a few easy questions. Are you and Steve brothers, friends or lovers?"

With a long delay, he croaked out, "We are half brothers. I am totally gay, and Steve is bi-sexual. As kids, we had sex a lot, but he grew to prefer women, especially older ones. I think he had a mother issue."

Luke growled, "Congratulations, son, for your first honest answer."

"You grew up in Dallas. Tell me if your first kill was there?"

Roy's face was frozen with shock. He choked, "I never killed anyone." "Oh, Son, that was your first lie. Would you prefer a dislocated finger or the duct tape as your consequences?"

With a quick move Roy's thumb was dislocated before he answered.

Luke whispered, "You took too long to decide."

With another quick move, Luke relocated the thumb. Roy's face was red with pain and blood trickled down his chin from biting his lip.

Doug's viper-like voice hissed, "Next time, it's my turn, big guy. Think about how that duct tape feels as you black out gasping it into your nostrils, begging for air."

With sweat pouring down his face, his eyes wide with pain, Roy's strained voice confessed.

"We had an older neighbor, Linda Lou. She hit on me repeatedly. I had a long fling with her. She humiliated me verbally until one day, I ended it and her." Steve wasn't involved."

"Was Steve ever involved?"

"Well, kind of involved. I told him about the feeling of excitement that I had felt watching Linda Lou die. We decided to do it again, this time with Steve being involved. Steve flirted endlessly with the older ladies at the spa where we were training, trying to identify a candidate. He finally found one, Sarah Leslie Lee."

"Okay, keep it up, Roy. You are doing just fine," came a growl from deep within Luke.

"She was loaded and was a flirt and cheat. Her husband was an overworked diamond salesman in Dallas who neglected her. She always found reasons to leave him while she whored around. She was very into redeveloping her aging body, and after a couple of flirtatious workouts, suggested that Steve join her on a three day bike trip to San Antonio. Every night, she had Steve over to her tent and gave him a good sexual workout."

"This went on for weeks after the trip. She would buy him gifts and sneak him into her home for his service work. After a while, Steve was tired of her. He wanted to end it, but couldn't tell her to her face. We decided I would end it. We entered her house one evening together on one of their rendezvous. She was naked and, as usual, dragged Steve to her bed. I watched the entire disgusting process from a shadow."

"After he was finished, she went into the bathroom and I simply hit her head on the bathroom tub. She looked like a slip victim after I poured a lot of wine around. Steve started to cry and moan. He simply couldn't hurt his old lovers."

Did you or Steve kill again?

After a long pause Roy continued, "Steve loved to find these rich older ladies. He would find them in the spas, work out facilities and bike rides. He would flatter them, massage them, and cater to their needs like a love struck puppy. Then he would fuck them endlessly, use their money and take their gifts. After a few months, he would get bored and ask me to tell them to leave him alone."

"We changed our process so he was never present. I would have him call and set up a sex-filled night. We were about the same size so I would put on a black wig and come in and after a little fuck and suck time, I disposed of them."

"Stupid old gals thinking they could keep a young man satisfied. They were just groping to hold on to their youth. They were so stupid. They deserved to be put away."

"You are one sick piece of shit, but that response was truthful," I interjected. The room was deadly quiet. "My big friend with his hand on your neck thinks that confession was truthful. How did you kill them?"

Roy squirmed and looked around for help. "I have said enough. I want to know who you are. Where is Steve?"

That comment was startling. "Listen, you rotten piece of garbage, I ask the questions. Got the picture?"

Roy gave me a defiant glare. With that, Doug pulled his small stiletto and carved a two inch crease in Roy's right cheek.

I was speechless at this unrehearsed but effective move. Doug hissed, "You heard the man; how many more and how?"

Roy's eyes were darting. He stammered.

"At first we weren't very clever. The slip and fall routine wasn't good enough. They might not die as easy as the first two. Our third victim, Hanna, had a husband who ran a drug store. While Steve was sneaking into their house for a nooner, he stole her keys to the drug store. I started to do some reading on the internet. I went in one night and took all of the potassium chloride and a few needles."

"We experimented with a couple of drunk, homeless guys. Steve was always there, but was squeamish. I found out that if it is injected a large dose it will cause a heart attack. I also found out that injecting it into a vein behind the ear is the quickest route to the heart. After a couple of clumsy kills of three old women, I found out if you inject it in the small scar area behind the ear left behind by a face lift, it is virtually not detectible. Nobody gets suspicious since older people have sudden heart attacks all the time."

Roy actually had a smirk on his face as he told the vivid detail of how the victims looked up in total fear as their hearts erupted and their minds went black. His pleasure grew as he started to describe in detail the next three kills. They were all wealthy friends of his grandmother who had befriended the boys when their mother left them to run off with her latest rich, younger husband; a country singer named Marty McCollum.

"Where did you hide all the jerseys from the bike rides?"

Roy gasped. "How did you know?" His voice went to a falsetto level. "How? How?" He was frozen. Luke reached over and waggled a small-beamed flashlight into his wildly gyrating eyes.

"Relax. Look at the light. I will help you relax. You can re-live the pleasure of killing all of them. Enjoy every moment again. Feel the surge of power once more. Feel the energy pulsing through you."

As Luke slowly moved the light around, Roy's eyes followed it. I saw a calm look appear on Roy's face as if his fear and tension had flown to another world. Luke nodded to me and signaled to continue my questioning.

The process went on for an hour without pause. Luke had waited for the exact moment when Roy was nearly catatonic with fear and had taken control of his mind. The stress, pain, fear and drugs blended into a huge truth cocktail.

Roy spewed forth graphic details about the deaths they had caused; five wealthy friends of their grandmother, six spa customers in Dallas, four in Omaha, five in Des Moines on their first visit, two wealthy patrons who loved private home massages in Minneapolis and six more in Des Moines on their most recent stay. Of these thirty-one victims that he discussed, we had only identified twelve.

"Did Steve ever kill?" I asked.

"Steve never could handle the older women situations, but Steve had a jealous side. He was always upset that I might leave him alone. Every time I got seriously involved with another man, my new best friend met an untimely death. He used simple methods; a couple of mysterious robberies with a fatal stabbing, a strangulation by a faked hanging, a fall from a five story parking garage and an accidental shotgun blast from a prized Beretta over and under."

"He also threw a garbage bag filled with rocks into ones rider's spokes when he was racing downhill. I heard he was quite a sight flying over the cliff into the Mississippi. Funny thing was, I wasn't even involved with that guy. In fact, I hated him. He had dislocated my finger."

He was becoming very groggy, so while we had his attention, I asked, "Why were you at the Knowlton house last night when we grabbed you?"

"Steve had fallen for her big time. She acted even more aggressive than her sister, Rita, during RAGBRAI. But, she clearly had not fallen for Steve's act. In fact, Steve was getting frustrated. She kept pressing him for more details about his relationship with Rita. She made a lot of promises about more great sex they would have, but usually found a lot of reasons to avoid the act. Steve was too dumb to lie very well. I don't know how much went on between them, but I was convinced she was getting close to our little secret. So I decided to end their relationship. I knew they were going to get together tonight."

"I knew she had to go, or she would figure it all out. Steve was still pissed with me for ending his affair with Rita too soon. Tina had to go."

"Yesterday, I heard him make a date to arrive at her house while her husband was away. She must have made a lot of promises, as he was almost giddy to get to her house. I decided to beat him there and left early. As usual, I used the wig, and snuck into the Knowlton house thinking that another old lady would be waiting with a smile, a high level of horniness and no clothes. Instead she was fully clothed and armed with a Smith and Wesson revolver. She screamed that I had killed her sister and fired at my shadow as I came up to the bedroom. Luckily, she wasn't a good shot and only hit me with a grazing wound in the shoulder."

After another hour, Roy was exhausted. We all were. To our amazement, he kept asking for us to get Steve as he was really the bad guy. We were amazed at the thought process a twisted mind can go through to rationalize wrong doing. I thought at my age, I had seen it all. But, my entire life's experiences with liars and cheaters was like amateur night at the east side strip club compared to this deranged fruitcake.

No remorse was ever displayed. His justification for eliminating aging and worthless lives spewed from him, without a blink of an eye or feeling of regret. He was void of any feelings. He was a true killing machine who found great pleasure in the power and adrenaline rush each kill provided him. To our amazement, it was clear he had not killed Steve.

We shut down the process, moved Roy to the vat room with ample duct tape on his hands, feet and mouth. As we gathered around the huge limestone table in Matt's kitchen, on cue Luke's big hands trapped Matt's right wrist in a powerful grip and pulled his left hand behind him.

Everyone jumped up in total shock. I looked, from three inches, into Matt's watering blue eyes behind his professorial glasses. His hair was even more wild than usual. His face grew red. His already chubby cheeks puffed wide as he gasped with surprise.

"Convince me why I should believe that the carving knife with your initials wasn't inserted in Steve's chest by you?"

NECESSITAS NON HABET LEGIM.
NECESSITY KNOWS NO LAW.

Lesson of Life–Nathan Wayne

Chapter Thirty-two

****

WAVES OF FEAR WASHED OVER ROY ROSE. The darkness of the room in which he was immured brought on endless bouts of nausea from the claustrophobic effect. The damp feel of the limestone floor and walls added to the nausea. Roy's skin began to twitch in spasms.

He knew he would be left here to rot. But why? All he had done was clean up a few of Steve's messy romances. Those old ladies were soon going to die anyway. They were just tramps and whores, the way they threw themselves at Steve. His shivers were hitting him in waves, he wanted to scream, but his mouth was closed tight with duct tape. He could hear voices talking outside the cold, black room that imprisoned him, but their sounds were too muffled to discern.

Suddenly, he saw a brief glint of light from the door area. He tried to scream out for help, but the duct tape muffled the sound. He saw what appeared to be a small figure quickly passing though the sliver of light. He smelled the sweet smell of almonds. Strange, where would that come from inside a cave?

The smell grew stronger and stronger. Then he felt a sharp pain in his neck, below his ear in the carotid artery area. Then all was still and quiet. Suddenly, a violent, throbbing pain shot like electricity through his brain and stomach. His intestines released their smelly contents. His every muscle contracted in unbearable pain. His eyes saw flashes of color, as if he was inside a massive kaleidoscope. Then he heard through the pain, a whisper.

"This will take a long time. You can't imagine the pain that lies ahead. Arsenic is a bad way to go, but you deserve every minute of pain. See you in hell someday. You will be there before I arrive, so tell your Mom Susan her killer sent his regards."

WE ALL WATCHED MATT'S FACE. His eyes changed from fear and surprise at being held by Luke's powerful grip to a piercing stare at me. A smile suddenly developed, to our relief.

"Lee, I know if I were you I would ask the same thing. Everything points to me as the killer, and like all of you, I'm convinced Roy didn't kill Steve. But, I did not kill Steve Delong."

Luke released his grip from Matt's arm and neck, and gave him a big hug from behind with a wet sounding kiss on the bald spot on the back of his head.

"Your pulse didn't jump and your lack of any quick eye or eye-lid flutter provided you with a passing grade. You're innocent. But who did it?"

We all moved around Matt and gave him a hug.

It was nearly three a.m. With a yawn I said, "I think we all need to get a good night's sleep to clear our minds. Roy won't go anywhere. That duct tape job Doug performed would bind a bi-polar ape. We need some clear thinking to determine a smart course of action."

"We know Steve was a possessive, jealous killer; likely Matt would have been a victim. We know Roy is a serial killer, and Tina was his target. Roy is clearly without a speck of remorse for their killings. In fact, he seems to have rationalized how the victims deserved it. However, from a legal point of view, everything we have is inadmissible in court. In fact, if we told the law about it, we would go to jail for the rest of our lives. My legal conclusion is we are fucked."

"I, for one, don't want to risk having a six foot tall three hundred pound bunk mate in a 10x10 cell. Matt, you might enjoy it, but I wouldn't." Everyone laughed, including Matt.

We all agreed to go to our respective homes and rest. I arrived home just as the sun was coming up through the haze of humidity that hung over the valley below me. The golden finches were flitting about for an early morning feeding. The swallows were darting about, catching a few summer insects in mid-flight. An occasional howl of a lonely coyote looking for a pack or a mate punctuated the silence. I sat in my favorite deck chair and took in the beauty of another sunrise. What the hell had I done?

Six normally law-abiding, middle-aged men, with wealth, social status, reputations and everything to live for had broken enough laws to get them prison sentences that would exceed their life expectancies.

On the other hand, Matt and Tina were alive and likely our meddling saved them. Roy was an animal, and letting him back into society would be a death sentence for someone. Add to the dilemma, we were all convinced someone other than Roy killed Steve.

I woke up with a start, still resting in my deck chair. The heavy-feeling air around me was dead calm. My skin was clammy from sweat produced by stress and the feel of the sun growing hotter. Another ninety degree day with eighty percent humidity greeted me. I took a quick, cold shower and a swallow of liquid vitamin B-12 in an effort to invigorate a very tired body.

I picked up the phone. "Chief, will you check if there is anything going down on the death of Steve Delong?"

He agreed to get back to me ASAP.

I next called Morgan.

"Morgan, can you turn on that brilliant computer-savvy mind of yours at this early hour?"

"Lee, I have hardly slept. Glad you called. What do you have in mind?"

"Is it possible to open up yesterday's images from that street camera you controlled when we broke into the Hansel and Gretel house?"

"Great minds think alike. That's the reason I haven't been able to sleep. I pulled that data this morning and have it on a disc. It's going to show that Steve and Roy both came home from work about six. About seven, Roy leaves. Immediately, a hulk of a person steps onto the street from behind one of those large oaks. He is in a white Media-Com service uniform, like all the repair guys wear. The images are very poor in quality, but you can see him knock on the door. Ten minutes later, he comes out with his hat pulled down and casually walks down the street to a large old pickup. Before you ask, you can't see the face, and you can't read the license plate. Those cameras are so poor that you can't get any detail unless you are within ten feet of the lenses."

"Let's get call everyone and get back to the Cave. Bring the disc."

We all returned with very tired eyes and bodies, running on adrenaline. After watching the disc, we all gave up on identifying the killer.

I looked at each of my best friends and said something that I never thought I would say. "We have no choice, we have to kill him and dispose of the body."

Everyone was deadly still. The buzz of a horsefly was the only sound as we all stood looking at each other. Taking a life in combat is one thing as the enemy is after your life. You are trained to kill. You are expected to kill for your country, your fellow soldiers and for survival. Taking a life up close and eye to eye was something I could not imagine. Yet what were the options?

As we all glared at each other in total silence and shock, Matt came around the corner from the mixing room.

"Guys, the problem of killing him is no longer an issue. He is dead."

We all rushed into the room and found Roy's body. It was grotesque with vomit squirting out of the duct tape and his nostrils. Feces and urine oozed out of his jeans. His face was red and contorted with pain. He was very dead. As I bent down to check if his eyes were fixed, the faint smell of almond caught my attention. I didn't mention it, but looked up at Doug, who looked as innocent as a choir boy; he was looking up at the ceiling. He then gave me a wink. I winked back. Justice was served in a unique way.

We all withdrew to the kitchen and poured ourselves some coffee. We all were like zombies. Our subdued glances shifted from each other's eyes. We were speechless.

Then I broke the silence. "Shit. This guy was a piece of human garbage. He took away lives of many good and decent people whose only sin was trying to stay young and believing in young love. He did it without a day of remorse or doubt. His brother also took lives. I am not going to live out my days questioning what we did. Maybe I am too old and too callused for guilty feelings. Who cares how he died. My only concern is what to do with that pile of human waste."

Matt was the first to act. "My vats of chemicals for rail cleaning are in the mixing room. We can just throw him in and within twenty four hours, he will be gone like a fart in a whirlwind."

"Matt, are you sure it is that potent?" I questioned.

"Strength is not its shortcoming. It will eat up steel rails in its current state."

In a few seconds, our eyes met. A bond was struck between us. We moved quickly and chucked the mess that was Roy into the vat and hosed down the mixing room. In less than two minutes, the human killing machine that was Roy Rose had disappeared from the face of the earth.

I turned to my friends with a calm that surprised me. "I have two tee times at one on the South course. Anyone up for a little fun and games?"

" Luke, Matt and I will take you other three on for two hundred dollars each. From now on, Luke will check your pulse as you bring in the scores. As an honorable member of the bar, of course, I am exempt. I know you guys all cheat and with big Luke on my team, I will catch you." We all chuckled nervously and left.

I heard a repeated noisy gurgle in the vat as I left. "Happy trails, Roy."

LOOK AT THE JUDGE, A GUY WHO SPENT HALF OF HIS
LIFE IN SCHOOL. HE'S A LAWYER. THEN HE'S A LOWER
COURT JUDGE. THEN HE'S AN UPPER COURT JUDGE.
HE WORKS HIS WAY UP TO SOME BIG IMPORTANT
MURDER TRIAL LIKE THIS ONE, AND HE DOESN'T
EVEN GET TO DECIDE IF THE GUY IS GUILTY OR NOT.
NO, THAT DECISION'S MADE BY FIVE SALESMEN,
THREE PLUMBERS, TWO TELLERS AND A DINGBAT.

Archie Bunker

Chapter Thirty-three

****

**WE WERE ALL HITTING GOLF BALLS, WARMING UP OUR VERY
STIFF MUSCLES FROM DAYS OF BIKING ACROSS IOWA.** All of us
were nervously looking about, exchanging friendly, meaningless prattle
with many friends. We had not totally come to grips with handling the
emotions of being unremorseful felons.

Questions about RAGBRI, partying and womanizing filled every
conversation. We all gave our version of the event and added our own
lies to the womanizing portion. If our version of the trip were true,
50% of the women on RAGBRAI were conquered by the traveling
horde known as Team Old Grey Geese. Men simply cannot be trustful
on this subject.

We all tried to act involved in the process of preparing to golf. But
after committing enough crimes to get us all one hundred years of
hard time, that little white ball and that ever-frustrating game seemed
trivial.

The wind was calm for mid-August. The heat and humidity

were extremely intense and the heat rose from the ground in a way that distorted the horizon. Iowa this time of year is like living in a hothouse. Every move causes sweat to gush from your pours. The sounds of cardinals, blue birds, gold finches and robins filled the air, as they filled themselves on the lush berry plants that were bursting from the ground. The smell of freshly cut fairway grass filled the air.

The course was silent, except for the sound of an occasional "Oh shit", "Bite you, son of a bitch" and "Oh, fuck." This was all part of a golf course's sound and a normal and customary part of the on-course vocabulary utilized in the gentlemen's game of golf since its inception at St. Andrews.

With our minds still focused on the open question of who did in dirty Steve Delong, and not on the mechanics of golf, a strange thing occurred. We all played better and forgot our self- imposed mental restrictions on repeating a good swing.

On the last hole, Luke, Matt and I putted out with our best year's scores, only to find we had lost two hundred dollars to each of the others.

I asked, "Luke check their score and pulses."

Luke took one step, and they all got into their carts and quickly departed for the traditional game-ending beer.

"Come on over to my place at six. Luke, bring a couple of good wines, and don't try to sneak in a couple of your new, but cheap, wine experiments. I'll grab six good New York Strips, some fresh sweet corn and new potatoes from the Hy-Vee store as I go home. I've had my lawyer's cap on, and I think I have a few answers regarding what's bugging all of us."

Everyone arrived early and quickly fortified their beer buzz with a real man's drink. "Come on, Lee, stop with the dramatics and give us your best guess," Morgan chided.

"You lawyers are always like movie actors, trying to drag on the suspense, just begging to be asked for more of a performance."

"Let's look at the facts. Steve killed several of Roy's lovers and likely, Matt was going to be another trophy. Roy killed over thirty women, all because he wanted to help his brother end fading love affairs. Tina Knowlton was likely the next victim. These were two bad people who needed to be eliminated from society. Chief tells me that

Steve's murder investigation has hit a stone wall. They have Roy listed as the key person of interest and surprisingly, they cannot find him."

I took a deep pull on my Templeton Rye and waited for the suspense to build.

"Hurry up; you pompous prick of a lawyer. Of course, those two names are a redundancy," bellowed Luke.

"Luke, be calm and let me savor this moment of brilliance."

"We know Tina had motive. She had repeatedly slept with Steve. Steve wasn't real bright and with a little pillow talk, she likely had a feeling he was involved with her sister, Rita. Maybe she was luring him to her house to kill him. But, the theory that Tina was the knife wielding maniac doesn't fly as Steve was dead when Roy went into her bedroom. Someone killed him before that moment."

"When Doug and I saw the body for the first time, the head was nearly cut off with one slash, and he was gutted from his dick to his Adam's apple. Matt's twelve inch knife had been stuck to its hilt in his chest. Those cuts took one strong and angry person. The video that Morgan pulled off the surveillance cameras showed a big man enter the house at about the time of death. Remember how he quickly appeared from behind the tree when Roy left?"

"Now my five criminally active old friends, who do you think wins the prize for homicidal maniac of the year?"

"Will you stop with the lawyer dramatics before we all forget our friendship and find a vat of chemicals your size?"

"Okay, Matt. It likely was Herb Knowlton. He is huge and powerful. He likely suspected his wife of an affair. I believe he confronted Steve in order to scare him away. He didn't come to kill him as he appeared unarmed. Remember, Matt's carving knife was already at the Hansel and Gretel House."

"Herb most likely thought he caught Steve getting ready to go pay a nocturnal visit to Tina, and a fight ensued. Little did he know, Roy was the real visitor and Steve was likely just waiting for a visit later in the night?"

"Where do we go from here?" I pondered.

"Nothing I have outlined can be proven without us all spending hard time hitting rocks around a jail yard with a stick. I don't have a solution. But doing the right thing the wrong way and spending time for it doesn't appeal to this old lawyer."

Before anyone could answer, I stated my solution. "I, for one, want to leave it be and call off any further discussion of the past few days. Let's just walk away. Let's swear a pact of silence. We have eliminated two very bad guys without any risk to ourselves or the Knowltons. I have no remorse for the outcome. Sometimes the court system is too flawed to find justice. If fate gave us this chance to do justice, why screw it up and punish ourselves, as well as hurting two people who did nothing to bring this problem on?"

"So what if Tina had a middle-age crazy moment induced by a mid-life hormonal surge and was less than faithful. Well, maybe she was more like a little tramp for a week. But why make her pay any more for a minor transgression that hurt no one? Herb is a big, proud, hard-working guy who is likely sorry for taking a life, but proud of defending his family. Let's leave it be. Forget this whole thing; let's move on. We have long and good lives ahead of us."

"The outcome was accidental justice. It feels good," Doug concluded with an unusual emotional quiver in his delivery. I thought a long time and looked deep into his unblinking dark brown eyes.

"You're right, Doug. I, for one, want to end this here and now. Leave the Knowltons to work out their marriage issues. Let's leave this as an unspoken escapade and lesson as to how justice can be delivered in unexpected ways?"

We all agreed, and that is nearly how it ended. Almost.

Chapter Thirty-four

****

LATE IN THE FALL, MATT RAN MORE TESTS ON HIS VATS OF CHEMICALS. He was relentless in trying mixture variations in his quest for diluting the destructive potent nature of the cleaner. He avoided the vat where Roy was dissolved. But, one day his curiosity took control, and he discovered that Roy's vat mixture was sufficiently diluted to avoid destruction of the rails and wood ties. In fact, the content had developed an unexpected adhesive quality. This adhesive attribute allowed the chemical to be dripped onto the tracks, with little spillage, and eliminated the previous accompanying damage to the wooden rail ties.

Repeated tests proved that adding two hundred pounds of protein, fat and calcium was the solution to this long-frustrating problem. Unfortunately, Roy Rose will never be recognized for his contribution to science.

Matt sold the product to the Union Pacific as per the contract we had signed. He started using hog carcasses, rejected by slaughtering houses for human consumption, as a Roy substitute. He was actually paid to dispose of the hogs. Matt was now recognized as an environmental hero for the innovation in waste disposal.

With the contract I negotiated for the use of this product, Matt's first quarterly check was in the seven figures. He hired Tim to use his logistics knowledge and reputation and they started to market the product with every railroad and subway in the country. The returns were quick, as part of the royalties was based on a projected savings in fuels. Matt was a hero for his contribution to the country's move to obtain fuel efficiencies through his new product, TRACK-OFF. Gay guys get all the big awards.

Since I owned part of Matt's business, because of my usual over-reaching fee arrangement, my balance sheet also had its own stimulus program. Matt and I decided to form a foundation to develop and staff the Caves at Madison County Incubation Center for Novice Entrepreneurs. The size of Matt's cave was easily expanded. The need for insulation and material for walls and footings were obviously eliminated and this allowed quick cost efficient expansion.

Mindy Brokowski was now Doug's live-in friend and they were inseparable. Doug's "consulting trips" had stopped. He was enjoying trying to introduce Mindy to new experiences and all the good things of life. Without saying it, he was obviously moving towards sharing the rest of his time with her.

Doug and I never spoke of his unique talents, especially the smell of almond which permeated Roy's corpse. I knew he was a loyal friend, and also never to make him an enemy. His well-developed talents petrified me.

Mindy turned out to be the prize novice entrepreneur. She developed a concept to further dilute Matt's TRACK OFF product. Under her business model, the product would be diluted into various levels to remove paint, deep stains from grease or asphalt or just clean very dirty hands. Each product was diluted for the desired results and sold as separate products. The success of TRACK OFF would be the focus of the marketing campaign.

After a few failed steps and burned hands, Matt's genius mind got the various dilutions figured out, and Mindy started marketing before production even commenced. She sold CRAP OFF to every major home supply company on a mind-boggling scale. It's amazing how a beautiful young, flirtatious, long-legged lady can get into the buyer's office when a middle-aged, knowledgeable male couldn't get an appointment.

Tim O'Brien again came to the rescue and developed the logistics to have the product prepared by outsourcing manufacturing to chemical companies and obligating them for timely delivery to buyers in every region of the country.

As the year was ending, I spent considerable time with R.F., wrapping up the details of his new business's first year of operation. His commodity timing business had predicted every swing of the grain markets as if he had access to the government reports before their release. I smelled Morgan's computer skills at work.

R.F. steadfastly denied any wrong doing. He gave out big bonuses, including the biggest one to Herb Knowlton. He and I also agreed to very significant donations to Luke's foundation for the education of disabled veterans.

Luke continued to consult with the military on selected issues involving interrogation methods. He was tireless in building resources for the foundation for education of disabled veterans. Because of our funding, he was able to involve nationally prominent educators. He named it for the sergeant who had saved his life. He had a mission, and he was energized again.

My last piece of closure to this bizarre series of unexpected events ended with my visit with Herb. I had given the name of a divorce lawyer to Tina with the counsel to move slowly and be patient. I lectured here that twenty-eight years of marriage should not be quickly thrown away. I found out she agreed, and Herb was the motivated party.

I found Herb with his big bonus check in his hands at the year-end annual meeting of R.F.'s new venture.

"Herb, you need to give me a hundred dollars as a retainer."

He looked at me with a blank stare that I knew masked a very smart person. His huge frame and simple farm boy looks were deceiving. He handed me a hundred dollar bill.

"What's on your mind, counselor?"

"Tina called me for a divorce lawyer referral. I gave her the name of the meanest, most unethical lawyer to ever crawl out of law school. She specializes in cutting the nuts off of male plaintiffs. Tina told me she did not want this process to go forward; that you're the plaintiff as you suspect she had an affair on the RAGBRAI trip. Since I am now your lawyer, whatever I tell you is privileged, as is whatever you tell me."

His stare became more intense and the veins on his neck started to show.

"You have a great wife, two good kids, a business that will make you rich, and Tina is rich with Rita's estate. Why mess it up? I have never seen a friendly divorce. The process is ugly and tends to take on a life of its own. They get mean. They become a lawyer's game, and the clients lose themselves in the combat and forget when it's over, they have lives to live. Before you answer my question, think about this hypothetical."

"Suppose a big middle-aged guy got jealous of his wife's suspected relationship with a younger man. Suppose that man made a call to scare off that young stud. Suppose that guy forgot there are surveillance cameras on many streets in that area of town. Suppose that young man was found dead from an unknown assailant's knife. Suppose that young man's half brother and gay lover was the key suspect and was not yet found. Would that smart middle-aged man start a lengthy legal process that could bring out possible ties by him or his wife to that dead man?"

Herb chewed his lip. He looked down. His big head moved from side to side as I heard a sniffle. He raised his head. His crew cut, blond head was huge, as were the gray eyes that held a tear in each corner. He cleared his voice and in an unusually voice, softly spoke.

"Counselor, you are quite a cupid. I think the answer to your hypothetical is that that big guy should bury his pride, admit he loves his wife and put this entire matter behind him. Confessions are seldom good for the soul. Wouldn't you agree?"

"Herb, you're a genius. You pass the test. Now, go out, fire your divorce lawyer after you dismiss the petition. Then, buy a dozen roses, a big rock on the end of a chain and a good bottle of wine. Go home and give her a big hug. Tell her she is your soul mate and you will never look back, only forward. Soul mates are rare; don't lose yours."

He started to leave. "Oh, by the way, I left out three facts from that hypothetical. The surveillance tape accidentally got wiped clean. Roy has gone to a place where he will never be found. I was on that RAGBRI trip and saw Tina and her group every night. She was perfectly behaved. I never saw her with any young stud. Does any of that change your mind?"

Our stares lasted a minute. No one blinked. Then he broke into a huge laugh. He gave me a bear hug with a sloppy kiss on my forehead and left. Again, a couple little lies did a lot of good.

I picked up the phone and called Millie to discuss a late dinner at my home and an early breakfast the next day. She was continuing to fascinate me, and to become a real friend. This relationship might last.

I GUESS SOME PEOPLE NEVER CHANGE, OR THEY QUICKLY CHANGE AND THEN QUICKLY CHANGE BACK.

Homer Simpson-The Simpsons

Epilogue

****

DOUG VALLI SETTLED DOWN TO SIP A TUMBLER OF KING LOUIE COGNAC BEFORE GOING TO SLEEP. He gazed pensively through the window as the large snowflakes from a late December storm fell in an ever-increasing volume. The landscape below the balcony of his Owl's Head Townhouse was filled with trees now totally barren of their leaves. His view of the large rambling evergreen- filled park below was now wide open. He could see the silver eyes of deer moving about in search of food. Their grazing areas were fast becoming a mounded white blanket. The occasional break in the clouds allowed the full moon overhead to produce a ballet of dancing shadows with ever-changing forms.

Mindy had collapsed in their bed. A couple too many wines had mellowed her bubbly, energy-filled personality. They had enjoyed an early evening at their favorite pre-civic center event venue. Splash Grill's owner catered to the pre-theater crowd and always had unique seafood appetizers and new wines for the regulars. Mindy had quickly overcome her small town taste deficiency and had acquired a passion for scallops, escargot, and salmon in any form with any sauce. Her taste in white wine had progressively moved up the quality and cost chart.

The night's pre-theater food was as always, unique. Doug had spent the time reviewing the background of the cast members performing in

"Jersey Boys." He talked excitedly about the credits of all of the actors, noting their many experiences on Broadway and commented on their impressive resumes. Mindy tried desperately to absorb his rambling, enthused dialog, and occasionally slowed him down with numerous questions, which showed she was in many ways still a twenty-five year old small town woman.

Doug had become captivated by her boundless energy to learn about any subject. In reality, as he sipped the cognac, he realized he was, for the second time in his life, deeply caring what someone else thought, what they did, and what they felt. He was captivated with the smell of her perfumes, the smell of her freshly cleaned body and her naked touch. He noticed what she wore to work or to any event. He couldn't wait to share his day with her or to hear of her day. The L word even occurred to him.

After pouring a second King Louie, Doug opened up the recently arrived packet for one more review. It had been sent through a very indirect series of routes: Palermo, to Berlin, to Rio, to Cabo and then to Des Moines.

The cover letter, in perfect handwriting, started with regards from Antonio to Arturo. "Consider with care taking one last consulting venture. The pay is handsome; the risk of failure is significant. We know of your desire to retire to your small town life, but struggle to understand your thinking. We still wish you would reconsider. Buy a villa on the bluffs of majestic Taormina, find a young Sicilian woman, and wake up every morning absorbing the view of the ocean below, after she has satisfied you. Blend in with your family once again. Live the life that your wealth and our power can provide."

The file was filled with details of the subject of the consulting venture. Kurt Garcia had been a playboy for the early portion of his adult life. His jet-setting activities with the young beauties of the seventies were documented in numerous magazines and gossip columns. Kurt disappeared from the public eye when his German-born father, Hans, was assassinated by a car bomb. His Mexican mother was killed three days later from a sniper shot as she walked beside Han's casket.

Kurt had disappeared from the public's eye as he had quickly thereafter taken over the monstrous drug programs of the family. His parents' deaths were quickly vindictive, as entire families of rival gang members were found in back alleys, old rivers beds and trash containers in multiple parts.

Kurt had thereafter taken the drug trafficking business to a new level by eliminating various levels of the marketing process. It took a logistics genius to control the continuous flow of traffic by small planes, small boats and cars. Benjamin Perez was that genius. His mathematics degree from MIT and ten years in the US Air force provided him with both the training and the equipment necessary to accomplish this task.

Kurt surrounded himself with dozens of ex-seal bodyguards and security devices that were cutting edge. He was paranoid about his life. He never married and changed female companions on an every two week basis.

Kurt's trafficking in meth had found a surprisingly lucrative market in small town America. The prospects of a bleak life with limited job and social opportunities that prevailed in these dying towns made them a perfect market for a quick, cheap drug that had an immediate addictive affect. It was as simple as any pyramid scheme. First hire a marketing person who could locate a team to infiltrate each state as part of the immigration flow of cheap labor. Get the team members jobs in the many factories that sought out cheap labor that they could dominate and control. Provide the team with perfect papers to prove their legal status and equip them with free samples to hook the locals. In a few months, the user base would grow and Kurt's factories could step up production and the flow to small town America. The marketing crew would then move on to the next site, leaving behind a distribution system operated by locals who were also the biggest users.

The report indicated the client had lost a daughter to Kurt's system. She had tried a meth sample on a dare at a small town graduation beer bash. Within years, she was out of college and hooking to support her habit. Her family had tried all the traditional cures, from Hazelton to Betty Ford, with abject failure. They had tried the hard love approach, and the daughter was killed in the streets of Des Moines by a local distributor who caught her cheating on the quantities of her deliveries.

The client had spent endless amounts of his large farm wealth in paying for the detailed background work that was a normal part of

Antonio's justice delivery system. Now the time was at hand for the completion of the assignment. Antonio wanted and needed the most experienced consultant in his stable of talented professionals.

The challenge of the assignment was to eliminate Kurt's logistics genius and then his marketing directors in the four primary distribution regions of the United States; the rural northwest, the rural southwest, the rural southeast and the rural Midwest. The process would likely draw Kurt into quick reactions and mistakes. The completion of the discharge of these marketing heads had to done in a quick fashion which would allow little time for considered reaction. It also had to be done in a fashion that signaled a takeover attempt.

Luckily, one of the most prolific of the marketing directors was located in Iowa. Jesse Marvin was living in the Loess Hills of southwest Iowa, near the town of Pisgah. His production and distribution operations were hidden by the rolling hills and deep gorges. The lack of population and law enforcement made it easy to handle production from deeply constructed cave warehouses. The numerous dirt roads through the area allowed vehicles to move in multiple directions to other secondary roads that crisscrossed the area.

Jesse never lost product, and his labor was easily accessed from the local population that he had addicted during his first visit to the area. If any of his production staff went off the deep end, it was also easy to convince his family that a trip to the city to find work had occurred. Those deep caves had lots of room for ex-employees.

Doug laid the file aside. The thrills of the planning and the performance of the ultimate solution to an assignment were causing his adrenaline to flow. His consulting fee was huge. However, his life was never better. He had discovered emotions that he had long ago buried and forgotten. He had often tried, to no avail, to force Mindy to choose to leave him. His long talks about the reality that there was a forty years different in age did not slow her passion for him. Being twenty-five and sixty-six sounded bad now, but it would really be awful when the ages were forty-five and eighty-five. He was always glad she never left, as she was now a crucial emotional part of his every day and every thought.

As he entered the bedroom, Doug looked out at the near blizzard snow. The view inside the room was only lighted by the glow of the embers from the dying oak logs. The snow-covered landscape below was mesmerizing. So was the view inside the room. He could not take his gaze off Mindy, who was cuddled into the down-filled pillows and covers. As he watched her, her eyes opened sleepily, gazing out of her toasty nest. She raised the blanket and exposed her willowy, youthful body, and she motioned for him to join her. "Come on, my old Grey Goose, this young hen needs your body to warm her on a cold night."

As he slid in beside her, he knew this decision would be a difficult one. Logic told him to pass on the engagement and stand fast on his retirement. He had been very lucky and was very rich. But the pulsing of his heart and the feeling of rejuvenation through delivering justice for pay one more time were exhilarating.

Like those Grey Geese in Nathan's poem, maybe he needed one more flight.

LaVergne, TN USA
05 August 2010
192117LV00003B/1/P

9 781449 059903